"Not Garfield," Fiona FitzGerald whispered, looking over Monte Pappas' thick shoulder as they scrutinized the seating list. A sweet-faced young woman suitably festooned in the costume of a colonial dame had handed them the list along with a toothpaste-sincere smile.

The Pepsi company had pulled out all stops for this annual bash of ingratiation for the celebration and benefit of the Congress and the diplomatic corps, a high-profile wingding, a not-so-subtle thank-you for helping or, alas, not interfering with spreading the international cheer of feel-good bellywash. Fiona, influenced by Monte Pappas' Public-Relations-Man cynicism and her own extensive Washington experience did not wish to think such spoiling thoughts. But how was it to be avoided?

The company had hired the hallowed plantation of George Washington's Mount Vernon, no less, put up a giant tent on a side lawn adjacent to the main house to hold more than 350 people and was laying on a five-course gourmet supper served by an army of white-gloved waiters on tables set with gleaming china and topped with elaborate floral centerpieces. Each table was designated by a Presidential name written in impeccable calligraphy on white board. For whatever inexplicable reason, although Fiona knew that such things were carefully orchestrated, they had drawn President Garfield.

There was a ten-piece band and a dance floor laid down in the tent's center and a large area set aside for the cocktail hour, a set piece of Washington entertaining devoted to the usual networking, influence-hustling and double-cheeking.

Some surely might have thought it defamatory for this national shrine to be invaded by the bellywashers and their freeloading minions, but this, as Monte had pointed out so aptly on the horse-drawn carriage ride from the Potomac river dock to the tent, was the age of corporate "Kultur" and thus the bash was a singularly appropriate exercise in one-upmanship. Besides, he had added, "Who else could afford it?"

They had glided into the Mount Vernon dock on charter boats moored on Main Street, which was closer to Capitol Hill, taking the slow ride the few miles downriver while a band played dance music and the bartenders merrily poured champagne. The April air was damp with the gamey odor of the awakening earth and there was more than a hint of a spring rain.

For Fiona, a Senator's daughter, weaned on the heady and subtle sweetness of Washington milk, the event went beyond the genre, and no amount of cynicism could dampen the sheer wonder and chutzpa of the idea. All right, so it was charmingly decadent, perhaps even a tiny defamation of this historical icon. But, hell, it was, after all, a slave plantation in old George's day and, therefore, not politically perfect by today's political standards. So what was wrong with such a choice spot for a bit of vulgar fun?

The rooms of the mansion house, with the exception of the entry foyer, were verboten to guests, and an impressive multitude of gleaming white johnny-on-the-spots, reached through a tented corridor, were arranged in a picket line adjacent to the main big top. It struck her that in-house johns were not a feature in old George's day and, therefore, the facilities were historically appropriate, which represented a saving grace of sorts.

There were moments, and this might be one of them, when she felt somewhat superior to the situation, a trifle too all-knowing and cynically cocksure. Monte Pappas, a gun-for-hire on any political campaign that could pay his price, wasn't shy about catering to and embellishing this attitude. He had, after all, adopted it as his everyday business pose. Fiona had already penetrated that part of him and seen the vulnerable sweetness under the facade, which titillated her motherly and less-platonic instincts.

Other Books by Warren Adler

The War of the Roses
Random Hearts
Trans-Siberian Express
Mourning Glory
Cult
The Casanova Embrace
Blood Ties
Natural Enemies
Banquet Before Dawn
The Housewife Blues
Madeline's Miracles
We Are Holding the President Hostage
Private Lies
Twilight Child
The Henderson Equation
Undertow

Short Stories
The Sunset Gang
Never Too Late for Love
Jackson Hole, Uneasy Eden

The Fiona Mysteries
American Quartet
American Sextet
Senator Love
Immaculate Deception
The Witch of Watergate
The Ties That Bind

Available in all formats as eBooks and Print on Demand wherever books are sold online and off.

Visit www.WarrenAdler.com and join the Warren Adler Book Club

Senator
Love

by Warren Adler

STONEHOUSE
PRESS

For Sunny, again.

STONEHOUSE PRESS

ISBN: 1-93130-463-7 Trade Paperback
ISBN: 1-59006-015-6 Hardcover

Inquiries: www. warrenadler.com

"So ask me," he had challenged her as they stood on the rail of the charter boat watching movie-set Washington twinkle past. "Why do they do it?"

It was his invitation, and she was only "and guest," and he was entitled to her version of the answer.

"Influence," she said.

"And *ego,*" he instructed. "Never forget ego. For one shining moment the Chairman gets to beat his breast in front of the power elite. The message is: 'Look at all my marbles, people. See 'em. Count 'em. Respect 'em. I'll throw some in your game if you be nice. And if you take them, by God, you better be nice to me.'"

"So what else is new," she replied.

"Who's talking new?" Pappas said, his arm enveloping her, touching her shoulder, squeezing lightly. She could feel his breath as he bent over to kiss her ear. Of course, he was executing his version of a seduction. This was, after all, their second official date, although they had known each other casually on the social circuit for years, part of her non-cop life.

He was dark, stocky and, as they say, forensically speaking, well nourished. Even in his tux he looked lumpy—his cummerbund did not seem like a good idea. But she liked his shifty, street-smart moves, especially his know-it-all throwaways that sometimes passed for wisdom, and in the context of when said, often seemed to cut into the heart of some simple truth.

The darkness of his beard suggested that his slightly inflated soft body was covered with a carpet of tightly matted jet-black curly hair, although she did not broadcast her curiosity. Put him down for a maybe, she decided. At the moment she preferred to keep matters on a plateau of sophisticated Washington banter.

Under the tent, they headed for one of the bars, threading their way through layers of familiar political and social faces. She knew some of them, stopping to chat as she moved through the crowd, offering her face for the occasional double-cheeker. Monte, too, worked the crowd in his own way, pressing the flesh, offering a wink or a bear hug where appropriate.

It was the Washington social way, peculiar unto itself, as comfortable to her as an old glove, despite her chosen profession. Always she marveled at the contrast, the Jekyll-and-Hyde aspect of her life, never quite knowing which part of it was the truth of herself.

Monte brought her champagne, taking a neat scotch for himself. It looked like a double. They moved to a quiet spot to survey the scene.

"Why the sigh over Garfield?" Monte asked.

"One of the bumped-off ones," she replied.

"Hope there's no symbolism there," Monte said, casting his gaze about in mock fear. "I need every client I can get." He could tell she was confused.

"It's Sam Langford's table," Monte explained. On their first date he had told her that Sam was a client, that he had run his two winning Senatorial campaigns.

An inveterate political watcher, a habit from her youth as the daughter of Senator Edward FitzGerald, Fiona knew who Langford was. Twice Senator from Florida, a comer, bright, handsome, fashionably conservative, terrific speaker.

"He's about to stretch himself," Monte whispered as they moved toward the table. She recognized Langford standing near an attractive woman and chatting with a young couple.

"The big banana?" she asked.

"Why not?" Monte shrugged. "He's got it all." He lowered his voice to a mood-changing mutter. "Maybe too much." Then raised it again on a note of optimism. "Be a great shot for yours truly."

"Here he is," Langford said as he spied Monte, "the Greek Oracle."

Dimples, Fiona thought. He has cute dimples and thick wavy light-brown hair going gracefully to grey, she remarked to herself. And blue eyes to boot. Not too tall, but flat-gutted and athletic looking.

Introductions were exchanged. The attractive woman beside him was Nell Langford, his wife—tall, blonde, squeaky clean and smiley.

Taken right off the shelf marked "obedient political wife," Fiona decided instantly. Somehow her smile seemed overly joyous in contrast to her
eyes, which were sad and wary, confusing Fiona's first impression.

The younger man was introduced as Bunkie Farrington, who then
introduced his date, a Bonnie something. Bunkie! The name itself
seemed a definition of the man. He wore a high-collared tux shirt
and a red bow tie. Blondish, balding, ferret-eyed, mid-thirties, his
entire demeanor said, "Color me preppy forever." Instantly she knew
she had him pegged. Langford's political lackey.

Odd, she thought, how some men telescope their personas so accurately. Or was it her cop training? She could hear his credo: "I'd go
through the fires of hell for that man," meaning Langford, as if he were
joined to the man's hip. By this, he surely reasoned, there would be the
big payoff for old Bunkie. She sniffed him, figured him for a shade
over 25. He stank of ambition. The aroma was always gamier at that
age. He had just handed the Senator and his wife two drinks taken
from a silver tray carried by one of the ambulatory white-gloved waiters. Only then did he serve himself and Bonnie something.

"Pappas says you're a cop," Langford said.

"Rest easy, Senator, you're not under suspicion."

He roared his laughter, then looked at Monte. "There's your
man," he said, pointing to the bulging middle behind Monte's cummerbund. "He's hiding the jewels in there."

"*Sam,*" Nell said with disapproval too genuine to be good natured.

"Not her bag, Senator," Pappas shot back, masking his wound.
"She's homicide."

"Heavy," Bunkie said, his interest elsewhere as his networking,
predatory eyes scoped the tent. In a flash he spotted prey, moved out
and led a distinguished-looking bemedaled gentlemen to the
Senator's side.

"You know Ambassador Blackburn," he said as the Senator proceeded to press flesh. Of course, they knew each other casually, but
this was simply another moment for the Senator to show the flag to

a representative of a powerful country. The two men chewed over the small-talk amenities appropriate to the event and parted.

"Grist for expanding one's experience in the area of foreign affairs," Monte whispered. "He's the Brit."

During the exchange, Bunkie continued to survey the crowd, found another victim, zeroed in and struck. Senator Sam never moved, the idea being to bring the mountains to Mohammed. Sun never sets on good old Bunkie, Fiona thought, noting her instant dislike of the man. With good reason, she decided.

His persona was a Washington category, the preppy sycophant, sucking up power and warmth from Langford's rays, a staff man outside the line of real legislative work. An image of what was surely his daily dress code popped into her mind. Polka-dot bow tie on a buttondown striped shirt. Pants held up by suspenders decorated with ducks. Patterned long-shorts underwear. As a kid he would have scared the shit out of a cat with a cigarette lighter. Going too far, she decided, reigning in her bile, her thoughts drifting back to present tense.

"My name is Kessel," a man's voice said behind her in a clearly Germanic cadence. "And I've been assigned to Garfield."

"Hans," Senator Langford said, putting out his hand while an arm crept about the man's shoulders.

"The Austrian Ambassador and the lovely Helga," Monte whispered with an air of unmistakable contempt. Langford planted a double-cheeker on a spectacularly beautiful lady in a pink sheath gown. Around her neck she wore a dazzling ruby necklace with matching earrings. A diamond bracelet hung around one wrist and an assortment of rings decorated graceful white fingers.

The woman's eyes sparkled with pleasure as she beheld the Senator from behind high cheekbones, holding the gaze longer than what might be considered appropriate.

"Does it show?" Monte hissed.

"The jewelry?"

"You know what I mean."

Before she could reply the answer was irrevocably telescoped in Nell Langford's barely perceptible lip tremor as she nodded toward the Ambassador's wife. An attempt at smiling would have created jagged fissures on her face.

"I was so happy when I saw the seating list," the Austrian Ambassador said. Fiona cut a glance at Bunkie, hoping for a wink. None came, of course. He did not even acknowledge her look. But she knew it was he who had arranged the seating. She was puzzled by the Ambassador's pleasure over the seating.

The band began to play soft dinner music and the guests began to straggle to their seats. The Austrian Ambassador took his place beside Nell, and Helga glided gracefully to a seat to the right of the Senator. Bunkie flanked her on the other side. Beside him, responding to the appropriate male-female protocol and much to her distaste, came Fiona. Thankfully, she had Monte on her right.

An army of white-gloved waiters fanned out to place the salad and pour the white wine. Fiona suspected that they would pay some lip service to the "turn" between courses, although she decided that old Bunkie would be deliberately attentive to Helga to cover for the Senator's being overly conspicuous in his ministrations to the lady.

"Damn fool," Monte whispered in her ear. "Bastard's got an Achilles' crotch."

"An occupational hazard," Fiona sighed, remembering her father and her mother's pain.

"This one's got a political death wish," Monte said. She could tell he was genuinely annoyed. "He'll blow it. I know he will. A need-to-conquer syndrome like poor Gary Hart." He shook his head. "Zip it up, schmuck," he muttered under his breath.

"Maybe he wants to get caught," Fiona said, spooning out traditional cop philosophy.

"He gets caught, I get nada," Monte sighed. "Sad case. Man's got it all. Looks. Brains. Good projection. Articulate." He shook his head.

"Seems he's done all right so far, despite his . . . ah . . . predisposition to being a satyr," Fiona said.

"The media x-ray is a surfacey thing in a Senatorial campaign. In a Presidential it goes to the bone." She looked at him archly, catching the inadvertent pun. Finally he laughed and took a deep sip of his wine. "Look at me," he chuckled, "so concerned with another man's sex life." He sighed theatrically. "No justice anywhere. He feasts. I starve. Maybe there's more to it than just business." He paused. "Like jealousy."

She patted his hand and shook her head. "You men and your penis envy," she chuckled. He laughed.

"Maybe we can share the joke," Bunkie said.

"We are sharing it," Monte said, noting that there was no love lost between the two men.

"Won't work out of context," Fiona said as Bunkie shrugged and turned back to Helga.

Plates were exchanged. An elegantly displayed fish course followed. Then perfect pink filets along with the French reds. Vegetables were served with consummate skill. It was, she realized, an orgy of overstaffing, a pampering, obviously a well-rehearsed and executed event. Someone would surely get a bonus.

Rich was always better, she decided, feeling again the profound, guilt-tinged kinship with her colleagues in the cops struggling to get by, usually with two paychecks and always with constant financial anxiety. In this environment, she would suffer severe bouts of second thoughts about her choice of career. Was she really the alien she imagined, the daughter of power and privilege slumming in a blue-collar ménage?

It was a question posed with ever-diminishing frequency. The cop hook was in her, the idea of it, the challenge, the danger, the adventure and, yes, the contrast. Despite the sometime pettiness, the turf and racial anxieties, the ego and emotional thrashing and bashing, there were psychic satisfactions in her job that were, well, enriching and worthwhile. Having her own "fuck-you" money made it even more fulfilling.

The grass only seems greener, she smirked to herself, her gaze washing over this acre of privilege. Anyway, she decided, as the soft French red titillated her palate, this ain't all bad.

Between courses the band played dance music and the dance floor filled with whirling couples.

"Ironies are everywhere," Monte whispered. She followed his gaze. He was watching a stately woman dancing with a ramrod-stiff grey-haired man in a two-step that reminded her of dancers in an old movie. No talk passed between them as they concentrated on the band's rhythm.

"The first Mrs. Langford," Monte said. "Can't get them to go home once they've seen Paree." Voluble sober, Monte seemed to be growing even more loquacious with his wine intake, which was considerable. Problem was that the waiters, to keep the assemblage well watered, were pouring heavy, leaving no glass untopped.

"Tough when they lose their status," Fiona mused, remembering her mother after her father had died.

"There's some cache in being an ex-wife. You get to keep the name, for example." He lifted his chin. "Like her."

"And she goes to the best places."

"She deserves it," Monte said, bending closer to her ear. "Old Sam certainly unloaded her wagons. Now it's little Nell's cross to bear." Fiona looked over at Nell, whose pose was of one deeply interested in what the Ambassador had to say, while her eyes drifted frequently to take in the sight of the Senator and Helga. On the surface, it seemed to Fiona as quite innocent. Bunkie and Helga seemed to be doing most of the talking.

"Ten to one Sam and Helga are locked in an undercover crotch hold," Monte said.

"A regular gambler," Fiona said.

"I don't gamble," Monte smirked.

"Considering where he wants to go, you'd think he'd know better," she whispered, surprised at her judgmental tone.

"Can't kick the one-eyed monster," Monte sighed, taking another deep sip of wine. She turned to look at him, slightly puzzled, until she realized what he meant, then, like a doe-eyed virgin, she felt herself blush.

"Sorry to put it that crudely. The man's incorrigible. Like tonight. Blatant stuff. In a minute he'll be asking all the girls to dance, little Nell for openers. You included. A red herring for what he really wants."

"How does he manage it? A man in the public eye?"

"That's old Bunkie's job. He's the staff man in charge of nooky. Plays the role, though. Beard, pimp, arranger. Also does the kiss-off routine when things get too hot. Valuable job in this town."

"And nobody knows?" Fiona asked.

"We try to keep it in a tight little group."

"Then why are you telling me?"

She turned to him. He shook his head and smiled.

"You're a cop. I trust you."

After a while the Senator stirred and asked his wife to dance. As Monte had predicted, then came Bonnie-something, who had barely uttered a word. On cue, Fiona came up on the dance card. Actually, the Senator asked Monte's permission in the old-fashioned way. Monte shrugged his consent. Fiona snickered her distaste. I dance with whomever I please, she told herself pugnaciously, then let the Senator lead her to the dance floor.

Close up, she felt the tightness of his body, his absolute sense of confidence in the way he held her. His dance technique, a bit heavy on the pelvis, was a blatant flirt.

Actually Monte had spoiled her discovery. The Senator was a natural seducer. She would have liked to find that out for herself.

"You're the prettiest homicide detective I've ever met," he whispered, pulling her closer for the compliment. Was he making a move? she wondered. "Maybe someday you can tell me how you do it."

"Do what?"

"Find the killers."

He twirled her around the floor, chuckling. Despite the warning bells, she felt strangely comfortable in his arms. She even felt, she allowed herself to admit, tiny tingles in the right places. Son-of-a-bitch had the stuff, she decided, providing him with a nickname on the spot. Senator Love. Hands-down that was it. Senator Love.

"Odd work for a politician's daughter, cops," he said as they moved around the floor. The sexual statement made, he moved to a more cerebral subject. Even his way of putting her on hold was a class act. Often, he would nod and smile at the other dancers.

"What did your father do?" she asked.

"A minister, actually."

"Well then," she said, leaving the idea unfinished. He quickly caught the innuendo.

"We do only the possible and leave the miracles to God."

Peripherally, she could see his first wife as she two-stepped toward him. Inexplicably, she found herself resisting his lead as if the confrontation was to be avoided.

"Hello, Sam," his ex-wife said as she whirled past. Close up she looked bigger than life, big bosom, a round face. Pleasing plumpness filled out the skin, holding back any discernible wrinkles. She was a picture of strength. Hardly an *ex*-anything.

"Frances," he acknowledged, offering a thin smile. She felt a snicker of contempt escape his lips. No love lost, she decided. But the greeting seemed quite civilized.

"You have any children?" Fiona asked, embarrassed suddenly by her oblique curiosity.

"Just two. Eight and six," he said, offering no details. None with the other, Fiona thought, oddly relieved. The band stopped and he led her back to the table.

"Now," Monte said as the band struck up again.

The Senator and Helga got up to dance. It seemed a cue for all the others. The Ambassador and Nell, Bunkie and Bonnie.

"Bad knee," Monte smiled, explaining himself.

"Really?" Fiona asked.

"Time to watch the fun."

They watched. Helga's slender body melted into the Senator's, although above the waist the dance had the illusion of decorum.

"Surely not tonight," Fiona asked.

"Never at night," Monte clucked. "That's his modus operandi. He's a matinee man and Bunkie's a past master of scheduling and timing. Easier to elude detection."

"Does little Nell know?"

"Oh, I'd say she might suspect about the sport fucking. It's the serious stuff that she's on the lookout for." He looked at the Senator and Helga intent on keeping their pose casual. "Like that."

"Must be exhausting work," Fiona said.

"Keeps her on her toes."

Fiona watched them. Without Monte's running revelations, she might have missed it. They didn't appear obviously improper. Not unless the idea was put into your mind. Her gaze wandered to the Ambassador and Nell, talking as they danced. Occasionally, on a turn, Nell looked toward her husband and his partner. Was it a look of curiosity or anxiety? For a moment, her eyes narrowed as she watched them, as if she were making a great effort to pierce the invisible veil in which the two seemed shrouded.

At one point in the dance, the big woman, the ex-Mrs. Langford, sailed past. She, too, seemed to be observing the Senator and his partner. When she passed him, she offered a smile. But the Senator was oblivious, his attention directed exclusively to Helga Kessel. Fiona watched her smile hold, then fade as she swung out of his line of sight.

The poor bastard is on display, Fiona thought, her sympathies suddenly with the Senator. In deference to this idea, she allowed her eyes to wander elsewhere, but only for a few moments. Senator Love drew her gaze back to him like a magnet.

II

"Hard night, FitzGerald?"

It was Cates' clipped exaggerated Bahamian British singsong pouring into her ear from the instrument that lay beside her on the pillow. She had heard its ring through the fog of sleep, a relentless assault on her attention.

She managed to squint into the red digital face of the clock perched on the antique dresser.

"Six in the a.m., you bastard," she moaned, still disoriented. "We're cops, not obstetricians."

Four hours, she calculated. That was all she had slept, a deep pass-out kind of sleep.

"We got old bones," Cates said. She wondered if he was enjoying the intrusion. She had told him she was going to this party, had expected a late night. They weren't due until three in the afternoon. All signs had pointed to a routine day, late shift. In the background she could hear the relentless cacophony of heavy rain banging against the house.

"Do me a favor, Cates. No cryptic. Not now."

Wine invariably translated into morning headaches. She imagined there would be other poundings among last night's assemblage, but inclusion did not comfort her. They simply poured too hard and she had not had the will to stop her lapping. Poor Monte's loquaciousness had been cut off abruptly at its source. After he had passed out in the back of their cab, she had had to half-cajole and half-cart him into the house, where he was now sleeping it off in the downstairs den.

"Literally old bones, Fi," Cates said, abandoning his torturous singsong, getting to the serious nub of things, his usual demeanor.

15

"Why us?" Fiona said with a sigh, feeling the sour backwash in her mouth, remembering further. She supposed that in a day or two her judgement would be that she had had fun at the Pepsi bash. Even the sudden squall that had crashed down on the party had failed to upset the festivities. Apparently the host, rather than send the guests home on the river in the hard rain, had managed to organize a giant fleet of cabs and limos to return all guests to Washington, albeit two hours later than scheduled.

All that talk about Senator Langford's sex life had been interesting, of course, although at the moment it seemed quite inconsequential to her life.

"Again the obvious. It's the eggplant's bigoted sense of demographics. The old bones are on your turf." He sucked in a deep breath and she pictured his delicate nostrils twitching, always a sign of his inherent disapproval. Like her, his Bahamian ancestry, accent and faintly mulatto skin tone assured his fish-out-of-water status in their inner-city, black, street-smart environment.

"So once again. Cates, I got to carry you on my lily-white ass."

"My fate, Fi," he whispered.

Her turf, in the eggplant's mind, was the clearly defined bounds that housed the power elite. At first she had railed against this pigeonholing, demanding equality of assignment. There was logic to it, of course, considering her background. Also resentment, although she had earned a grudging respect when she broke the hard cases.

Lifting her naked body, she sat upright on the bed, determined to gather her wits and attain some degree of professionalism. She could hear his breathing at the other end of the line.

"Where?"

"Woodland Hills. Just off Rock Creek. Yesterday they were bulldozing for a swimming pool. Apparently the rain did the rest."

The chill on her naked skin revived her somewhat.

"How much time?"

"Pick you up in ten," Cates said with a hint of a smile in his voice.

"Make it fifteen," she said.

"I'll split the difference," he said as she slammed the receiver into its carriage. She padded across the room into the shower and turned on the cold taps, screaming herself into alertness.

One thing she could say about the eggplant, he got his priorities right. A homicide happening in certain neighborhoods like Georgetown, Woodland Hills, Cleveland Park and upper Massachusetts and Connecticut Avenues to the District line—the hallowed Northwest quadrant—put the ball in her personal court. Parts of Capitol Hill were on a par and certain pockets elsewhere as well. Everyone knew exactly where. It was a class and money thing, well beyond race. In D.C. this was where, as he put it, the "powah resahded." And, as everyone knew, the "powah" must be served.

The rain had continued through the night and looked certain to be one of those long, soaking spring rains that cast a different tone of light on the city, putting everything, from the wedding-cake buildings and monuments to the people themselves, into sharper definition.

She watched the windshield wipers make little progress against the slanting rain as Cates drove through Rock Creek Park, respecting her need for silence. The normally benign creek was churning white water beside them as Cates hurried the car to the Woodland Hills area, where the wooded backyards of the western line of large homes backed up to the park.

They spotted the site by the police cars parked along the shoulder of the road and the uniforms poking around in the wet tree-studded land that dipped sharply upward toward the rears of the houses.

They got boots and slickers from the trunk of the car and, getting handholds on stubborn brush, maneuvered their way up the slope to a plateau carved out of the hillside. Yards away loomed a large house, three stories high from the rear, with a wide stone terrace edged with a gracefully winding stone balustrade. Obviously the owners planned a large pool and deck. A bulldozer stood idle at the bottom of the muddy hole that would one day be the pool.

Flannagan's technical boys were already on the job, but all that seemed called for was to bag the bones and check the area for related artifacts. Large floodlights had been set up to enhance the rain-shrouded grey light. A police photographer snapped a series of photographs showing the bones, which were still intact.

"It's all here, the skeletal remains," Flannagan said. Fiona could see them clearly visible in the strong light, which also defined the heavy rain. "Can't be sure of the sex," he said, squinting upward and winking, his usual prelude to some gross joke. "Not without skin around it."

"Or how long it's been there," Fiona muttered, ignoring his remark. She was standing at the edge of the excavation and looking downward at the skeleton. "Bag some earth around it as well," she told him.

Cates jumped from the edge of the excavation to the bulldozer then moved toward the far wall of earth where the skeleton was lodged.

The body looked to be buried at the furthest end of the lot about four feet deep, and the area around it now formed a shelf about halfway down the excavation. Apparently the men digging the hole had used shovels to unearth the full length of the skeleton after it had been uncovered by the action of the bulldozer.

"Get it to forensic," Fiona said. "At least we'll have the sex. I hope they can tell how long it's been there."

Cates, standing at the bottom of the muddy excavation, inspected the bones from stem to stern. She watched him move suddenly, his hand reaching out. Then he called up to the photographer.

"Get down here and get this," he said, rain splashing about his head. His boots were three feet deep in water and mud.

"What is it?" Fiona asked.

The police photographer, using the bulldozer as a bridge, scrambled down and, following Cates' finger, took his pictures. Then

Cates fiddled with one of the bones and with his pencil lifted an object and put it in a plastic bag. Fiona waited for his answer.

"A slave bracelet," he shouted up at her, holding the plastic bag to the light. "Name of . . ." He squinted at it. "Looks like Mabel."

Cates scampered up the bulldozer again and jumped to where Fiona was standing along the edge of the excavation. He showed her the plastic bag.

"Very narrow. Looks like gold," Fiona said, her mind finally ratcheting forward, concocting theories. Her head had cleared. She was working. All other considerations vanished.

"Nothing else visible," Cates said.

The kind of bracelet suggested a younger woman. One riddle quickly solved. She couldn't quite make out the engraving in the poor light.

The men began to bag the skeleton with great care and Fiona and Cates wandered to the terrace, where an older couple watched the proceedings. Both wore matching red flannel bathrobes, which gave the illusion that they were twins. Actually they were a married couple named Parker. He was ruddy with cherub cheeks and bushy grey eyebrows. She was a washed-out bleached blonde, and the gloomy greyish light was not kind to her wrinkles. They both looked angry, as if the messenger was somehow the cause of this dilemma.

"It does take the enthusiasm out of the project," Mrs. Parker said. Mr. Parker shook his head and sighed in agreement. He seemed to be muttering under his breath.

"How long have you been living here?" Fiona asked.

"Three years."

"Probably before your time," Fiona said, asking, "Remember who owned the house before you?"

"Matter of fact I do. Fella named Prescott. Worked for Cap Weinberger. Assistant Secretary of Defense I think he was, an early Reagan appointee."

"About 1980 then."

"Might have been second wave, maybe '83."

"And before that?" Cates asked.

"How the hell should I know? We were out of the country. I was Ambassador to Kenya. Democrat. Carter appointee." He hadn't cracked a smile. "This country's changed, I tell you. Bodies in the backyard. Got any idea who it was?"

"You know a Mabel?" Fiona asked. Parker looked at his wife, whose wrinkles seemed to have multiplied in the harsh light.

"Soft and able," Parker said with an air of disgust. "Goddamned house cost me two mil."

"Gives me the creeps now," the woman shivered. "How can I ever go into the pool now? How awful. How absolutely awful."

Fiona, who had been taking notes, snapped her notebook shut. She could see their point. She started back toward the excavation and the way they had come.

"What do we do now?" Mrs. Parker called after her.

Fiona turned.

"Build the pool," she snapped. "And call us if you find any more bodies."

III

"I hate old bones," Captain Luther Greene said.

"Ups the statistics of open cases," Fiona acknowledged.

Captain Greene, known affectionately—and often derisively—by colleagues, supporters and foes as the "eggplant," had been drumming that point home now that politics was in the air again. The Mayor, getting ready to run for a third term, needed better statistics for his law-and-order stance, much better. The crack and gang wars had escalated, driving the homicide rate through the roof and scaring the hell out of the voters.

By definition, it was homicide—violent, brutal and ugly. But, in fact, it was really urban combat, not the kind of homicide that challenged the imagination, offering a puzzle of motives and a mysterious cast of suspects. Still, every murder counted in the statistics. They were rising ominously. The Mayor wanted them cut. And he was the boss, lord of influence and promotions, career maker and breaker.

The eggplant had assigned her and Cates to rummage through some of the recent open unsolveds and a number looked very promising. He needed them to stay on that track. It was a political necessity.

The eggplant was a political animal, often too political, which partly accounted for the negative aspect of his sobriquet. Cops, in general, despised political pressures. Unfortunately, few cops could move up the ladder without understanding these realities.

The eggplant understood. In fact, despite his vanity, short temper, sarcastic arrogance and obsessive ambition, he held the respect of his co-workers since, above all, he was professionally talented and instinctive and often wise and cool under pressure.

Yet someone, long gone, had pasted the nickname on his forehead and it had stuck. It had no relationship to logic, since he wasn't lumpish like the vegetable, although at least one variety matched his color. The connotation, of course, was not altogether flattering, although at rare times it carried with it an air of genuine affection.

They were sitting in his office. Against the grey backlight of the window behind him, his body was in silhouette, his face featureless. Rain pelted the dirty windowpane.

"Any media interest?" The eggplant sighed gloomily. An avid self-publicist, he normally might have liked the idea, except that the payoff and timing just wasn't there. It was, Fiona knew, tough as hell to solve a case that appeared this old, and they did not need another open case at this point in time.

"We'll see how it plays," the eggplant said.

She knew his shorthand. He meant that if the media paid little attention, they could shove it into the background and concentrate on the more contemporary cases.

"Might even be a natural," the eggplant said hopefully. It was clear that he wished that the skeleton had never been found.

"Known to happen," Fiona said, struggling for neutrality.

"Maybe they couldn't afford burial expenses," the eggplant muttered, chuckling.

"Not in that neighborhood," Cates said.

"Never know. Big front. No cash. We live in bullshit land," the eggplant countered.

His telephone rang and he picked it up, but not all the way. The huge index finger of the hand that held the telephone shot up.

"You keep me 'apprahzed,' hear," he said, scowling. It was his traditional cautionary warning. Nothing behind my back, nothing out of channels. Keep me "apprahzed." The word literally defined the eggplant's limits.

Then he moved the instrument to his face and turned his attention to its message, waving them out as he began to speak.

There was no point in mounting any argument. The forensics weren't in yet. She had called Amy, Dr. Benton's assistant, to put in her oar for priority treatment. Although she enjoyed a strong and respectful relationship with the Medical Examiner, she was sparing in her request for special favors.

They had also sent the ankle bracelet down to the lab to be cleaned off and checked out. The fact was that, despite the eggplant's indifference, she could not choke off her mind's search for theories. A body buried in the backyard of one of the fanciest neighborhoods in town, uncovered after years. A tantalizing mystery there. A human being, a wife or mistress, someone's mother or daughter or sister, buried like rancid waste. Attention must be paid. Her mind spun with possibilities.

She knew what was happening. Always when a case intrigued her beyond the routine, ideas and speculations began to grow in her imagination. She knew, too, that each new fact would create parameters, inhibit the growth of extraneous theories, narrow down the choices.

There was something else, too. Despite the scant details, she felt a growing sense of identification with the victim. A life cast away like a piece of garbage, a brain holding a dark secret in its memory, a secret that needed burying forever. Only nothing was forever. Nothing.

Monte Pappas called her in mid-afternoon.

"I'm completely, totally, irrevocably embarrassed," he began.

"They were pouring pretty heavy," she said. "Forget it. I was half in the bag myself."

"I'm still at your place. My head feels like a rock and I've shot the day. Whites, reds and scotch. For me it's a deadly combination."

Luckily for her, although she felt slightly fatigued, the mental deflection of the case had chased any lingering hangover.

"Never mind. All is forgiven. Help yourself to anything. My tent is yours."

"I really owe you one, Fi. I was awful."

"It's okay. Don't flagellate."

She waited through a long pause.

"Bet I talked too much," he said, as if he were testing the waters, waiting for her response.

"You did talk," she chuckled. "I won't deny that."

"Did I say . . . I mean . . . anything that could be, you know . . ."

"Used against you in a court of law?" she bantered. She knew, of course, what was troubling him. He had, indeed, talked more than was discreet about Senator Langford, but in that context, he had nothing to fear from her.

"You did give me a snootful about . . ." She smiled. "Senator Love."

"Oh Jesus."

"Just between us girls."

"That name. Gives me cold shivers. Blank it out, please. And not on the phone."

She wondered if he was joking.

"Are you really concerned about my discretion, Monte?" she asked, surprised by her own reaction. His paranoia carried the cutting edge of insult.

"Fi. Fi. I don't know what I'm saying. That's a double apology I owe. Please. I have a tendency to overreact on that subject, considering its importance to me."

"I'd say you are being a bit hysterical," she said. She might not be having a hangover but she felt more testy than usual.

"Dinner Friday, Fi. It's important to me. I . . . I thought we were doing well together before this . . . nonsense."

"We'll see," she said. The fact was that she did enjoy Monte Pappas' company, his know-it-all manner and cynicism and the pretense of toughness he had adopted. Getting people elected, she had learned from experience, required a kind of dispassionate ruthlessness. In this respect, she knew, he was not a natural. Poor Monte had visible soft round edges, which was why she liked being with him.

"You're not mad?" he coaxed.

"Mad-mad maybe. But not angry-mad, no."

Her other line lit up. She put him on hold.

"I've read your bones, Fiona," Dr. Benton said. "Come on over."

"Got to go now," she said, switching back to Monte. "We'll touch base later about Friday." It was Wednesday. She hung up.

Dr. Benton was waiting in his office, his fingers held together in his classic cathedral style, an indication that he was in deep contemplation. She loved to see him in that pose, his cobalt blue eyes intense in his dark face, the genetic result of two hundred years of intermingling Cajun blood.

He was a man of rare privacy and wisdom, and on more than one occasion he had helped her cope with her own demons. He had his as well, the bitter loneliness of life without his beloved Dorothy, whose memory was his shrine.

His relationship with Fiona was profound enough for Cates, despite their partnership, to absent himself when he correctly read her need to be alone with him. This was one of those occasions.

She stood in front of his desk, waiting for him to acknowledge her. Finally, he pushed himself out of his chair and looked out of the window into the gloom of the relentless rain. His body spoke for his fatigue. Lately, there had been an endless parade of bodies.

"No more than 20," he said, still not turning. "A woman, five foot three, perhaps 110 pounds. From the rupture of the cartilage in the neck area, I suspect that she was strangled." In his verbal explanations with police officers, he deliberately eschewed highly technical terms, although his written report always used impeccably precise anatomical nomenclature.

Finally he turned to face her. The grey light could not hide his weariness.

"I think it's the rain. It depresses me. I buried Dorothy in the rain."

She had suspected the real source of his sad mood. To counter it she offered him a broad smile. He had often told her that her smile was like a dose of sunshine. He shrugged, responded with his own half-smile then moved back to his chair and put his feet on the desk.

"How long ago?" Fiona asked.

"A dozen years at least. Late seventies. Probably 1977 or '78." He shook his head. "Within a year is the best you can do."

She had hoped that the woman might have died later. More than a decade was a long time. Harder to track.

"What about race?" Fiona asked. Considering the turf, it was a proper question, but it carried baggage and implications. The majority of the open cases were black. Most of the crime in fact had a black connection, not uncommon considering the demographics. In this case the relevance was also based on neighborhood. More precisely, on what is commonly referred to as "class."

"I can tell you this," Dr. Benton said, obviously aware of the implications. "The woman was buried naked. There is absolutely not a trace of clothing anywhere among the bones. The dental work also is not very extensive and could prove difficult for establishing the body's identity. Unless, of course, you have something reasonably definite and needed a confirmation. All in all, probably a healthy young lady. This will be a tough one, Fiona."

"Tougher than you think. The Captain is indifferent."

"Priorities, Fiona. There is a traffic jam in here." Again, he made a cathedral of his fingers.

She considered again the eggplant's earlier reaction. Further pursuit depended on piquing his interest. If the case was too esoteric, with little media coverage, that would be an impossible chore, especially in today's political climate.

"Too bad." She sighed. "I was beginning to identify."

"An occupational hazard to be avoided," Dr. Benton said.

"Like you do," she said.

"Do as I say, not as I do," Dr. Benton said. He also had his lapses of objectivity. She saw his mood changing to black again.

"With each new abomination, I grow more reverential toward human life. And more hateful toward the abominators who deprive others of the experience. It always hurts to see injustice rewarded, especially through default and disinterest."

"It's not over yet," Fiona said.

"Dear Fiona. Always to the highest mountain. The bones have testified. Slim pickings for a crusade."

"Not necessarily, Dr. Benton. Whoever did it forgot something," Fiona said. As always with Dr. Benton she saved the best for last.

"No one's perfect," he sighed.

She explained about the ankle bracelet. He turned away and contemplated his cathedral, raising his eyebrows finally in what she knew was a gesture of optimism.

"When it came from a boy they used to call it a slave bracelet. I got one once from a high school boyfriend." She chuckled at the sudden shard of memory.

Then she remembered that the one found on the skeleton had been engraved with the name of Mabel, which might have implied that it was bought by the woman herself, more of an ornament than a symbol.

To truly qualify for a slave bracelet it would have had to have the mark of the boy on it like the one she had once received from her high school sweetheart. "Forever, love Larry," had been engraved on the surface worn closer to the flesh. And you wore it because it said you belonged to him, a more passionate kind of symbolism than say merely being "pinned." She snickered at the concept, then realized that her reaction was not only politically contemporary, it embarrassed her present sense of self. How dare I let anyone ever own me, she thought militantly. It took a few moments for the anger to clear. It was, nevertheless, a strong clue for identification purposes.

"The computers should be able to narrow down a missing Mabel of that age and description for those years," Dr. Benton said hopefully. "It's quite possible that justice might be served after all."

"I'll transmit your rallying cry to the eggplant," Fiona said. "This day pure justice is not his highest priority."

By the time she got back to the squad room the sense of exciting expectation that had carried her through the day had begun to ebb. Her head throbbed and she felt her mood changing rapidly.

She met the eggplant coming out the door of his office. He looked at her briefly, nodded indifferently and moved toward the corridor. It was obvious that his level of engagement about the case was nil. Nor did she have the energy to attempt to put new life into it. She'd do her duty, the minimum.

Cates lifted his head from the files he was reading and watched her as she came forward to her desk.

"He ask about it?"

"About what?"

"The bones, for crying out loud." Her level of irritability was rising. Fatigue was taking its toll.

"Not a word," he said. It was obvious, too, that his mind was busy elsewhere.

"Just another murder waiting to be solved," she said with disgust. She looked at the files on Cates' desk. "We can barely keep up as it is."

She felt her energy flagging, but mustered just enough to tell him what Dr. Benton had discovered. He listened intently, then went back to reading the files on his desk. Suddenly he lifted his head.

"The lab came back on that bracelet," he said. He pulled it out of his desk drawer, still in a plastic container, but now sparkling like new.

"Oh," she said, only mildly curious.

"We had it wrong. Must have been the light."

"Had what wrong?"

He took it out of its bag and held it between thumb and forefinger, dangling it.

"It wasn't Mabel. It read My Bet."

She held out her hand and he dropped it into her palm. She took it, felt it. It was almost weightless and very thin. She read the engraved letters.

"My Bet," she said.

"Somebody's Bet," Cates said, nodding.

A new wave of disgust rolled over her. The symbolism gnawed at her, sparking anger. Had that meant that the woman had given herself away, sold her soul?

In her business the dead often had a message for the living. She wasn't quite sure what that was, but this she knew: This girl was screaming through the dust of more than a decade, demanding her attention.

IV

Before she went home that night, she and Cates went over possible name variations for a missing-person trace, Bette, Betty, Beth, Elisabeth, Mary Beth and any similar combinations. They asked for a computer sweep for the years 1977 and 1978 and left it at that.

The next day they worked on the contemporary open cases and put My Bet on the back burner. Nor did the eggplant have anything to say on the subject. The *Washington Post* gave it a paragraph in the back of the paper adjacent to the obits. The site of the discovery was described as a backyard in Northwest Washington. The story ended with the line that "the police were investigating." Such scanty details reinforced the notion that, barring anything of real import, the case was heading into limbo.

They spent the afternoon chasing down promising leads on an unsolved case in a drug-related stabbing, picked up a prime suspect in Northeast Washington and brought him downtown. The man, who was the manager of a fast-food franchise, had been interrogated before and had been released for lack of evidence.

But timing and pressure had a way of working their synergism. The man, who at the time of the murder had managed to conceal his drug habit had, in an effort to kick his habit, signed up at a methadone center. Then he had dropped out, which indicated that he was probably back on drugs.

If the eggplant hadn't been pressing on the open cases at just that point in time, the man would have gotten away scot-free. As it was, they were able to squeeze the man through deprivation, and his confession came in record time. It encouraged the eggplant to press them to do more on these old cases, and he held a meeting in the squad room offering rare compliments for Fiona and Cates for their efforts.

31

It seemed to put the cap on his interest in the case of the old bones, as she was referring to it in her mind. Nevertheless, it continued to nag at her, overriding all her efforts to put it in perspective.

The fact was that remains, whether buried or simply cast away in remote places, were invariably young women under 21, a prime target of opportunity. A high percentage of these were sexually molested. Many were naked or seminaked, obviously subjected before their deaths to the most unbearable and painful humiliations.

As a woman, Fiona had been especially appalled by these statistics. Also, she had never become completely inured to the horrible sight of these young female corpses, their features etched forever in the death mask of horror, their unseeing eyes offering compelling evidence of their violation. Just to see them in that state was all the motivation that Fiona ever needed to pursue their murderers with all the single-minded purpose she could muster. Despite this obvious kinship, Fiona felt that a great effort of will was needed on her part to force her objectivity when confronted with such cases, mostly to show her male colleagues that the gender of sisterhood did not set off an emotional vulnerability that might diminish her in their eyes.

My Bet, although merely bones, triggered even more of this effect and required even more masking of emotion. Indeed, the features that her imagination concocted seemed more horrifying than those recorded when her eyes actually bore witness to a violated female corpse with all the flesh intact.

She had arranged to meet Monte Pappas at the Jockey Club and had dressed in the ladies room and returned to the squad room, where she found Cates on the phone. He flagged her attention and mimed "missing persons." She was already late, but she waited until Cates had completed the call.

"Like falling off the roof," Cates said. "Actually a half-dozen female Bet possibilities, but one that fills the bill head-on." He read from a pad. "Betty Taylor, age 20, white, five-four, 110 pounds, grey eyes, raven hair." He shook his head and looked up and said: "Coming alive. Like watching a developing Polaroid shot." He continued. "Call reporting her missing came in from her mother, an Emma Taylor in Fredericksburg. Virginia. No trace. Gone with the wind."

"Not the wind, Cates," she said shaking her head.

"I got the mother's name and address." He shrugged and smiled. "Sometimes it's easy."

"Not often enough," she said.

He looked at her and smiled. "Heavy date?"

"More ways than one," she said.

As she turned, the eggplant was coming out of his office.

"Lookin' good, FitzGerald." He winked. He was always in a better mood on Fridays. He had spread the word among the division that his weekends were sacrosanct. If he had to be summoned, one had to be prepared to face the consequences.

"Thanks, Chief."

With him, Fiona knew, a compliment was as scarce as a snowstorm in July. In fact, he rarely complimented anyone on their appearance, especially females. For some reason, she decided to take advantage of his upbeat mood.

"We think we have a fix on our old bones," she said, glancing quickly at Cates, looking for support. She found none. He had turned away.

"Must we, FitzGerald?" the eggplant said, shaking his head. The sunny weather in his expression changed abruptly.

"Won't hurt to check it out," she said, trying to head off any impending storm.

"But it will, you see. It will hurt time. Time is more precious than riches. In this place, time is our most important commodity." He was starting to launch one of his sarcastic tirades, gaining momentum. "We have lots of recent travesties against women that need solving. There are more than enough modern-day killers to keep us busy. In fact, we need an army just to keep up with the traffic."

He was right, of course. But agreement would get her nowhere. "There's a lot of cache in solving an old crime. Shows we're on the ball." "Shows who?" the eggplant said with contempt.

"Him?" She moved her head in the general direction of the Mayor's office.

"He, too, has his head in the immediate present. Therefore . . ." He paused and focused a penetrating gaze on her face. ". . . Do you capish?"

"I understand Spanish, Captain."

"Funny lady."

What she understood, of course, was that the Mayor had given him his marching orders and he was marching. She could hear the crack of the Mayor's bark. "I win. You win, Luther." Winning for Luther was becoming Police Commissioner in the next administration. Inwardly, he may have railed against such manipulation and kowtowing, but he surely understood what running after such a carrot meant. So did Fiona. The idea of being thwarted could make him very mean.

"Who would know better about such matters, FitzGerald. You, a Senator's daughter."

Whenever he needed to batter her with stinging ridicule, he would pull that from his quiver of sarcasms. As always, it struck her deep and hard.

"Are you saying we shouldn't pursue this?" she said, the challenge in her voice clear.

"Did I say that?" The anger in the retort was meant to be intimidating. She realized suddenly that she had, indeed, picked the wrong time. Most of all, he seemed to resent her for forcing a change in his mood. All goodwill in his earlier expression had clapped shut and he stormed out of the squad room.

"Go ahead," she told the slammed door. "Doodoo on integrity."

"Let go, Fi. Poor bastard is between a rock and a hard place."

She waited until her anger subsided, then she motioned with her chin to the pad that lay on the desk in front of Cates. "Poor Betty Taylor might have some comments on that old chestnut."

V

Naturally Monte had arranged a good table in the front room of the Jockey Club. Martine, the headwaiter, fussed and fawned and Monte did a round robin of handshakes to those among the privileged and influential seated at nearby tables.

"Politics is perception," he said, smiling, satisfied that his restaurant clout and performance had impressed her. His mood was ebullient, jovial, a far cry from the whining cynicism of the other night. Yet he made it clear in his attitude and demeanor that it was all part of the game not to be taken seriously and certainly not to be confused with the real Monte Pappas.

She ordered a vodka martini. He raised two shaggy eyebrows and cocked his head, then doubled the order.

"Nevertheless," he said, "I've placed severe limitations on the intake. Tonight, I'm determined to get high only on the company."

The martinis came and they clinked glasses. She took a deep sip, hoping to let go of the anger that still clawed at her.

"And how was your day, honey?" he asked.

"You noticed?"

"Is the Pope Catholic?"

"I shouldn't take it home," she said. "I should be dispassionate. It's not professional."

"Passion is good," he chuckled. "At the proper time." The double entendre rode through the air like a Mack truck. He was so transparent, it was almost refreshing. Also boyish and unsure. He reminded her of a small, cuddly bear, all soft and furry. Yet his seduction attempt seemed more focused than the other night. Then he had been sidetracked by other concerns. Now he appeared eager

35

and obvious, although the objective was probably less of a priority than he allowed himself to believe.

She knew the type well from her days observing her father's political groupies. Politics was all, an addictive obsession, and the heat of the campaign was the orgasmic nadir of their lives. Even the winning or losing was secondary to the action of it, the involvement, the emotional roller coaster that struggled up the track to elation and bottomed out in depression. Up and down. Down and up. She was not surprised that he was divorced. Such men, or women, feared any relationship that inhibited their addiction. Often, perhaps more often than others, they needed the solace and validation of a truly human experience. Although never permanent, their relationships were, nevertheless, intense and sincere within their parameters of compressed time and tenuous involvement.

Perhaps that was why she was comfortable with Monte Pappas. She understood him. He was a classic specimen of the genre. Watching him across the table, his soft brown eyes observing her, his smile flashing out all the charm he could muster, his soft, slightly chubby fingers with their scraggly spines of black hairs nervously strumming the checkered tablecloth, she decided that, barring an unforeseen turnoff, she would sleep with him tonight.

"Things must be going well," she said, determined to erase the tension of her confrontation with the eggplant. Nothing must interfere with the broadcasting of her intentions. Although she knew what buttons to press for the political side of him, she had heard that Greek men were very complicated and acted only when they were absolutely certain that they would not be rebuffed. This required, she assumed, sending clear signals of consent, yet allowing him to feel that he was making a conquest.

"You betcha," he said, looking about him at the others in the small front room. He bent closer to her and lowered his voice. "We got him to kick it."

"Kick it?" She was confused.

"The habit," he whispered. She continued to be puzzled, definite-ly not getting his shorthand. His nostrils flared as he sucked in a deep breath. "The habit," he repeated. "He's mothballing the torpedo."

The image was strongly suggestive, considering where her own thoughts had headed, and it triggered her understanding.

"The Senator?" she asked. He quickly put a finger on his lips and shook his head. Only then did he nod and smile his confirmation.

She remembered his running commentary on the escapades of Sam Langford. Also, the subtle erotic manner in which he had danced with the beautiful Helga. And, if the truth be known, with herself.

"And just how did you accomplish his acceptance of this extraor-dinary feat of self-denial?"

She quickly fell into the pattern of shorthand that they had adopt-ed to protect the conversation from the ears of the adjacent diners. Paranoia was a rampant Washington disease, and an overheard con-versation, especially this one, had enormous currency.

"Read him the riot act." He lowered his voice still further and she had to strain to hear him. "I told him. Take heavy doses of saltpeter. Concentrate on one aberration at a time. Make love to the TV cam-era. He's a master of that as well. You just can't play in this game with your fly open. He has everything going for him. Good looks. Articulate as hell. Good-looking family. A great record. Dead-center on most issues. No rocka da boat. The election committee is being formed. The do-re-me is on its way. If we go, he has the whole pri-mary thing ahead of him and the press will go over his life with a hundred-power telescope. Like the honeybadger, first thing they go for is the crotch." He chuckled at his humor and took another sip of his martini.

"But can he hide his past completely?" Fiona asked, remembering her father's media wars.

"No. But he's been pretty cagey. And he's had old Bunkie to camouflage his peccadillos and 'Dear John' them when things got sticky."

The idea, perhaps the cavalier way in which he described it, offended her.

"And they all go quietly, I suppose."

"Let's say not disruptively. They haven't made waves, which means he's been lucky enough to escape the wrath of female outrage." He shrugged. "Maybe they figured they got their money's worth. On the other hand some of them might have gained a leg up to that elusive place where they were headed. That ring around the finger is not the only prize available in the pantheon. In this town women gain clout if they have a powerful scalp on their belt. Starfucking is a Washington sport with a paramutual payoff. There are lots of subtle ways to reward sexual cooperation. Sometimes even the act itself is reward enough. The fact is that, despite what you've read about exceptions, the general rule is that disengagement occurs more often than not."

She felt mildly offended by his observations, not because they were inaccurate. More because they contained some raw truths about the vulnerability of her gender peers.

"Don't dismiss the exceptions so easily, Monte. For five minutes of fame and some serious bucks, women have been known to succumb. Shall I tick off the careers that have been ruined by some who have not gone quietly?" They had become household names with remarkable staying power—Elizabeth Ray, Fannie Fox, Paula Parkinson, Donna Rice.

"Are you trying to ruin my evening?" he said, half joking. She could detect the tiniest evidence of anxiety.

"Not at all. I just wanted to scrape some of the smugness away. Women, I have observed in my work, can be quite vindictive. When they murder, for example, the victim is invariably a husband or lover."

She was teasing him with the truth and it appeared to be more than he bargained for. Worse, she worried that it would make him fear her, which, she knew from experience, could be devastating to his libido.

She reached out and patted his chubby hand. It felt soft and warm and comfortable.

"I'm not saying you didn't have it right. Just offering my own knee-jerk defense. The fact is that none of us can be sure about the motives of other human beings, male or female."

"You sound like a politician. Coming down on both sides of the issue." He chuckled and caressed her hand. She hoped that her warm flesh showed him the first happy signs of compliance.

"Anyway," he said, "we think we've got that part of it on hold." He pursed his lips as if repressing a sly giggle. "I can assure you, Fi, the double entendres are not intentional."

"Just good old-fashioned dirty talk," she said, squeezing his hand, "never killed anybody." Their eyes locked for a moment. Deliberately, she disengaged first, hoping he would see it as shyness, and restore his sense of aggression. Not yet, she cautioned herself.

"So the beautiful Helga has been dispatched," she said. Her voice had risen and she put a hand over her mouth. He looked about him to see if she had attracted any attention. It appeared not. "Sorry."

"Let's say the process has been initiated."

"And who does the doing?"

"Ve haf our methods," he mocked.

"Not the man himself?"

"We thought it unwise. He understands." He bent closer. "Besides, she has her own problem."

"The Ambassador?"

"He likes his job. Perhaps he has overlooked the affair deliberately to, copping another pun, save his own ass."

"She'll go quietly?"

"For her there is no choice."

"But what of love?" Fiona asked. Despite the sarcasm, she knew her question had the bite of truth. Love has been known to be a stimulator of bizarre and often counterproductive actions.

"Show me a single instance of a politician who gave up his ambition for love. I have observed that political ambition is always more
powerful than love. My theory has always been that if King Edward
the Seventh had real power he would never have given up his throne
for his ladylove."

"You have no romance in your soul," Fiona whispered. He raised
soft brown, imploring eyes.

"I'm only an advisor. My soul stays with me. Romance and all."

He signaled the waiter, who offered his ceremony of the specials,
which they declined. Then he took their order, a salad for starters
and grilled soles for both of them. They ordered a French white.

"Crazy, isn't it," he said when the waiter had gone, "that this issue
should transcend all the others."

She sipped further on her martini. "What were the grounds of his
divorce?" He did not take offense at her curiosity. Nor did she think
the question was out of order. He trusted her and needed to tell, and
she was, after all, a detective.

"Not too bad, actually. They just agreed to disentangle. You saw
her. They're not buddies, but they exchange pleasantries. Besides, he
was very generous and they had no kids. The woman understood.
Sam spreads it around. That's Sam. Accept it or get the hell out. She
chose the latter. He was single for a whole year before he met Little
Nell. Which means you could never accuse her of being the vixen
who broke up his first marriage. That's very important. Besides,
she's almost boringly traditional. Country club, white bread-and-
mayonnaise type."

"I saw a troubled lady."

"Very perceptive. Wouldn't you be, married to him? But Little
Nell gets high marks for dissimulation. She seems to go more for
appearances. Keeps her own counsel. That's the mark of a good political wife."

"She's also human."

"And being so, she knows the value of a long leash. Probably more upset by others seeing Sam playing pelvis touchee with the beautiful Helga. That's appearances, a different mad than jealousy. But she also knows that he has to keep it in the barn if he wants to be President. The fact is that, for now, at least, she's won. No more sharing for a while. Until he's President. Then he's got a whole army of Secret Service men to cover his ass. Like Jack Kennedy. He did more exercise of the venery in office than out."

"You say he was single for a year. Has to be media grist in that."

He looked at her and shook his head.

"The affairs of a single man are not the stuff of scandal-mongering. Sam's drive in that regard actually subsided. They tell me that the lack of danger inhibits the intensity of the activity." He nodded and upended his glass.

"That judgement, I assume, is based on personal experience," she said. Her own as well, she thought. It had to do, she had concluded, with time-frame and anxiety level. She had, after all, had experiences with married men, an unwise exercise at best, although the emotional and sexual intensity had been extraordinary.

There had been a touch of humorous sarcasm in the remark, but he responded with dead seriousness.

"Has to do with comfort level, Fi. Even in a bad marriage there is some security. Which leaves you the luxury of concentrating more on the other." A sudden faint blush dappled his dark skin. "A single person needs more than just . . ." His voice trailed off and he picked up his martini and finished it, avoiding her gaze. He had revealed the full extent of his vulnerability and at that moment it appealed to her. When he had put down his glass, she edged her leg closer to him, felt it touch along the side of the shinbone. He responded with his own pressure. Message sent. Reply received.

The waiter brought their salads and for a few moments they ate in silence. With the evening's agenda agreed to, they could both relax.

"I'm not saying it will be easy," he said, as if there had been no break in the conversation. He had never left his sphere of interest.

Par for the genre, Fiona knew. A manifestation of the addiction. Everything personal was also political.

"But I think we can mount a campaign with real legs. It's a long haul. The election is two years away, but you've got to start the ball rolling. He's a natural, don't you think? Hell, you know this business, Fi. Is that man not the perfect candidate?"

"I have only one question, Monte."

"What's that?"

"What does he stand for?"

"That's simple," Monte said, picking at his salad, his leg rubbing against hers. "He stands for getting elected." She could feel his eyes studying her.

"And if he does get elected what will he stand for?"

"Getting reelected," Monte said without hesitation.

"And after? There are only two terms."

"In the last two years of his last term, he will stand for assuring his place in history. He will graduate from politician to statesman."

It did not offend her. She had expected the answers. It was no different in her father's time. Except that he had finally risen above it, chosen crucifixion and martyrdom to political expediency, thrown in his lot with the anti-Vietnam war movement at the worst possible political time. It had defeated him as a politician, but he had regained himself as a man, although he had, despite the doctor's report, died of a broken heart. She had been quite young, but old enough to understand, and it had validated her respect for him, and his memory continued to enrich her life and give her the assurances she needed to fight her own daily battle for moral rectitude.

The waiter brought their sole, which was soft and tasty, and they washed it down with cold white wine. Throughout the dinner they continued to caress lower extremities.

It was only later, after he had followed her home in his car and they had made love in her wide queen-size bed and she had discovered that he was, indeed, soft and furry all over and quite cuddly, effective and endearing as a lover, that she broached the question that had probably nagged at her all evening.

"Why aren't you outraged?"

"About what?" he asked.

"About selling a straw man to the public for President."

"That's the best kind. No baggage. We can fill him with the right kind of straw. Make him salable. Package him to attract the widest possible segments. The campaign is won on simplistic symbol-mongering and television-picture opportunities."

"But what does that say about us? I shake my head in understanding. Not outrage, understanding. Are we such jaded, cynical and corrupt people that we acquiesce and go along? Know it's wrong, but go along?"

She wrapped her arms around him and fingered her way across his wide expanse of hairy softness. As she had suspected, he felt comfortable, warm, his body a kind of metaphor for generosity. She felt comfortable and secure and she could barely summon up a sliver of outrage.

"We're part of it," she whispered.

"Part of what?"

"The corruption," she sighed. "Of misplaced priorities and injustice."

"All that?" he muttered.

"I can't let it go," she said. "Those old bones were once a person. And that person has as much right to justice as anyone."

"You lost me," he whispered.

She was silent for a while, wondering if he was awaiting further comment or just drifting off into sleep. She said nothing, feeling the first faint signs of the return of her outrage. Then she heard his light snore of deep slumber.

VI

The gently rolling green hills of the Virginia countryside were capped with mist as the rain continued to fall, steady and relentless. She felt no sense of gloom nor did she long for the sun. It was, after all, a spring rain carrying with it the hopeful promise of fecundity and flowers.

Driving alone had never seemed therapeutic. But it did today. The grey mistiness gave her a sense of sweet isolation, as if she were gliding through a bank of soft clouds. She allowed the car more speed than was legal, finding comfort in the smooth movement and the reassuring sights of the swiftly passing dark green fields, the sturdy houses nestled in their stands of shade trees and the shiny hides of huddling cows.

She had acted out of compulsion, a reaction to the frustration of her expectations. It had been one of those deliciously languorous awakenings, a menu of tiny preludes, the extended hugging and cuddling foreplay induced by rainy days and the prospect of hours of exquisite leisure.

Their erotic needs satiated, she went downstairs to make one of those after-play Hollywood breakfasts, bubbling bull's-eye eggs and bacon, toasted bagels, assorted cheeses and coffee. She brought in the plastic-wrapped *Washington Post* and *New York Times* and set the table in the breakfast alcove with the yellow patterned dishes that her mother always used for special breakfasts.

Her inheritance of the family house had seemed a headache at first, and she had rented it out for two years after their deaths. Mother had followed father by little more than a year, a kind of poetic justice. All her mother's life she had stuck by the Senator, had followed, albeit kicking and screaming but, in the end, obediently.

45

Now the house had become her anchor, an oasis, a validation of her roots, an envelope of memories. An only child, she had treated the house as a sibling, a fact that had not occurred to her until she had lived away from it for a while.

It was not without its ghosts, defined not as white-sheeted visitors from the spirit world, but invisible puppet strings of parental attachment that were irrevocably stapled to her, to be tugged at and manipulated as the occasion arose.

Often, in the throes of some sexual acrobatics, she would find herself rationalizing the act, even as it were occurring, to counter her mother's disapproval. A practicing Catholic who reveled in verbalizing a catalogue of sinful don'ts, her mother in afterlife seemed far more tolerating than forbidding, although Fiona was not indifferent to the pull of the strings. By explaining these perceived sins to her mother, Fiona felt that she somehow had mitigated part of the guilt.

Indeed, just moments before she had begun this breakfast preparation, she had explained to her why she was on her hands and knees on the edge of the bed being done by this man resembling a bear, rearing and roaring on hind legs.

"It's only fancy fucking, Mom. Doesn't He want us to go to the limits of our potential, soul and body?" Surely she understood the soul part.

She had smiled to herself, just as she did in the recollection, and had looked out through the kitchen window. The rain had dyed the lawn and trees a dark green and the grey sky was seamless. The table set, she turned back to the burners on the wooden work island. On the far side of the kitchen was a butcher block counter on which was a telephone. A button was lit. He was making a call. The light disappeared quickly and he was downstairs fully dressed.

"I can't stay," he had told her, distracted.

"Problems?"

"Afraid so," he grunted. His gaze had taken in the table setting, the bubbling eggs, the toasting bagels. She moved toward him and kissed the bouquet of black curly hair in the V of his unbuttoned shirt.

"It's the weekend," she said foolishly, echoing a hundred complaints from other weekends when she had been the spoiler and others were on the receiving end.

"There are no weekends in politics," he had sighed, another recycling of her excuses. Duty decrees. She knew the drill.

He was transformed, no longer the horny bear. His mind was elsewhere, wrestling with the problem that had intruded.

"You shouldn't have called," she had rebuked, watching him wolf down her carefully prepared breakfast with little relish.

"Hell," he said. "I bought us the night."

He had finished his coffee standing, then put the cup on the table. For a moment, it crossed her mind that he might be one of those people who, once satiated and empty of desire, needed to rush away from the scene of their sexual enterprise. She had encountered men like that on occasion and had had episodes of such emotions herself.

"Hope your day is awful," she had called after him. He had wrapped her in his bear hug and they had lingered for a long moment. No, she had decided, he truly wanted to stay and she could feel the tension calling him away.

When he'd gone, she had stared at the table until her eggs had grown too cold to eat. Nor could she concentrate on the newspapers. She truly deserved this day of leisure, loving and release. She had reserved it in her mind. Indeed, last night and throughout the early morning, her body had seemed to demand it and acted accordingly, allowing her a feast of orgasms. Still, she knew that her appetite craved more. From self-pity, it was a tiny step to injustice.

From there it was a circuitous but logical path to arrive at the injustices that had to do with the circumstances surrounding the investigation of the old bones of the young girl.

It helped for her thoughts to sail back to this gritty reality of shop talk. For a detective, the puzzle was always in play in the subconscious. Little effort was required to bring it back to the surface and it came roaring back with all the force of the repressed anger that the eggplant's attitude had spawned. His priorities were misplaced. Time was not the issue.

It was, she decided, unjust to ignore the girl's remains and all that they implied. It was a travesty, an outrage. It deserved more than short shrift. It demanded her attention.

"It's my own time," she had said aloud, as if the eggplant was standing at her shoulder.

She fished a name out of her notebook, Emma Taylor, Fredericksburg, Virginia. It took a half-hour to find the right Taylor, mother of Betty. The long silence after the question told her the truth of it. Had she been too callous in the asking? she wondered.

"Did you have a daughter named Betty?" was the way she phrased it. It was too late to recall the tone.

"Ah *have* a daughter named Betty," the woman said, in a soft, polite, deep Virginia twang, yet offering a dash of indignance to mask the sudden pain of it. Fiona noted the not-so-subtle change of past to present tense.

Fiona identified herself, then tried to soften the blow somewhat, although she knew it was too late.

"We have some new facts . . ." she began, then waited, listening to the woman's breathing at the other end of the line. She imagined she could hear her pumping heart.

"Ah'll nevah undastand wah she just upped and disappeared into thin ayah."

The voice and inflection suggested the usual southern clichés. All the predictable images surfaced of a small-town woman holding onto appearances at all costs, playing for approval of the local ladies from the bridge club.

"You heard from Betta?" the woman asked suddenly, hope ascending in her voice.

"Not exactly," Fiona said, lying.

"Ah'd appreciate ya tellin me if ya do," the woman said politely. There was a long pause. "Ah'll nevah undastand," she sighed. "Somethin up thayah in Washinton jes turned her head in the wrong direction."

"I'd like to come out and see you, Mrs. Taylor," Fiona said.

"Ah would welcome that," the woman said. "Deed ah would." Another pause. "Not a day goes bah when ah don hope."

There was no point in a direct response. Instead Fiona got directions and hung up. She lingered for a long moment. Perhaps it had not been a good idea, after all. And yet something in the woman's voice, the inflection, not the words, troubled her. It was a trade-off, she decided. She detested playing the messenger of death. The fact that she would do so off-duty and unpartnered made it even more offensive. It was also too late for that. Her curiosity was too aroused to turn back. For a detective such an attitude was like raw meat thrown to a starving lion.

She rolled the car through a long curving exit from the main highway and found herself on the outskirts of Fredericksburg, a fair-sized town, yet light-years away from the Washington metropolis. Following the precise directions the woman had given her, she traversed the main arteries of the town and drove through what passed for suburbs, noting large houses surrounded by big lawns.

She had no preconceived notions of the kind of place in which Mrs. Taylor lived. No hint was given, except that the neighborhood where Betty's remains had been found had been very upscale, which suggested that she might have been used to such an environment. But that theory quickly dissolved. The neighborhood in which Fiona finally arrived was a sleepy southern ghetto, neat, look-alike small houses, each fronted by a miniscule patch of lawn.

No way of telling race, Dr. Benton had told her, as she pressed the old-fashioned door bell and listened to the now unfamiliar ring. A light-skinned Negress came to the door, tall, dignified and stately. Her voice was instantly recognizable.

"Miz FitzGeral," Mrs. Taylor said, leading her through a small hallway to a neat, well-cared-for living room. The houses of black people were familiar to Fiona, and, aside from the tension of her mission, she did not feel uncomfortable or out of place.

"Ah've made some coffee," Mrs. Taylor said. She was gone a moment, returning with two cups, a pot of coffee and a plate of chocolate-chip cookies. Because she moved with such self-absorbed intensity, Fiona was able to observe her without fear of being considered impolite. The woman's complexion was golden and seemed to glow from within. Not a wrinkle disturbed the symmetry. Chronologically she would be nearing 50, but there was no way of telling from her features. Her well-proportioned figure had thickened, but it was clear that in her youth she had been a knockout.

Mrs. Taylor poured the coffee with a sense of solemnity in the ritual and handed it to Fiona with a thin smile. Her eyes, Fiona noted now, were a startling bluish grey like her own, her greying hair naturally wavy. Only a somewhat larger flair to the nostril testified to the Negroid genetic share. It was then that Fiona had realized why she had made the mistake of picturing Mrs. Taylor differently. Her voice and inflection revealed only the slightest clue to her blackness. Outside of this environment she might have easily passed for white, but it was quite clear which side she had chosen, and she was obviously proud of her choice.

As she sipped the coffee, Fiona's gaze swept the room, arrested finally by the obvious. Betty Taylor's picture in full color. Undoubtedly a clone of her mother in her youth, a grey-eyed, golden beauty. She noted that the flare in the nostrils was less pronounced. Except for its environment, the woman in the photo might have had a great deal of trouble passing for black.

"That's Betta," Mrs. Taylor said. From where she sat she could reach the picture. She took the frame, studied the picture for a moment, then held it up for Fiona to get a closer look, although she would not release it from her own hands.

"She certainly was a beauty," Fiona said, once again regretting the tense. But a picture of the old bones had flashed in her mind. It was all she could do to keep her tears from coming.

"A dozen yeahs now," Mrs. Taylor said. "Mah husban's gone now. Owah son is up in New Yoke. A lawyah." She looked at the picture. "Betta was always a rebel. We had no choice but to let huh go to Washinton. To huh that was the big city." Her gaze drifted toward the window. "Ah knew she was too pretty to go so young. Much too pretty. Sometimes that is a cross to bear, Miz FitzGeral." Fiona's eyes, tearing now, drifted toward the window which revealed nothing but a seamless grey slab. Finally, under control again, she turned back to Mrs. Taylor. "But even a pretty bird must flah on her own. There was no way to keep huh in a cage. There was no stoppin huh."

Fiona saw the onslaught of memories invading the woman, reviving the pain of the old grief. Fiona had been through similar situations many times before. It had never been easy and only a great effort of will kept her emotions in check. Her experience had also taught her that the woman was deliberately postponing the inevitable revelation on the theory that any new information would be the awful truth.

It was, in a way, a *danse macabre,* a kind of game. Postponing the revelation also gave Fiona an opportunity to learn more before the curtain came down irrevocably.

"What did she do there? In Washington?" Fiona asked.

Mrs. Taylor, cooperating in the silent conspiracy, nodded, continuing.

"Worked for this committee in the Congress of the United States. Loved huh job. She wrote often. Called once a week. And then . . ." Mrs. Taylor's grey-blue eyes misted, but she was a woman who obviously considered control a virtue and she quickly recovered. "Later we blamed ourselves foh the estrangement between Betta and mah late husban and myself."

There was a long pause through which Fiona remained silent. She was certain that the woman sensed her daughter's death, had sensed it for years. Still she held back her own question. Now she was remembering, holding back the flood of emotion, like the Dutch boy with his finger in the dike. Fiona knew she would be more forthcoming in this state than later, when the dike burst.

"Somethin changed. She wouldn't tell us much. Even when she came home on holidays she told us nuthin about her life except that she still had the same job and she was happy. But we both knew, mah husban and I, that somethin had changed. Parents know their children. Wasn't that she was morose or unhappy. Not moody. She was quieter, like she feared sayin much to us. Betta always confahded. That was what made us think that somethin was being hidden from us. Oh we asked if she had any boyfriends. Mah husban worried more about that than anythin. She just smahled over that one, but she told us nothin and treated us as if we didn't have a raht to ask." She paused, shook her head then looked away and stared into space. "So we went up thayah to see for owah selves." The woman paused and cleared her throat. Then she saw that Fiona's cup was empty.

"May ah offer you moh?" she asked. Fiona declined, worried that the interruption might inhibit the woman's story. It didn't.

"We came up thayah without tellin Betta. It was a Sunday, ah remembah. We had her address. She told us she was livin with some girls in an apahtment on Capitol Hill." She shook her head. "We didn't expect to fahnd what we did. She was livin in one of them townhouses that had been converted to apahtments. She was sure surprahzed to see us. Not too happy, I can tell you. In fact, she was downraht mad, accusin us of spahin on her. The surprahz was owas, I can assure you. We saw no sahns of girlfriends and the place looked more expensive than she could afford. We had words and it was apparent that Betta wanted us to leave and we did." She shrugged and was silent, forcing Fiona to prod her.

"What did you and your husband think?"

"We may be small-town folks, but we are not uneducated and naive." She drew herself up stiffly in the chair. "Somebodah was helpin her pay for that."

"Did you confront her with that accusation?"

"We did. She told us to mahn our own business. Oh, she had become arrogant. While we wuh thayah she got a phone call and we heard words between huh and whoever it was. They're jes leavin, she told the person. And we had the impression that the person on the othah end was none too happy with the revahlation that Betta's parents had come to visit."

"Did you have any idea who that might be?"

She shook her head.

"Any intuitive ideas?"

Mrs. Taylor shot her a look of sudden disdain.

"We had ahdees." She was obviously having difficulty fighting off her reluctance.

"Like what?" Fiona pressed, but gently.

"She was involved with a waht man."

The woman said it flatly, but the accusatory passion was unmistakable. This, to Mrs. Taylor, was the real sin of the situation. Fiona knew that she would not explain this further. It was simply a fact of her existence. Born on the edge, she had made her choice and that choice was irrevocable for her and her progeny to the end of time.

"You had evidence of this?"

"None but what we knew to be true in owah hahts."

Fiona detested that kind of decree of truth without proof. Intuition was merely speculation. Many an injustice had been perpetrated by such self-induced fantasies. A hunch was not necessarily truth, although it was sometimes true. This was, however, not the time to debate the issue.

"Did you confront her with this?" Fiona asked.

"Mah husban was a man of deep prahd. He felt that Betta had betrayed owah trust in her. We just stohmed outta thayah. Ah do admit ah was also very upset."

"What happened after that?"

"Mah husban determined not to have nothin to do with her. You have to undahstan. She was his little girl, the apple of his ah, and she had betrayed him. We had no illusions. She was involved with a waht man. Bein kept by him in a stahl that she could not afford. She was his mistress." Her lips curled in disgust. "This was not the way she was brought up." She was, it was obvious, having difficulty mustering the heat of the old indignation, but she tried gamely to keep the pose for appearance's sake. Only her sad grey-blue eyes broadcast her defeat.

"You didn't try to contact her?" Fiona asked. She could tell that Mrs. Taylor was coming to the end of the line, unable to keep the illusion of postponement going for much longer.

"Mah husban fohbid it."

"Did Betty try to contact you?"

Her lips trembled. She was having increasing difficulty keeping herself under control.

"She did trah. But . . ." The woman swallowed and turned away. From the movement of her back Fiona could see she was taking deep breaths, determined not to fall apart. When she spoke, her voice was raspy. "Unda any circumstances, a lack of communication is nevah the raht course." The rebuke was meant for herself. "Add that to prahd and you have a disasta. Aftah a few weeks of trahin, and confrontin owah rejection, she gave up."

"But you did report her as missing?"

"Mah husban had a heart attack and died soon aftah. She had a raht to know that." The dike finally burst and tears ran over the rims of her eyes, down her cheeks. She used a napkin to blot them.

"Where did you think she went?"

"As far away from us as possible," she whispered, again managing control. "The police speculated that she had just run off. Her clothes were gone. She had not shown up to work. People called from the committee and such wonderin weah she was, but that stopped soon enough. The police said it frequently happens to a young girl in the big city. She'd be back, they told me."

The light had changed in the room. Shadows were deepening, but Mrs. Taylor made no move to put on the lights. In the darkness, there was no mistaking her race. She was a woman who knew who she was, who clearly understood her racial predicament. Fiona waited through the long silence, but it was apparent that nothing more was to be offered before the burning question was answered.

"Weah is mah baby?" Mrs. Taylor asked.

"I think she's dead," Fiona said, not meaning to offer hope. "I'll need the name of her dentist."

She heard air expelled, as if it were a scream whose fury could not find any way of exiting the woman. She could see the balled fists and whitening knuckles and imagined the pain of her long night of guilt, which up to then had been merely a prelude.

VII

She avoided the inevitable confrontation for most of the day, spending her time in the office continuing to go over the open cases, searching for overlooked leads. But her mind was elsewhere. Mrs. Taylor had unnerved her.

Earlier she had phoned in the name of Betty Taylor's dentist to Dr. Benton's office. Just procedure, she knew, feeling certain that the dental records would confirm Betty's identity. But considering the obstacle of the eggplant, she wanted the identification to be impeccable. In his present mood, he would challenge her on every tiny detail.

She also called down to a friend in records who brought up on the computer the details of the investigation. Wasn't much. They had treated it routinely, assuming that the woman had run out on her job and went off to find a new life somewhere else, a common occurrence among young people.

She looked toward the eggplant's office. He was berating one of his men, tongue-whipping him.

"Man wants his numbers," Cates said.

"Law and order. The old bugaboo," Fiona muttered. "Mayor's got a point, though. Better numbers in homicide will make him look good. Show the voters, especially the blacks who bear the brunt of it, that he's tough on crime. Not to mention that it's good money-raising fodder for the whites who think one day the black menace will invade their protected little compounds, guns blazing."

"Money and votes." Cates sighed.

"You're learning, pal."

Again she looked toward the eggplant's office. She felt Cates watching her.

"I wouldn't," Cates warned, as if reading her mind. She had told him of her visit to Mrs. Taylor. "Today is Monday."

It was an anomaly. The eggplant looked forward to his weekends, then returned on Monday, more often than not, gloomy and depressed. His barometric pressure seemed directly related to how his wife, Loreen, had treated him.

A pushy, domineering woman with antecedents that had deep roots in old black money and influence in the community, Loreen made no bones about disapproving her husband's present status and was forever prodding him to be more aggressive in his pursuit of the police commissionership.

Since this was ultimately the decision of the Mayor, his reelection was crucial to the eggplant and his wife's ambition. Hence the tension. Boosting the homocide statistics had serious personal as well as political connotations for Luther Greene.

"The press ignored it. No big deal. We've got it on the books. It's not that we're covering up a crime," Cates reasoned.

"It needs work and, therefore, approval from our Lord and Master," Fiona countered.

"So do these." he said, holding up the files.

She looked at Cates and shook her head.

"You're getting to be a real kiss-ass, Cates," she told him. An idea was emerging in her mind, a plan.

"Considering the manpower, he has a point about the more recent cases," Cates said. "Murderers are walking around. The streets are running with blood." He chuckled.

"This one's been walking around for twelve years."

"Why so personal on this?" Cates asked, obviously puzzled.

"Good question." She had been asking it herself. She thought about it a moment, then felt the compulsion to articulate something.

"She was expendable and she was dumped," Fiona said. "Could be I'm offended by the constant drumbeat of female abuse. Maybe

I'm relating too much. I know it's a problem. But I don't want to stop myself."

"Some things are out of your hands, Fi," Cates said seriously. She knew he had no stomach for admonishing her, perhaps afraid he might set off some Irish fireworks. All right, she was, as her father would say, headstrong. Tame it, he had warned. She was working on it, she promised him again and again.

"There's still a right and wrong," she said, watching his face. "Could be that someone who thought she was white found out she was really black and got very pissed off. As a black man doesn't that fry your guts, Cates?"

She knew it didn't, which was a problem for Cates. The fact was that he did not have the inner sensibility of the oppressed black. He had been born in Trinidad and had arrived in America as a teenager. By then, he had a fixed view of himself in relation to the white world, determined that he was an educated equal responsible for his own destiny, and let it go at that. For this reason, he was, along with her, a white woman, considered an outsider by his colleagues. She was merely reminding him of their alienation.

"Murder is beyond race, gender or nationality," he said, deliberately offering the warmed-over cliché. She got the point.

"All right, then," she said, springing the trap. "What about simple partner loyalty. Are you going to let me go in there by myself?"

He averted his eyes and she could see a nerve palpitating in his jaw. Without looking at her he shook his head. A minute later they were sitting in the eggplant's office.

Since she had been thinking about it all day, she was able to encapsulate the information before the eggplant could raise a full head of angry steam. He lit a panatela and blew a geyser of smoke into the already cigar-smelly room. In the pause of the long puff and exhalation she followed her plan.

"Somebody around here was incompetent a dozen years ago," she said.

It stopped him short. Incompetent was always a wounding word
loaded with racial implications. The fact was that the level of com-
petence was much lower twelve years ago, statistically speaking. It
was the time when the racial balance was in flux, on the verge of
moving to a black majority. There were those that blamed it on the
flux and others who ascribed more bigoted motives.

"And your evidence for such an accusation?" the eggplant asked,
nostrils quivering with repressed anger.

"It was just a surface job. Nobody really showed any interest."

"Can you be more specific?"

"They did no investigation, made no attempt to go beyond
the obvious."

"And what would you have done?"

"I'd have talked to co-workers, former roommates, her landlord."

"Why? Was there evidence of foul play?"

"Nobody ever looked."

"Why should they have?"

"Because she was a young beauty, living in a plush apartment,
obviously living above her means."

"And that would be grounds to assign manpower, spend the tax-
payers' money?" He puffed deeply on his cigar and the smoke came
out with his words. "Maybe she was a hooker. That would account
for the apartment."

She berated herself for her oversight. Worse, she had built her
case on Mrs. Taylor's intuition about Betty having a white lover,
thereby neglecting the obvious. The missed beat told him that she
was vulnerable.

"You didn't check?"

"No, I didn't." She stole a look at Cates, who, obviously seeing the
debacle, turned away. "Christ, Chief. I was with her mother yesterday." She paused and raised her hands in a cease-and-desist gesture.
"It was on my own time. Anyway, this was a good family. Her mother was a proud woman. I told her what we had found."

"And the ID was positive?" the eggplant asked. He was boring in on the obvious, magnifying the flaws.

"Except for the dental," she said defensively. "The Medical Examiner will confirm. I'm sure of it." She looked up at the eggplant's face. Was he intrigued? With him, it was impossible to tell.

"Suppose it doesn't check?" he asked.

"It has to."

The eggplant lowered his head and shook it in mock disbelief.

"Now we're stuck with it," he said. She observed the protocol and made no comment, knowing she had won a tiny victory. "Pretty clever, FitzGerald." He offered a sneer, but she could tell from his eyes that he was relieved that he had found a way to give his consent without surrender. What was most maddening to her was her inability to lay down a matrix of his logic system. He could feign stupidity with the best of them, could pose as a hardhead, while all along he would be creating networks of subtle new logic to test and challenge them. He seemed always to be probing, forever challenging, playing the flunky, even the stereotypical black incompetent to infuriate them, setting out decoys and red herrings to confuse them, leading them through minefields where only he knew the path of safety.

"Does that imply that you want us to continue?" she asked cautiously.

Despite the victory, she was annoyed at being bested. Her plan was to unleash a nasty racial weapon to force his hand. The woman was black, asshole. That's why they swept it under the rug. Twelve years ago, who gave a shit about a missing black woman? Even black detectives were singing whitey's tune.

"It implies," he said slowly, crushing the stub of his panatela in his overflowing ashtray, "that we are also stuck with the baggage of the past. There's lots out there who want to think we're incompetent, a label far more politically damaging than merely showing lesser homicide numbers." He lit another panatela. "We mustn't stand in the way of identifying the lady. That certainly counts as official

interest. If you get my drift." Then he turned away, his attention
now concentrated on some paperwork on his desk.

   As she and Cates left, she felt his gaze on her back. Perhaps he was
smiling as well. But she dared not turn back to find out.

VIII

The lab confirmed the identity of Betty Taylor through her dental work. She was sure it would. Indeed, she was certain that the eggplant knew it would as well. Considering the quid pro quo of the transaction, she assumed that, if she postponed telling him, her permission to pursue the case further was automatically extended.

"Madness," Cates said, as she attempted to explain it.

"Not when you understand the code," she told him.

It was enough to motivate him into a frenzy of investigatory activity. Once committed, he was a tiger at footwork and a whiz at details. He went off to the Hill to speak to the staff director of the committee that had employed Betty Taylor, while she called the District Building to track down the owners of the building in which the young woman had lived.

She was shifted through a tangle of bureaucratic ineptitude, from one bored clerk to another, none of whom were intimidated by her official position.

"All I want to know is who owned the building in the late seventies."

"I got to check the tax records."

"Isn't there a simple list of property owners?"

"There's a problem with the computer stuff for that period. We gotta find it by hand."

"How long will that take?"

"It's nearly four."

"So?"

"So I'm off at four."

"You sound like you're off now," Fiona snapped.

"You want me to get your answer or not?"

"Do you realize you're obstructing justice?" Fiona said. It was the kind of question that telescoped its response.

"Kiss my ass."

"The way you move it that ought to take a week."

Round and round. She hung up in disgust, but with a greater understanding of the eggplant's fear of being labeled incompetent.

Then she got a call from Monte Pappas.

"What are you doing?" he asked. Although it had the air of flippancy, she could sense the tightness under the forced levity.

"If you were giving the bureaucracy an enema where would you put the nozzle?"

"Can I substitute a person and keep the water going until he explodes?"

"My answer was the District Government. What's yours?"

Suddenly, all happy-talk pretense evaporated.

"Fi, I've got to see you."

"Nice to be needed."

She retained a lightness, hoping that it had another connotation. But she knew better.

"More than you think," he said. "Urgently."

"When?"

"As fast as you can, Fi. Can I pick you up in fifteen minutes?"

"That bad?"

She looked at the notes on her yellow pad, contemplated the frustrations ahead of her, regretting now that she had put the wheels in motion.

"You know where headquarters is. I'll be in front."

* * *

She was prompt, but he was already there, his Caddy glistening from the rain. She had barely opened her umbrella before she had to close it again. He had swung the door open and she had hopped in.

The rain had turned nasty again, vast sheets angling against the windshield, winning the battle against the wipers. The grey skies were darkening into night.

"Hope you got your ark ready, Monte," Fiona quipped. His mood was gloomy, but he managed a polite grunt of acknowledgment. He made a sharp turn into the tunnel heading for Capitol Hill.

"I appreciate this, Fiona," he muttered. In profile he seemed to be biting his lower lip.

"What are friends for?" she said, hoping that the light touch wasn't off-putting. It didn't matter. He seemed to be ignoring it, lost in his own thoughts. She let him brood. Finally he spoke.

"I don't know how to handle this, Fi," Monte said. He took one hand off the steering wheel and gripped her arm. "It's your expertise."

"So far it's an endless prologue," she said.

"There's something else." He cleared his throat. "I need your word on this. Complete silence. No one."

She thought about that for a moment and searched for a way to say it.

"I render unto Caesar."

He nodded as if he understood. Then he seemed to be mulling it. "Fair enough," he said. He rubbed the back of his hand against his mouth.

"She's disappeared," he said, shaking his head. They were out of the tunnel and into the rain again, heading in the direction of the Capitol dome, lit now, a welcoming beacon in the downpour.

"Who?"

"Helga Kessel, wife of the Austrian Ambassador."

"The beautiful Helga, mistress of Senator Love."

Again, he ignored the attempt at a lighter touch. And yet, the subject matter belied his obvious panic.

"Who needed this?" He shook his head. She had turned to watch him and he had met her gaze briefly. A headlight illuminated his troubled eyes. "It was supposed to be all handled. Sam had taken the pledge. Clear sailing. Then this."

"There's missing and missing," Fiona said.

"I know." He expelled air through his teeth. "It's bizarre. He . . . Sam . . . gets this call no more than two hours ago. The Ambassador himself, Hans Kessel. Remember him?" She nodded. "Says they should meet at the Dupont Circle subway stop. Something urgent. Sam, naturally, calls Bunkie, who follows him."

"Not you?"

"I come later. I'm the fireman, you see. When I get to it, it's already a conflagration." He sucked air through his teeth. "Assholes."

"So they meet," Fiona prompted. He was obviously too upset to focus logically. The explanation seemed painful.

"A brief talk. Kessel is panicked. The lady has vanished. As near as he can see no clothes missing. No notes. Nothing. She had gone out yesterday. He wasn't sure where. He let it go by one night. Maybe he's had some experience along these lines. When nearly another day went by, he got the message."

"Why Sam?"

"He knew. The son-of-a-bitch knew that Sam was diddling his wife."

"Was he hostile?"

"No. Nor irate. He's a European, if that explains it. He and Sam have a common cause." He turned toward her. "Not what you think," Monte sighed. "A morbid fear of embarrassment. He's also a diddler with political ambitions back in Austria. Takes one to know one."

"Did he have any ideas where the woman might have gone?"

"None. That's the point. He asked Sam that very same question."

"So what's the bottom line?" Fiona asked, her mind spinning with scenarios. Maybe the woman was teasing both of them, scaring the shit out of both of them, getting even. Fiona could empathize with that.

"You're the bottom line, Fi," Monte said.

The car sped through the rain, turned and proceeded on Independence Avenue.

"We're all way out of our depth. To report this thing could spell political sudden death for Sam and Kessel. It will come out. That's a given. Unless we can find some way to keep the lid on." He looked again toward Fiona. He slapped his chest. "We don't know how it's done."

"You think I do?"

"You're a cop. She's a missing person, for crying out loud."

"Could be just a game's she's playing."

"Some game."

"She got dumped. She was pissed off. Could be her way to twist your you-know-whats."

"We wish," Monte sighed. "That kind of pain we can live with." He grew silent. "But for how long?"

"Longer the better."

"Okay, she was dumped. But this is beyond the pale."

"No it's not."

She tried to soak up the woman's humiliation, calculate the anger and thirst for vengeance. Unfortunately, she could not sustain the indignation. The woman was a damned fool to get mixed up with a married politician. Served her right. The sense of sisterhood faded. Helga was a diplomat's wife, for chrissakes, she knew the score.

"How was it done?" she asked. "The Dear-John?"

Suddenly Monte slapped his thigh. The noise startled her.

"A comedy of errors, Fi. Wrong all around. Bunkie Farrington was the messenger. I swear the morons are in charge. It was decided." He took his hands off the wheel to use them for emphasis. "I am equally at fault, knowing Sam's penchant for avoiding scenes. A sycophant panders, Fi. And it was I who said those immortal words: No more. Cut it clean, said Bunkie. He had done it before. He said he was good at it. It was the one time Sam should have done it himself."

"Real class," Fi said, disgusted.

"I think I could have stopped it. Now I pay. You are my ace card. No. My only card."

He pulled up in front of a townhouse. A man in a raincoat and hat sprung out of the shadows. She heard the click of car locks and the man came in the back door of the car.

"You remember Bunkie, Fi," Monte said. Fi turned and Bunkie grunted a response.

"Not my idea," he mumbled.

"Bunkie is hostile, Fi," Monte said.

"It grows," Bunkie said. "In this town, knowledge expands geometrically."

Monte drove toward the Potomac, ducked under the highway, then found a parking space on Main Avenue. The rain had thinned out the tourist traffic and the dinner crowd had not yet begun to descend on the wall-to-wall restaurants along the river. They sat in the car, motor running, the rain pelting the roof and windshield.

"We're all going to drown anyway," Bunkie said gloomily.

"It was Bunkie here who was the last of our group to see the lady."

"No big deal. We met for cocktails at the Ritz-Carlton. She was already primed. I merely read her the drill. She said she understood."

"She wasn't upset that the Senator wasn't there to convey the sad news?"

"She said she wished it would have gone that way, but that she understood. This is no kid. She's in the game. I told her the Senator was running for President, for crying out loud. She was a liability and she knew it. I told her the Senator was broken up about it, but had to make this decision. Went smooth as silk. She was cool."

"Just like that. No emotion?" Fiona asked.

"She's a diplomat's wife. She wasn't a receptionist or some dumb cunt in the typing pool. She had a mind."

"I'm glad one of you did," Monte muttered.

"We were clean on this. I did a surgeon's job. I know it."

"How do you read it then?" Fiona asked.

She had turned slightly in the front seat to see him, but his features were undefined. His shoulders moved, a gesture of frustration and confusion.

"She thought it over. Looked at what she had and what she had just lost, then just cut out. That's the only explanation that makes sense. Women do that. It's not rational. But they do it. I think she just got pissed off and cut out."

"Kessel said she took nothing except the clothes on her back. Nothing."

"No jewelry?" Fiona asked.

"Only what she was wearing," Monte said. "Nothing else. Sam said Kessel was emphatic about that and that was what was scaring the shit out of him."

"Maybe she wanted no part of anything," Bunkie suggested. "She wanted to break clean. It happens."

"Ever happened to you?" Fiona asked.

"Not quite that way. I rather shy away from emotional glue," Bunkie said. Bet you do, she thought. Cold-blooded bastard. She turned again to Monte.

"Kessel is dead-certain about her taking nothing?"

"I just told you," Bunkie interjected snidely. She ignored him. Monte looked at his watch.

"We'll know in ten more minutes. We're meeting the Ambassador."

"Monte thinks it's important that you two get acquainted," Bunkie said. He shot her a look heavy with sarcasm.

"You've done this little chore before?" Fiona asked Bunkie. "The bearer of bad news?"

"I've got a complicated job," he said morosely. They waited through the silence. "He's got this insatiable dick." More silence. "Shit. Yeah two three times. Only when they get serious or pushy."

"Did his wife know?" Fiona asked, her mind set in detective mode, mentally lining up the suspects. Force of habit, she told herself, amused with the idea.

"Know? Hard to say. She'd have to be there, wouldn't she?" Bunkie said. "Suspect? Goes with the territory. The fact is the Senator is a family guy."

"Mrs. Langford never raised the issue?"

"Not to me," Bunkie said. "I'd say though that he has plenty to spare."

"Plenty of what?" Fiona snapped.

"It can rise to any occasion," Bunkie sneered, as if his surrogate duties included the Senator's brag.

"So you also watch," Fiona said with obvious contempt.

When he didn't comment, Monte pulled the car away from the curb and started westward up Independence in the direction of the Washington Monument. It was slow going, the rush hour was in full bloom.

"I still don't know why we had to bring her into it," Bunkie said.

"She's a pro is why." Monte said. He patted Fiona on the thigh. "When you report someone missing what happens?"

"Goes into a data bank," Fiona began, explaining the process. "Available to one and all, up to and including the G-men."

"They ever find anyone?" Bunkie asked.

"Sometimes. Unfortunately, it takes more manpower than is ever available. It becomes a lesser police priority as time goes on." She thought suddenly of Betty Taylor's remains. "And harder to find them."

"In this case, the best course is to do nothing," Bunkie said. "That's my call on it from the beginning. The lady will turn up. She's probably already shacking up somewhere in Europe. I figure a woman with that kind of looks can find someone to stake her on a new wardrobe, some baubles, and the price of an air fare. The more I think about it, the more I say we're panicked for nothing."

Monte headed the car around the Lincoln Monument back up Twenty-third to Georgetown, then up Wisconsin Avenue, pulling into a Seven-Eleven parking lot. He did not turn off the motor and after a while another man jumped into the back seat.

"This is Detective Fiona FitzGerald," Monte said. "You remember her, Mr. Ambassador."

"I do," he muttered.

Turning, she could see him in the reflection of light from the neon Seven-Eleven sign. It cast a green pall over all of them, making them seem like frozen victims of some exotic catastrophe, like a poison gas attack.

"We've filled her in, Mr. Ambassador," Monte said.

"Nothing official?"

"Absolutely not, Mr. Ambassador," Monte said, cutting a glance at Fiona for confirmation. "She's merely acting as my friend and advisor."

"I feel ridiculous," the Ambassador said in his Austrian accent, speckled with British pronunciations.

"Her passport, Mr. Ambassador?" Fiona asked with some sense of urgency. "Is it still in your residence?"

"Yes," he said. "That was my first thought, too."

"He knows everything?" she asked Monte.

"Just about," Monte said. He turned toward the Ambassador. "We deemed the stakes too high for secrets." It was, she knew, an ambivalent word, with too many meanings for precision.

"So you see the problem here, Detective FitzGerald," the Ambassador said. She wanted to ask him deeply personal things like how he could ignore, and possibly sanction, his wife having a love affair with another man in their official circle.

It occurred to her that he might have actually encouraged the liaison for his own political reasons, as if the beautiful Helga were a kind of bribe, a sexual favor offered in exchange. For what, she wondered. Except for the Waldheim flap, Austria seemed so benign, so distant from American political machinations. Nevertheless, she made a mental note to find out what committees Sam Langford served on. Again she thought of the remains of Betty Taylor. Cates had spent the day on the Hill checking on the Committee that had employed the unfortunate woman.

"Detective FitzGerald has just explained to us, Mr. Ambassador, that any missing report would go into a data bank, accessible to any official group."

"Internationally as well?"

"Of course. In the case of your wife, Interpol will hop on it. Not that this means that anything will be done. Although in this case, the impetus will be there. For the press as well."

"It will be like being up against a firing squad," Bunkie muttered.

"Wonderful," the Ambassador said gloomily. He had lowered his head. Suddenly he looked up and turned to Bunkie. "For your Senator as well." In the darkness, she could see Bunkie's eyes, which seemed to suck the greenish light into them. It made him look ominous, hateful. Iago thwarted, she thought suddenly. His aura stank of resentment. Incompetent strangers, he must be thinking, had pissed on his dream.

"You never had words over this . . . this affair . . . with your wife?" Fiona asked.

"Angry words?"

Fiona nodded.

"No." He sighed. "We have a rather unique marriage."

"Did she have any other lovers?"

"I doubt it. She genuinely adored the Senator."

"She told you this?"

"Of course."

Gamey stuff, Fiona thought. Maybe it was a turn-on for both of them.

"Wasn't this . . . politically speaking . . . the affair itself . . . dangerous?"

She marveled at his value system. Was it decadence or naiveté?

"One expects discretion in these things," he said simply. "It is the danger that provides the interest."

She stole a glance at Monte, whose eyes looked upward in exasperation.

"Did you know about Mr. Farrington's visit?" Fiona asked.

"Yes," the Ambassador said.

"Your wife told you?"

"Yes."

She turned to Bunkie.

"Did you know she told her husband?"

"Not until he told me," Bunkie said.

"Did the Senator know?"

"We keep him out of this," Bunkie said. He talked in the direction of Monte. "Leastwise you could have clued her in."

"The point is we, the Ambassador and us, are in it together," Monte explained. "Everything is on the table now."

"Allies for the common good," Fiona said, hoping her revulsion didn't show. Self-interest makes strange bedfellows, she knew. It was a cliché of the political life. Unfortunately the human side of it was repelling.

Helga's elegant question-mark posture materialized in her mind. She saw her bejeweled and graceful as she danced, melding into the body of Sam Langford, gliding with him in a sensual pas de deux. If it was love you wanted, lady, you should have steered clear, she told her silently, remembering her own titillation.

"Have you checked everywhere?" Fiona asked the Ambassador. "Friends? Relatives? Even acquaintances?"

"I have been on the phone for twenty-four hours. I've used every euphemism I know, stretching discretion to its furthest point. I have racked my brains for some sign of this action coming. Anything. There was simply nothing to predict this. No harsh words. No subtle hints. Yes, we went our separate ways. Our only rule was discretion. We understood our responsibilities completely. I am absolutely certain that Mr. Farrington's explanation was accepted with total understanding. We are quite mature about these things. The fact is that I'm baffled. She had no reason to disappear. Not on her own."

"When did you see her last?"

"I told you. Yesterday morning."

"When?"

"At breakfast."

"How was she dressed?"

"Her dressing gown."

"What did you talk about?"

He thought for a moment.

"Events of the day," the Ambassador said. "We read the papers at breakfast."

"How do you read them?"

She was trying to get a picture of that last moment of his observation.

"I start with the *New York Times*. She starts with the *Washington Post*. We sit in the breakfast room. Our cook serves us and leaves. We have a pleasant view of the garden through a bay window."

"Now you're getting it," Fiona said.

"What sections does she read first?"

"Style. Women love the style section. My wife is a social animal. She likes to read the party coverage, the reviews. I have to read the more serious material. The editorials, for example."

"Does she read the more serious material?"

"Not often."

"Is this important?" Bunkie asked.

"Probably. She is a trained interrogator," Monte said.

"I don't mind. Really," the Ambassador said. He was quiet for a moment and she let him think.

"I'm trying to get you to remember that last moment. What was on her mind?"

"Real estate," he said suddenly. "Real estate was on her mind. It is a topic of conversation in Washington, the value of real estate. The extraordinary appreciation. She was thinking of investing in real estate." He paused again. "Yes. She always read the classified for the real estate."

"Had she made any investments?"

"Actually, no. But she was interested. Occasionally she mentioned having gone to look at something." He shrugged. "You see, the wife of an Ambassador has a problem. She cannot work, except as a volunteer. In Austria she owned a fashion boutique, but sold it when we married. She liked the idea of travel, the diplomatic life, but she was an active woman. She had a head for business. Real estate interested her." He nodded. "Yes, I remember. She did read the real estate classified yesterday morning as well."

"And then?"

"I left the table, showered, dressed and went off to the Embassy."

"You never saw her again that day? Or spoke to her on the phone?"

"No. It was quite a busy day."

"You don't know where she went?"

"No. Nor did any of the servants."

"She didn't take the car?"

"No."

"Have you found her wallet? Do you know what she wore?"

"I did not find her wallet. And, frankly, I did not keep track of her clothes. She went out. That is evident. Then she disappeared."

She heard the rain dancing on the car roof, Monte breathing heavily beside her.

"Sometimes we never know what motivates people," Fiona said. "Even those we love most."

"I think she just got fed up about something," Bunkie interrupted, "and decided to jump ship. Maybe she had it up to here with everyone. With all of us. Maybe the only person she was comfortable with was herself. She'll either come back in her own time or she won't. Doesn't mean we have to call out the cavalry."

Despite her distaste for Bunkie, he appeared to have the most logical attitude on the subject. Never trouble trouble till trouble troubles you.

"Got the picture, Fi?" Monte asked.

Like a half-developed Polaroid, she thought. There were unseen complexities here. Wheels within wheels.

"Who else knew?" she asked. Kessel and Bunkie exchanged glances, revealing a commonality that had escaped her. Was it a sub-

tle conspiracy? Or simply the kinship of fear? No explanation necessary. They knew what she meant.

"No one," the Ambassador said. "Only me."

"That's difficult to do," Fiona pressed. "People observe. They have
eyes." She shot a glance at Bunkie. "Where did they see each other?"

"My place," Bunkie said.

"There are neighbors, repair people, delivery men."

"Is this relevant?" the Ambassador asked.

"I'm not sure."

"Then why ask?" Bunkie snarled.

"Because it's important," Monte snapped.

"Okay, you want to know," Bunkie said with exasperation. "We
had this routine. I have one of these garages. Electronic doors. I
picked her up in different places. I got this one-way reflective glass
in my car. No one can see in. I just drove her into the garage. The
Senator walked the two blocks. They did what they did and I picked
her up and dropped her off."

She looked at Kessel, who showed no reaction.

"You really had it down," Fiona said with grudging admiration.

"Bunkie thinks of everything," Monte said with sarcasm.

"Politics teaches. Remember Gary Hart," Bunkie said.

"If it was such a good system why stop?" Fiona asked Bunkie, who
ejected a bitter laugh.

"When the media turns on its brights, even the cockroaches
scramble," Bunkie said. "Nobody's perfect. Everybody gets careless.
Worse, they were beginning to have ideas."

"Romantic notions?"

"More or less."

"You saw that?"

"Part of the job," he said with surly arrogance.

Again she looked at Kessel. Again no reaction.

"And did you also see that?" she asked Kessel, only gently.

"She is a romantic," the Ambassador said. "But, above all, practical. She also understood the security aspects. I am certain she told no one."

"Surely they used the telephone," Fiona said. "Embassies are often tapped."

"We have a safe line," the Ambassador said, showing the briefest glimpse of international intrigue. It crossed her mind that perhaps the Ambassador and his lady had conspired in this for reasons that had more to do with the relations between governments than people. In that case others surely knew. Many others. Intelligence agencies and their ubiquitous agents. The CIA. Fantastic scenarios suggested themselves.

"Maybe your government was tapping," Fiona said.

"I am quite sophisticated about these matters, Detective FitzGerald." She saw his face flicker into a small smile. "Security is sometimes a double-edged sword for a diplomat. It can actually strengthen the ramparts of discretion. Mrs. Kessel was also sophisticated in this and I assure you that I had no knowledge of the mechanics of her liaisons. Nor would I inquire. She was free to indulge as long as it did not interfere with my mission or our marriage."

"Sounds like a conflict of terms," Fiona said.

"I know," the Ambassador answered. "But you would be surprised how common such arrangements are."

Not as much surprised as offended, she offered silently. By rights, considering her experiences with politics and the police and the social hurly-burly of the Washington high-life, she should have been more jaded, more cynical, more tolerant of such oblique values. It surprised her that she wasn't. Happily so, she told herself.

"What about Nell Langford?" she asked, wondering how truly accepting Little Nell might be of such an arrangement.

"I told you. Nell suspected everyone. Came with the turf," Bunkie said. "But she could never know. Not really know." He paused and sucked in a deep breath. "What you see is what you get."

There were reasons for these questions, she told herself, although she resisted the full amplification to herself. Of course she knew that she was triggering greater anxieties, perhaps preparing them for the worst.

"So you're all saying that nobody other than you truly knew the score?"

"Now you," Bunkie said.

Beside her, Monte stirred.

"So what do you think we should do, Fi?" he asked.

"I know what you can't do," she said. She turned to the Ambassador. "Aside from the emotional trauma, the not knowing, I think the best course is to wait. No sense stirring the sleeping dogs." She paused, letting the message sink in. Wait for what? they surely were speculating. She had the answer to that, but she held off for the moment.

"We didn't need you to tell us that," Bunkie said.

She looked at the Ambassador. "Ever happen before?"

"Never."

"Is she the kind of woman who might do this . . . well, for the sake of annoyance?"

"No," the Ambassador shot back. "Not Helga. She is not a woman who could indulge in recrimination."

"What about for fun? To tweak you all."

"Not Helga."

"Would Helga do anything if . . . if she were hurt?"

He made a strange sound, a kind of joyless laugh.

"You must understand. A beautiful woman in her prime is not like other women. My wife has many wonderful qualities. But at heart she is a narcissist and, if you know the breed, they are totally self-centered."

"Did she have enemies? An unrequited lover, perhaps?"

"Not to my knowledge." He thought a moment. "Or hers. She would have told me."

"Do you love your wife, Mr. Ambassador?"

"Of course."

For a diplomat, he was surprisingly open and unguarded. But then, his value system was outside her frame of reference. She suspected that he was cooperating because he was genuinely alarmed and, although ambitious, less frightened about his career dangers than the Senator and his men.

"I assume each of you has considered and discussed the other scenarios," she said. Their silence told her that they had, encouraging her to continue.

"If she's been kidnapped for ransom, you'll hear. If she's been taken hostage you'll hear that, too. If she's been kidnapped for other aberrational reasons, sex, for example, you'll probably never know until she's been released." She paused for a long moment, repressing something she wanted to say, then continuing. "That is, if she's released." She said it quickly, not willing to linger over the point. "On the other hand, this may be all her doing and since she knows it is highly unlikely that you would contact the authorities, she might simply, barring those behavioral patterns that the Ambassador rejects, be enjoying some self-motivated bizarre type of freedom. Freedom from her own identity. It happens."

Fiona shrugged. She had tried to be precise. Of course there was a puzzle here and they all knew it. But she clearly understood the role that Monte had cast her in and which she had accepted. She was here for reassurance.

"So we wait," Monte said.

"Was there ever another choice?" Bunkie said morosely.

"I just want her home," the Ambassador said. It was the nearest thing to a cry he had uttered.

"I'm sure it will turn out just fine," Monte said, much like the boy whistling in the cemetery.

Ambassador Kessel got out of the car and ran through the rain to his own. Monte maneuvered the car out of the Seven-Eleven lot and drove south down Wisconsin Avenue.

During the drive back to his house, Bunkie dozed and Fiona stared straight ahead, mesmerized by the steady hum of the windshield wiper as it beat away the rain. It had slackened somewhat but not much. Far from over, she told herself.

When they reached his townhouse on Capitol Hill, Bunkie got out. Instead of making a run for it, he tapped the window on the driver's side and Monte brought it down.

"I still think we didn't need her," he said, not bothering to look toward Fiona. Without responding, Monte raised the window and gunned the motor.

"How come the Senator wasn't here?" Fiona asked when they were underway.

"He doesn't do this."

"The dirty work?"

"That's the deal."

"Even when things go sour?"

"Especially then."

She thought of her father. No way, she decided. Her father wasn't a creation made out of straw and polls. He would have done the right thing.

Monte headed the car back toward police headquarters. She had toyed with the idea of inviting him home, but then he foreclosed on it himself.

"Now I've got to hold Sam's hand," he sighed. "But I'd rather hold yours." Reaching out, he took her hand and held it up to his lips. "He'll be disappointed."

"How so?"

"Nothing definitive really happened. We agreed to wait is all, hold off informing anyone. For him that's nebulous. He likes resolution. Something happening that inspires the need to interact."

"A real man of action," she quipped as he headed the car back to police headquarters. They drove in silence as he continued to hold her hand. Fiona's thoughts drifted.

"In a way, he's right, Monte," Fiona said, breaking the silence.

"Who?"

"Bunkie. About not needing me."

"Not needing you? To me you were essential. Maybe I needed you to get me through this. I hate it. The whole idea of it. I'm a professional. This is not part of my act. I needed you."

"I know you needed me, Monte," she said, moving closer to him, caressing his arm. "I didn't mean that. I meant something else."

"What?"

It had to be said. She owed him that.

"You won't really need me until the body turns up."

IX

"I had a problem," she told Cates the next morning, explaining why she had not been there when he had gotten back from the Hill. It wasn't exactly a lie. She could tell he didn't buy it.

She wished she could discuss it with him. It had haunted her all night and needed airing. Had she given her promise to Monte too eagerly? Giving one's word had always been sacred to her, even as a child. Long ago she had made it the bedrock of her value system.

"Remember, Fiona," her father had told her, in a preachier moment, perhaps when his own integrity had been challenged. "All you own is your good name and your word. Everything else is borrowed."

His loans against such a wise homily had been large and then, in one swoop, he had paid them all back. But her father was more of a gambler than she. Thy good name and thy word shall comfort thee. For her it was a form of religion, which was why she had concocted her "render unto Caesar" remark. She assumed Monte had gotten it. If it was inside the law, no sweat. But outside—another matter entirely. Which was why she had tossed and turned all night. However bizarre the lifestyle of Helga and her husband, nobody walks cold turkey. Something goes along.

Cates, perhaps noting that she seemed spacey, pulled out a file from his drawer and opened it. At that moment the eggplant arrived carrying a very wet big black umbrella, which he leaned against the wall outside of his office. He surveyed the squad room, grunted a greeting, went into the office and closed the door behind him.

"Foul weather. Foul mood," Fiona said. She looked at Cates nursing his pout behind the file. "The suspense is killing me, Cates."

"He's got a point," Cates said without looking up. "The longer, the harder. Lots happens in thirteen years." He shut the file. His

83

pout had switched to an expression that meant strictly business. "The Taylor girl's record with the committee was nothing to write home about. She wasn't too punctual and she had more absences than she should have had. Then one day she didn't show up."

"Anybody remember her?"

"Except for one older secretary, those that were around then were mostly vague. The picture jogged them. They had recollections of her prettiness. Beyond that, she barely made a dent."

"Except for the older secretary," Fiona prompted.

"She remembers more. Mostly because Betty was, according to her, trying to pass. The woman, Miss Phillips, is one of these faded, white, old maids. An observer type, you know, encased in fat. Not part of the main social stream. Work is her only life. And gossip about the staff and the House members, past and present. You know the type. Says Betty and she were friendly when Betty first arrived. Remembers her as bubbly, enthusiastic and pretty much able to field the young men that knocked on her door. Then three months into it, she said Betty suddenly changed."

"In what way?" Fiona asked.

"No more bubbly. She got quieter. More secretive. Went to lunch by herself. Became more of a loner. That was the heart of her memory. How Betty Taylor had changed. It left an impression."

"She have any ideas why?"

"Not really. At least she didn't say. They're careful up there. I couldn't tell if she was telling the truth. She's Hill smart. Doesn't want to upset things for herself. She beat a fast retreat when I pushed too hard."

Mrs. Taylor had it right, Fiona was certain. She knew what it meant to have that kind of beauty. Some of the older cops of both races called it high yellow, a genetic alchemy that spawned a golden complexion and made extravagant what was already beautiful. Its mention, too, had a decidedly erotic tone, as if the tone itself was a rare aphrodisiac.

And so the beautiful butterfly was let out of the cage. The salivating predators, as always, were waiting. The Hill was a cauldron of sexuality. Power, too, has its erotic attractions, its Pied Pipers of seduction. Experts at manipulation, they could play the siren song in whatever key was necessary. Titillating stuff, especially for a girl from the boonies, a golden beauty just out of the cage.

"Got a list of staff and members for that year?"

"My new friend promised it today," Cates said. His earlier annoyance had evaporated. "She's ordering a book from that year from the Library of Congress."

Cates' thoroughness was always a marvel to Fiona. Of course, he still needed seasoning, the kind that spiced the palette of logic, but that would come with experience. He had been assigned to her by the eggplant after Jefferson had been killed.

She still missed the big black bastard, which was the way she preferred to remember him, at full strength with all the surface meanness showing. How slyly he disguised the litmus of his sensitivity, the bigness of his overflowing heart. Cates was different, harder in a way than Jefferson, more cerebral and under control, hiding his hurts with more skill, less volcanic and nerve-wracking, yet equally reliable when it counted. The eggplant, a giant mass of impenetrable complexities, was a shrewd and unerring marriage broker when it came to partnering.

"I also checked out the apartment," Cates said, looking into his notebook. There was, of course, an implied rebuke in the revelation. "I was up there," he explained."It's only a couple of blocks away."

She didn't press the point. Turf was never a problem between them. Besides, she had failed in her search.

"Place had sixteen units. None of the existing tenants had lived there more than six years. I spoke with the managing agents. Place was sold twice since then. They told me to check at the District Building."

"Rots a ruck," Fiona said, remembering her battle with the District bureaucracy. "I was diddled on the telephone merry-go-round. What do you say we go down and kick some ass?"

They started to put on their raincoats, then heard the eggplant's voice behind them. Later she would tell herself that she knew, even before any words were exchanged, she knew in her gut. He crooked a finger and summoned them into his office. But he did not sit down. Instead he went to the map mounted at one end of the room, squinted at it then tapped a dark finger on its surface.

"Here. Cleveland Park."

His nostrils quivered when he turned and faced them.

"I'm afraid you'll have to put the old bones on hold for a while. We have something for you more contemporary."

They waited, not responding. He walked toward the window and looked out of it.

"The rain, you see, it's turning the ground to mush. And spitting up ladies."

X

A retaining wall had given way and the ground behind it rolled like volcanic lava to the yard behind it, stopped only by the foundation of the house on the lower elevation. The body of a nude woman, not long dead, popped to the surface midway between the house and what once was the retaining wall.

Fiona and Cates had slogged to the body in high boots. The nude body was on her back and there was no mistaking who it was.

"I figured," Fiona sighed. Cates looked at her with bewilderment. "It's Helga Kessel, wife of the Austrian Ambassador."

"You knew her?" Cates asked with some surprise.

"You might say we broke bread together," Fiona replied.

"Jesus, this is big." Cates whistled.

"Bigger than you think," she muttered. Cates cocked his head, puzzling.

Kneeling, she inspected the body. It seemed childlike, smaller than she had appeared in life, but well proportioned in scale. She noted that the grey nipples on the woman's breasts were larger than most she had seen. The long blonde hair was caked with mud and the eyes were open and slightly bulged. The head seemed unnaturally attached, indicating the probable cause of death was through strangulation.

From the position of the body and the way in which the ground above had broken, as if someone had bitten through a chunk of a nut-filled caramel candy bar, it was apparent that the body had been expelled from its burial site under a stand of trees that edged the higher property.

The similarities of disposal between this body and that of Betty Taylor was not lost on Fiona. She exchanged glances with Cates.

87

"It's our week for coincidences," he shrugged.

"Mustn't jump to conclusions," she cautioned, waving her finger in mock rebuke. She was rebuking herself as well. But it didn't stop her mind from reaching across the years.

The technical men and the uniforms slogged through the mud of the scene and the body was bagged and carried away through a path that ran beside a detached garage at the end of the driveway of the lower house. Following it, they confronted a young woman holding a baby, both dressed for the rain. She was standing in the open side door of the garage. They showed their badges.

"It was like an explosion," the woman said. "Suddenly the ground gave way."

The woman introduced herself as a Mrs. Carlton. Cates played a game with his fingers for the benefit of the baby, who smiled in appreciation. Beyond the woman, Fiona could see cars and vans pulling up. The media. She watched Flannagan's boys quickly load the body bag into the police van and speed away. Watching the media swooping down on them like a wild herd, she suddenly thought of Monte and his worst fears. Sorry, guy, she muttered to herself. It's now Caesar's problem. To whom I render.

"Do you think we could duck in here for a moment?" Fiona said, leading the woman into the interior of the garage and closing the door.

"It's important that we get as much as you can remember."

The woman nodded, apparently eager to tell her story, and dived right into it. The baby continued to watch Cates distract it with finger exercises. Its nose was running, the mucus dripping from its chin.

"When I heard the explosion," the woman said, "I ran upstairs to get the baby, dressed him and got out of there as fast as I could. I came out here and saw that my whole lawn was gone and there was a lady's leg stuck up in the air. I swear it was unbelievable."

"Who lives there?" Fiona said, pointing to the house visible behind the thinned-out stand of trees, a number of which, although still upright, were denuded to their exposed roots. About half the upper yard had disappeared into the lower one, now a mass of mud, bricks and broken trees.

"Mrs. Gates lived there until a month ago. It's been empty. For sale." The woman shook her head. "I never trusted that damned retaining wall. Never. My husband used to pooh-pooh my anxiety. Wait'll he sees this. Who knew that we would have the worst bout of rain in a hundred years." She turned to Fiona. "You think our insurance covers this?"

"I suppose it depends on whose wall it is," Fiona said, sorry that she had volunteered.

"Shit. I think it's ours. It was there when we bought the house. The fucking rain. It never stops." She hiked up the baby in her arms, then felt his bottom and sniffed him. "Now he's made a poopoo." She looked at Fiona with angry mouse eyes. Her hair was straggly and she wore no makeup. "Can you blame him?"

"Did you hear or see anything uncommon coming from the Gates' yard in the last two days?" Fiona asked. "More specifically, the night before last?"

Cates stopped his finger exercises. She could feel him studying her.

"All I've heard for the last few days is the sound of the rain. God's pee. Why us?"

"Have you seen anyone around the Gates' house in the past two days? Anyone at all?"

"On this level, all I could ever see was that damned retaining wall."

"And from upstairs?"

"Trees. In winter I could see the house. They were a retiring couple, the Gateses. Wasn't much outside life there."

Through the dirty garage window she could see the media people clustered in a knot near the driveway, needling a nervous rookie uniform, who probably had said more than he realized.

"You got a phone in here?" Fiona asked.

"No," the woman snapped in a surly tone. "And I don't want you in the house." She looked at her mud-splattered boots.

"A woman's been murdered," Cates interjected.

"That's her problem," the woman shot back. "You gonna pay for my clean-up?"

"Used to be a genteel neighborhood," Fiona said.

"I know. Grover Cleveland came here for his summer vacations. If he knew how much it costs to live here now he'd be rolling in his grave."

Fiona looked out again at the cluster of reporters.

"No hotdogging," Cates said. She knew what he meant. The eggplant had made an ironclad rule. No one from homicide ever talks to the media. Except him.

They thanked the lady and moved out of the garage. Getting to their car was like running a gauntlet. And they ran it. The reporters and cameramen were on their heels, first cajoling, then cursing as Fiona and Cates locked the car doors.

"No shit," the eggplant said into the car radio after she had identified the corpse. He lowered his voice. "You're positive?"

"I met the lady," Fiona said. Briefly, she confronted the dilemma of her knowledge, then mentally postponed it.

"You do get around, FitzGerald."

She coughed into her fist and looked at Cates. "I'm locked in the car and surrounded by the animals of the media." She held the microphone pointing at the window.

"Hear?"

"You tell them anything?"

"Not me," she said in a mocking tone. "I obey the rules according to . . ." She paused deliberately. He knew what they called him behind his back.

"The eggplant," he chuckled.

"The thing is," she said, "if we don't say anything, they'll think we're hiding something, something big."

"Makes sense," the eggplant muttered.

"So what should we do?"

He was silent a moment. Of all his duties, he loved playing the star. Only he could be cast as Mr. Hot Dog and beware anyone who had the audacity to steal his limelight. Fiona noted that the media people had grown bored with their harassment and were heading toward the house.

"Tell them," he said, "that I'll be holding a press conference up here in say, three hours." He paused and cleared his throat. "We'll need a real positive ident before we send this one up."

"Looks like a strangulation," Fiona volunteered.

"I'll push Benton on this one. I want every fact to be letter perfect. Tell the world we're pros."

She knew he was already giving things a political spin in his mind. A diplomatic murder had cachet, took the pressure off the escalating killings in the crack wars.

"Shall we notify the Ambassador?" Fiona asked, knowing the answer.

"Do what you have to. Come in with enough time to brief me. I want to go out there smart as hell."

She waited for his ten-four, but it didn't come.

"Get your jollies poking around graves," he said. She caught the shorthand. He was making the connection. Then he signed off.

The media people were huddled in a circle around the woman and her baby. Television cameras, like small cannons, were focused on them. The baby had started to howl.

She banged the car's horn to get their attention. They came running and she opened the window a crack.

"Greene's running a press conference in three hours," Fiona snapped. A barrage of questions began and Fiona gunned the motor.

They drove around the corner and pulled up in front of the house where the yard had caved in. Planted in front of it was a For Sale sign. Haber and Weston, Real Estate.

Constructed mostly of wood with cupolas, gables and an outdoor porch, the house had an expansive Victorian feel, suggesting more leisurely times in a bygone age. It was well set back from the street with a fence of high hedges along its property lines that assured its seclusion and privacy. A car could easily be driven through the driveway and disappear behind the hedges, totally out of the field of vision of neighbors on either side.

Determining that the house was locked and, indeed, empty, they moved to the yard. A walkway of wide stone slabs led through the trees to the point where the ground had given way.

Fiona speculated that the body was dragged along the stone walkway to a point under the trees. A grave was dug, probably an easy job, owing to the softness of the ground because of the rain. Then the body was thrown into the hole and covered up. It was obvious that the cave-in had literally buried any useful clues and the rain had undoubtedly washed away others. They moved over the stone walkway searching for any indication that a body, a person, a shovel had come that way. Nothing. Here, too, the rain had done its job well.

"Good choice?" Cates mused.

"Except for the rain. Might have been here forever."

"Nothing is forever," Cates said.

Somehow Fiona detected in this remark the very essence of Cates' determination. Here was the black boy from Trinidad, with shiny ebony skin stretched over Caucasian features, speaking in the clipped accent of the island, as different from the native blacks who populated the MPD as she was, the white woman.

Like her, he thrived on obstacles and divining strategies to outflank them. Unlike many of his fellow detectives, he had a degree in criminology from Florida State, although he was careful not to flaunt it.

"Being philosophical today, Cates," Fiona said, mildly teasing, yet knowing that few remarks could penetrate Cates' uptight sensibility when he was immersed in a case. He was too focused for idle bantering and definitely not one for personal revelation.

Fiona knew very little about him. He was 30, had emigrated with his mother as a teenager. He still lived with her in an apartment in

Northwest Washington. He had admitted, in a rare moment, that he had a girlfriend who was studying to be a doctor in a school in upstate New York. As far as she could tell, Cates was faithful to her. He was also obsessed with making good at his job, and as Fiona's junior, eager to learn anything she could impart.

"Not philosophical, Fi," Cates replied. "The fact is that in due course everything is revealed."

"Depends how long we live."

Cates nodded, refusing to take up the cudgel, lapsing into silence.

They drove to the Austrian Embassy and Fiona opened the door.

"I've got to do this alone," she told Cates.

"Is that wise?" Cates asked. Despite his deference, she knew he was questioning her motives.

"I know the man," she responded.

"Sometimes that could inhibit objectivity," Cates responded.

"That's a pretty rigid evaluation, Cates."

Cates shrugged, obviously avoiding any confrontation.

As she left the car, she chose to turn away quickly, unwilling to confront his expression nor her own motives. Call it a postponement, she assured herself. Was there enough evidence yet to scuttle a man's career?"

The receptionist was surprised when she was let in immediately. The Ambassador, impeccable in a dark blue suit and discreet striped tie that hung in a Windsor knot from a starched collar, came out from behind a carved oak desk and greeted her in perfect diplomatic fashion.

He ushered her to a seat in a conversational setting in one part of the spacious office.

"Can I get you anything?" Ambassador Kessel asked. She could tell from the elaborate way he had chosen to illustrate his exterior calmness that he suspected her mission. He seemed different from the anxious person she had been with just yesterday, more polished, but calmer, as if he had already sensed her mission. She studied him carefully for signs and possibilities.

He had, after all, given her a picture of their marriage that was deliberately planted to illustrate his indifference to his wife's unfaithfulness. Perhaps all that had been merely a ploy to set up a future denial on his part. Nevertheless, she did not wish to appear callous and indifferent.

"I think I've found her," she said, her words hesitant, hoping by her somber mood and delivery to telescope the message.

"She's dead," he whispered, swallowing deeply. He had gone pale and clasped his hands between his knees. He lowered his head to hide his eyes and shook it from side to side.

"How?" he asked. It seemed a genuine effort for him to expel this single word.

"Strangulation, I think. The Medical Examiner is checking as we speak." She then explained the circumstances of the discovery. Each revelation seemed a physical blow. "Why Helga?" he asked in a voice now muffled by grief.

"That's exactly what we're trying to ascertain, Mr. Ambassador."

"She loved life, perhaps too much," he sighed.

Although the color had not come back into his face, he seemed to have gotten himself fully under control. She noted that the knuckles of his clasped hands were white. Suddenly he looked around the office. He seemed furtive, then he leaned over and spoke in a whisper.

"Will it be awful?" he asked.

She shook her head.

"I mean the aftermath." A nerve palpitated in his jaw.

"I'm not sure." His meaning seemed clear to her, but she could tell that her response hadn't satisfied him. "I'm afraid there will be a great deal of media coverage and wild speculation. There's no escaping that. You are, after all, the Austrian Ambassador. And she was a beautiful woman."

"I understand." He nodded to buttress his reaction.

"My boss is holding a press conference. They will be crawling all over this place, looking for stories, pictures, anything. I would suggest you keep as far away from them as you can."

"Will he tell them everything?"

"He doesn't know everything," she said pointedly. Then, after a long pause, she asked gently, "Do I?"

"I don't know what to say. It is all beyond belief."

He sucked in some air through pursed lips, then expelled it in a gesture of disgust.

"Can it be avoided?" he asked tentatively. "The other aspect?"

"Depends," she said, wanting to be sure he understood fully. "If it's not connected."

"Do you think it is?"

"I hope not."

She was sincere, even hopeful, but dubious. The image of Monte's apprehensive face flickered in her mind. She chased it away, although she determined that she would be the one to break it to him.

"These things have a way of spilling over everything."

He cocked his head and unclasped his hands, as if to illustrate his surrender to events.

"You're absolutely certain it was her?" he asked.

"Unfortunately I have to take you in to confirm it."

He put his hands in front of his face. His shoulders shook, although no noise escaped his lips. His grief seemed genuine, but she forced herself to suspend judgement. She had been fooled before.

XI

Monte, looking wary and very nervous, slid into one of Sherry's torn naugahyde booths. Fiona watched him across the chipped formica table. Of course, he knew that something devastatingly important was happening. No question about it. He was a man prepared for the worst. She introduced Cates and the two men shook hands.

"He has to be in it now," Fiona explained. "He's my partner."
Monte shrugged, obviously a man waiting to hear the worst.

Earlier, she had told Cates of her involvement with Monte, leaving the implications for him to deal with.

"We dated," she told him, watching his eyes dance away from hers.

"It happens." He shrugged. But she knew there was more going on behind the response.

"Some might say it's a conflict," she said cautiously. "Might interfere with my objectivity."

Cates kept his eyes from confronting her. He was obviously evaluating the revelation, being deliberate, checking it against his own standard and, of course, its effect on his career. It was a measure she understood.

"When you swim in your own pool," Cates said after a long pause, his glance meeting hers, "you're bound to meet familiar fish."

"Bon mot, Cates?"

"I was looking for a good way to say it."

"Say what?"

"That I trust your judgment, Fi."

It embarrassed him to say it and again he turned his eyes away.

"Fair enough," Fiona said, offering a thin smile. She wanted to bend over the table and kiss his cheek, but she held off, worried about any misinterpretation.

Sherry came over and filled three coffee mugs. They waited until she finished her chore and waddled away.

"She's been murdered."

It did not need to be said twice. Unlike the Ambassador, who had gone white, Monte flushed red.

"Fuck," he said.

She watched the anger wash over him. His large brown eyes flickered with pain and his chubby fingers tapped the formica table. She wished she could have broken it to him by herself in a private comforting way, cuddling him in her arms like a big teddy bear. In his game, she knew, a threatened career held all the terrors of a threatened life.

As quickly as she could, in much the same way as the eggplant had briefed the press, she gave him the details. In performance, the eggplant always rose to the occasion and she was proud of him, albeit grudgingly. She considered herself far less skillful. It was impossible for her to coat the pill.

"Those lice will find a way to connect Sam," he said, meaning the media. He could not stop shaking his head in disbelief. "Could be an absolute disaster politically." He started to slide outward from the booth. "I've got to tell them before it hits."

"I'd be circumspect, Monte," Fiona said, her words cautioning. He stopped his slide at the edge of the booth.

"I don't understand," he said, searching her face.

"They're suspects now."

"Jesus." He paused. "Me, too, I suppose."

"Only technically," she admitted.

"Jesus. Jesus K. Christ. I can't believe it." He leaned against the backrest. "Fi. Me?"

Fiona exchanged glances with Cates, who was present as both col-
league and witness. Again she wished she were alone. But that
would be unprofessional, compromising and insulting to Cates.
Besides, she respected his judgement and she badly needed another
opinion for her actions.

"It's our job, Monte. Everyone who has even the most theoretical of
motives is automatically a suspect," Fiona said, putting her hand over
his. He moved it away. She knew Cates had noticed. It didn't matter.
She was certain he knew there was something more between them.

"And what is mine?"

It didn't need to be explained, but she did it anyway.

"Politics. You were running Sam's campaign. High stakes and
good reason. The woman could upset the goal. Perhaps she was
becoming a nuisance and she had to be taken out."

"By me. Monte Pappas. A killer. I can't kill cockroaches." He
reached out, wrists together. "Cuff me."

"It's a scenario. It's the way cops think. I'm letting you in on the
process."

"Maybe you should disqualify yourself. You've got a conflict of
interest." He expelled the words in a fit of temper. Of course, he was
angry. He had a right to be. But not at her.

"I have an interest, not a conflict," she snapped back. I care about
you, you prick, she shouted inside herself.

"You wouldn't be here if she didn't care," Cates suddenly interjected. They had exchanged glances.

"You keep out of it," Monte said, still testy.

"I'm in it, Mr. Pappas," Cates replied calmly. "So are you and
nothing can change that. Nothing."

"Don't blow it, Monte. He's on our side."

"You mean we have a side. You're both cops. You can't be on anybody's side," he said, his eyes shifting from one face to the other.

"Maybe what happened has nothing at all to do with the Senator
or his staff," Fiona began, deliberately showing him a note of hope.

"Thank you," he mumbled.

"That's the benefit of the doubt, Pappas," Cates said. "Be grateful."

In her heart-to-heart with Cates she had told him of Monte's trust in her. Trust was a commodity of enormous value in the cop business. Indeed, in life.

"We don't know that anyone in your tight little circle killed this woman. We intend to find out, no holds barred. But we can promise that we will do everything in our power to"—she remembered how they had put it—"to be discreet."

"How can you do that? The very act of investigation sends the message. The stink will be in the air and the media will follow it. And it will lead directly to the Senator. You've just supplied the motive. Mistress of Presidential-hopeful murdered. Two and two make five to those vultures. Grist for the mill."

Sweat had sprouted on his upper lip and he paused to wipe it away with the back of his hand.

"Depends on how we handle it," Fiona said gently. They hadn't yet put the eggplant into the loop. He had rushed away from the press conference for a meeting with the Police Commissioner, which gave them both the excuse of postponement. But she was obliged to keep the eggplant "apprahzed," especially when a case involved a politician, and he, in turn, was obliged to keep the Mayor "apprahzed," which meant that the involvement or noninvolvement of the Senator was at the mercy of conflicting agendas.

Before leaving for the meeting with the Police Commissioner, the eggplant had told them:

"Tomorrow in my office. First thing. I want theories and options." He had lifted one of his well-cared-for ebony fingers and pointed it at them. "No surprises," he had warned. In his shorthand it meant that he would hold them responsible for anything the media might ferret out, whether they knew it in advance or not. He would be particularly intolerant, in fact, inflamed, if he discovered that they were withholding information from him deliberately. On this latter issue, they were forever vulnerable.

"Help us move fast, Monte," Fiona said. "This could be a totally unrelated thing, and a quick absolution of your principals might get everybody off the hook without a mark on them. Fact is that nobody on our side wants to fuck over a potentially powerful politician . . . if it's not necessary. We have to see Sam, Monte. No way out."

Monte looked down at his fingers, mulling it over. When he looked up again, his gaze had softened. He reminded her of a big curly-topped baby on the verge of tears.

"More coffee?"

It was Sherry, looking as shabby as ever in her bageled stockings and stained cardigan pulled tight over her overample figure. As always, she wore battered and stained once-white Reeboks. Without waiting for an answer she filled their mugs.

"As the doctors say," Fiona told him when Sherry had walked away. "Cut out the cancer before it spreads."

"You mean now?"

"We're wasting time," Cates said.

"I'll try. Sam's first instinct will be to stonewall," Monte said, biting his lip. He slid out of the booth but did not go for the phone. "There's something else." He shook his head. "He doesn't know you were in it."

Naturally, she thought. They were the clean-up boys. Despite her knowledge of the system, she was developing a strong distaste for Senator Langford.

"Then explain to him how lucky he is," Fiona said, watching Monte's face. Their eyes locked. In that moment of shared intimacy she tried to convey her feelings. I'm your friend, but I'm a professional. Trust me. I will not hurt you unnecessarily. Such words could not be said without compromising herself, not even if she was alone. Understand the level of my involvement, she begged him. Not quite love. Friendship, perhaps. More than fucking buddies, though. He was, she knew, an honorable man in a dishonorable profession. For that reason he reminded her of her father.

"He is lucky," Monte said, nodding to emphasize the point. He looked toward the battered phone on the wall and its halo of hastily scrawled numbers. "Hate phones," he muttered as he moved toward it, groping in his pockets for coins. He couldn't find any, then came back. She had a quarter ready.

"For want of a nail," she said. He smiled and their hands touched, then lingered, and she knew the subliminal message had been conveyed. Trust me.

"For his sake," Cates said, watching Monte punch in the numbers, "I hope he's a good salesman."

"He sold me," Fiona said, feeling a hot blush rise to her cheeks. She broke into a broad smile. "Did I say that?"

They watched Monte talking into the phone, holding his voice down to a heated whisper. She knew he was begging, imploring.

"A tall order," Cates said.

"Depends," Fiona mused. The story's promise was lurid media fare. They would make a beeline into the lady's secret life, certainly the sexual part. Depended on two things. Had anyone outside the inner circle known? Discretion was relative. There were the little people to consider, the casual observers, the secretaries, messengers, receptionists, waiters, doormen, maids, the inanimate and neutral who bore witness and could come forward. And, of course, the unknown confidants. Like herself. Now Cates. Soon the eggplant. Then, maybe, the Mayor. Everyone would have to look to their agendas.

Monte's body language told her that he was having trouble. At one point he leaned his forehead against the wall in frustration. Then he slammed the receiver back on its hook.

He was agitated when he returned to the booth. The flush was heavy on his cheeks, congealed to two dabs of bright red, like rouge.

"Asshole," he said.

He slid back into the booth and reached for his coffee mug. It looked tepid, and oily circles floated on the surface. His hands shook as he raised it to his lips. Showing the extent of his distraction, he drank half the mug in one gulp.

"For a telephone paranoid, you talked fairly long," Fiona said.

"It's not easy arguing in code," Monte muttered.

"Why are we sitting here?" Fiona asked.

"He wants to consult Bunkie. He's scared shitless. I gave him this number."

"No time for that, pal," Cates said. "We're in a race. Any media calls yet?"

"So far no," Monte said. "Asshole thinks Bunkie can fix it."

They were silent for a long moment.

"Maybe he already did," Fiona said.

Again silence. Monte was the first to stir. He slid out of the booth and stood up.

"You guys coming?" he asked.

XII

"Godammit, Pappas," Bunkie said, his heels clicking along the marble floor of the Senate Office Building as he came to intercept them. "I told you no." He looked around him furtively, then faced them, talking between clenched teeth. "He doesn't want any part of this. He told you that, for chrissakes."

"He can't duck it, Bunkie," Pappas said coolly as Bunkie's feral eyes darted between Fiona and Cates.

"Now him," Bunkie said, pointing his chin at Cates. He turned again to Monte. "You had to get her involved. Shit, Pappas. All your brains are in your cock."

She fully expected Monte to explode and it took all her discipline to keep herself under control. Monte's reaction was to smile, although she noted a touch of malevolence.

"These are the police," Monte said. She had seen him suck in a deep breath, pull in his stomach and square his shoulders with that Boy-Scout pride that made him so loveable. "They are involved in an official investigation of a murder." He paused and again exchanged glances with Fiona. "And you are one of the primary suspects."

The blood drained out of Bunkie's face and his body seemed to cave in on itself. He had all he could do to control his lip tremors.

"Me?"

His gaze danced everywhere. The long, wide corridors seemed endless, deep caverns to nowhere. Occasionally, someone would emerge from one of the large oversized doors that opened on to the corridors, but they seemed dwarfed by the huge expanse.

They let him stew his way through a long pause. Of course, he was a prime suspect, but he could barely comprehend it. She attributed that to his lack of insight and his egoistic and therefore narrow

105

focus. It was obvious that the consequences of such suspicion was occurring to him now at an exceedingly rapid rate.

"We can stand here and talk," Cates said, prodding him. He seemed to be unable to make a decision. "Or we can take you down to headquarters."

Movie talk, she knew, but effective. Bunkie managed to muster his own movie retort.

"I'll call my lawyer."

"Be my guest," Fiona said pleasantly.

Bunkie stood rooted to the spot.

"Mulling it over, right, Bunkie?" Monte said. "You want to expand the group go right ahead."

"All right, we'll talk," he shrugged. "But not here. And not in the office, okay?"

"Geography wasn't our primary interest," Fiona said.

Bunkie led them through the long corridor. They came to a polished set of double doors, one of which was lettered "Committee Room" in gold. He opened the door and they followed him in.

Dominating the room was a huge half-moon oval rostrum for the Senators and theater-style seating in front of it for the spectators. Along the side were loose chairs, which Monte drew into a circle for them.

By then, Bunkie had recovered somewhat, although his pallor was still ashen. He was, as Fiona had suspected he did when she had first seen him, wearing flashy suspenders with a garish duck pattern, a matching bow tie and a clashing striped button-down shirt. On his feet were tasseled overshined loafers over red polo socks. All in all, perfect casting for the preppy political loyalist.

Without any more preliminaries, Fiona dived right into it, her eyes fixed on Bunkie's, although he would not lock into her gaze.

"She was found this morning, apparently buried in a hole behind a house in Cleveland Park. Medical examiner says strangled."

He muttered "shit" under his breath and nervously scratched at one arm. Cates filled in additional details. His face became a kaleidoscope of disgust, as if he were being dragged through a cesspool.

"The point is, hotshot," Monte added, after Cates had finished his lurid story, "that Fiona and her partner here are going to try and keep their investigation quiet. No guarantees." He cut a glance at Fiona. "That is no small thing, considering the circumstances."

"Look," Bunkie said, trying to gather the remnants of his courage. "It wasn't us. Not me. Not the Senator. Do we look like murderers?"

"Murderers don't look like murderers," Fiona said.

"Jesus, you were coming to the office. People have eyes. Ears. They watch and listen."

"You refused any other options, Bunkie," Monte reminded him. He looked down at his hands for a long moment, then lifted his head and smiled. "Bunkie baby," he said, "you piss them off, they can haul your ass in, also the Senator, make a big deal, lots of noise." He puffed his cheeks and expelled the air. "Over. All over. Finis. Presidential shot." He made a chopping motion across his neck.

"Damage-control is all, Monte," Bunkie said helplessly. "I know we're clean. Langford wasn't even in the loop on this. These people already know too much."

"Not nearly enough," Fiona interjected, showing a flash of anger. This Bunkie, she thought, had to be cut down to size.

"Let's stop this bullshit, Bunkie. Where the hell is the Senator?" she said.

"He'll really be pissed," Bunkie mumbled.

"Being a Senator doesn't make one immune to being a suspect in a murder," Cates said.

"True even for a Presidential candidate," Fiona added.

"Don't be an asshole, Bunkie," Monte said.

"Okay," Bunkie said. "I can see me as a suspect. Crazy. But I can see it. I don't like it. But I do understand. Really. I understand." He was being patronizing now, changing tactics. "I'll answer anything you want."

"Will you?" Fiona chirped. "How noble."

She studied him. He was the quintessential Washington cliché. The flunky zealot, ambitious to the point of aberration, who had attached himself to the great man like a Siamese twin. The extent of his dedication was total. No task was too demeaning. That had been confirmed the other night. The perpetuation of Sam Langford on his journey to political power was Bunkie Farrington's reason for living. But would he kill, if he had to? Yes, she decided.

"How long have you been with the Senator?" Fiona asked, telling him silently: *Assume the position, pal. Spread 'em wide.*

"Fourteen years. Right out of Yale. When the Senator was in the House."

"How long did it take you to get this close to him?" The implication that there was something rancid in the idea of it was deliberate. Once again he showed his total lack of insight.

"Very quickly," Bunkie said with pride. "We hit it off instantly. We have a compatibility of political ideals."

Whatever they are, she thought. Fiona, not wanting to deal with the trite, did not pursue this. Monte had addressed the question with more honesty and panache on their first date.

"You told me the other night that you had"—she watched him gathering his concentration—"arranged things for him."

He turned to Monte.

"You had to bring her the other night. You couldn't leave well-enough alone."

"That's the point, Bunkie. Nothing was well-enough. A disaster was unfolding. We needed all the help we could get. Now we need her more than ever."

"To sniff around? Accuse us?"

"You're pushing, Bunkie. They can get real nasty."

"I'll bet."

She turned to Monte.

"One phone call we can sink this ship," Fiona sighed. "This jaboni is going to blow it."

"Better listen, schmuck," Monte warned.

"Just want you all to know I'm not going to lay down just because you're leaning on me." He was obviously hiding behind a fairly flimsy macho facade. "So what was the question?" Bunkie asked.

"She didn't ask any question," Cates interjected.

"You've done this before?" Fiona asked.

"Now that's a question," Cates said.

"Done what?"

"And that's no answer," Cates shot back.

"Been a pimp, for chrissakes," Fiona said with irritation.

"I resent that," Bunkie shouted. The sound of his own voice apparently set off a retreat. After calming himself, he spoke again in a lower tone. "Hell, he is a magnet for women. He didn't need anyone. They love him. I just kept him out of trouble."

"Like with Helga Kessel," Cates pressed.

"She got all that the other night," Bunkie said, shoving a thumbing toward Fiona. His voice was getting shrill again. "And the Ambassador told her that she took it like a trooper. In fact, it didn't seem to mean diddly squat to the bitch. Her being murdered had nothing to do with us. Not with me and not with him." He pointed with his chin in what was undoubtedly the general direction of the Senator's office.

"After your little Dear-John drink you never saw or heard from her again?" Fiona asked.

"Why would I?"

"That's not what I asked, Farrington," Fiona snapped.

"No. I never heard from her again." Arrogance was becoming surly impatience.

"And the others? Did you hear from them again?"

"What others?"

"That's for us to ask and you to say," Cates said.

"What the hell do you think I am?" he protested.

"We've established that," Fiona said.

Suddenly he shifted in his chair and turned to Monte, pointing a finger in his face.

"You talk too fucking much, pal. The Senator's about had it with you."

She wondered if they had gone too far, jeopardized Monte's relationship with the Senator. To keep that cool had been her primary objective. But she could see that the relationship between Monte and Farrington was tense at the best of times.

"You're overreacting, Bunkie," Monte said calmly, illustrating to them that he knew how to unload Bunkie's wagons. Nevertheless, Fiona decided to take a new tack. No sense throwing the baby out with the bath water.

"Let's get down to the cream cheese, Farrington. We figure that Helga was strangled sometime during Monday. She was probably buried during the night, probably that same night . . ."

He seemed to brighten with optimism.

"Monday." He offered a wry chuckle. "I was with the Senator the entire day. From eight until nearly midnight."

"Just you and him?" Cates asked.

"Most of the time with a roomful of people." He looked around him. "In this committee room as a matter of fact. He was taking testimony on waste disposal. I was with him the whole time, including lunch. We ate in the Senate dining room."

"And after?" Cates pressed.

"Back at his office. We were with his AA in the office until nearly nine. Then we went over to The Monocle for dinner and hung there until midnight." Calmer now, he cut a glance at Monte. "Never stops, does it, Monte?"

"You're a very dedicated man." Monte harrumphed.

"And then?" Fiona asked, still in pursuit. "After The Monocle."

"Sleepy-bye. Remember Bonnie at the Pepsi thing? She was up at her place waiting for a cuddle. Doesn't talk much, that one, but, boy, is she expressive in other ways." He was gloating now, changing his tone yet again. He seemed relieved.

"And the Senator?"

"Back to home and hearth. I called him at seven in the morning. He was there. Nell will back that up. It pisses her off."

"What does?"

"Our . . . well, the closeness of our working relationship."

He was getting to her.

"Jealous of the office wife," Fiona snapped.

"Sorry, I won't be baited. Call it what you want, lady cop. Fact is I'm clean as a whistle on this."

"We'll be checking it out, Farrington," Cates said.

"Clean may be too strong a word," Fiona said, annoyed at his final return to arrogance. He had probably seen her back off. Yet she was certain that his story would check out, although she had hoped for more intimidating leverage to cut through the bullshit. Now he would feel more confident about stonewalling.

"They do have an alibi," Cates said, picking up the rhythm of her thoughts.

"I'm relieved," Fiona said. "Aren't you relieved, Monte?"

Monte was confused. His gaze washed over the other three.

"He really had me worried," Fiona said.

"Me, too. I would want nothing to reflect on the integrity of a dedicated public servant."

"I think Captain Greene would be proud to make that announcement." She smiled pleasantly. "Chief of Homicide. Loves publicity."

"What do you mean, 'announcement'?" Bunkie asked, his brow wrinkling.

"About how clean you and the Senator are," Fiona said.

"No longer suspected," Cates echoed.

"You're kidding," Bunkie said, struggling to emit a laugh. "This is a joke, right?" They watched him squirm. "You know we're not without recourse. Senator Langford is very powerful. I wouldn't fuck with him if I were you."

"Above all, I wouldn't let you be me," Fiona said.

"No way," Cates said, meaning himself as well.

They got up from their chairs and started for the door. At the door, Fiona turned.

"Coming, Monte?"

He got up, totally confused.

"I want to catch Captain Greene in time. Might make the evening news."

"You're bluffing," Bunkie shouted.

"Put a little pancake on Farrington. He looks a little peaked for TV."

They went out through the double doors, exchanged glances then started down the corridor. They heard his footsteps clattering behind them. They accelerated their pace.

"I'll make a deal," Bunkie said, breathing heavily. They stopped.

"I'm all ears," Fiona said.

"Give us a break, will you? I've handled this badly."

Monte, who had followed Bunkie along the corridor, reached them.

"He's a good man," Bunkie begged. "All right, he's got this problem with the girls. But this is just a coincidence. Something outside our orbit. Be fair. That's all we ask." He turned toward Monte. "Right, Monte? All we want is them to be fair."

"They've agreed to that, Bunkie. That was the point," Monte said.

"Okay, then. But please. Just the lady. One-on-one."

Fiona hesitated, reluctant to comment. The ploy was too obvious, laughable. Throw him a female. He'd have her bamboozled in the blink of an eye.

"It's the best way," Bunkie pleaded. "Too many of us will spook him."

Fiona weighed the offer. She'd danced with the man. Now she remembered her reaction. Nevertheless, she resented the implication.

"I know him, Sergeant FitzGerald," Bunkie said. "He couldn't kill anybody. He's innocent on this. We're all bystanders here."

"Settle down, Farrington," Fiona said. "If we reaffirm both your alibis you could be in the clear. Fact is, it has to be done."

He looked pitiful, but she felt no sympathy. They were clever, these bastards. They could fawn on cue. She looked at Cates.

"Any objection?" she asked.

Both she and Cates knew the question was solely for effect. It was one of the hallmarks of their partnership that they both check their ego at the squad-room door. The name of their game was detecting, finding the bad guys, not gratifying their egos.

"Hereby registered," Cates answered, also for effect. Then he stood up and began to move away. She hurried after him until they were out of earshot of Monte and Bunkie.

"Pappas is okay, but the other guy stinks to high heaven."

Quick to judgement, she thought suddenly. Could she strike Monte off the list so cavalierly, despite Monte's own protestations? As if in counterpoint to her thoughts, Cates continued.

"People who want things badly enough are capable of anything." He paused and his voice dropped a few decibels. "Especially politicians."

"For a comparative newcomer to this town, I'd say that's pretty cynical."

"Bad attitude, right?"

"It does cut into your objectivity," Fiona said. Not that her objectivity remained pristine. *Do as I say, not as I do,* she cautioned him silently.

"I have a confession then," Cates said. She braced herself for the revelation. Sometimes, she knew, things had to be articulated to make sense of one's thoughts.

"I'd love Farrington to be the one," Cates said. "Shifty bugger."

"That's called emotional involvement," she replied with a touch of rebuke in her tone.

"I know."

"Objectivity means keeping all of our options open. At this stage everybody is fair game. Everybody remains a suspect. Everybody. We call that an open mind, Cates." She smiled, taking the sting out of the admonishment. "Consider yourself spanked."

He shrugged and offered a thin smile.

"For my own good, right, Fi?"

"Right."

They had, she knew, picked up the investigatory rhythm of the case, moving now in perfect tandem, thinking in synch, communicating in their own special shorthand.

"I'll also follow up on the real estate. Touch base later."

"And I'll duck the eggplant until we catch up. We'll pull it together before the meeting."

He nodded and started to move away, stopped suddenly and turned.

"What was that old movie expression? Yeah." He nodded. "Keep your powder dry." He was being cryptic, but she knew his meaning. He was genuinely worried.

"It's okay, Cates. I'll keep my legs crossed."

His lips curled upward, not quite a smile. With one finger he waved goodbye and she watched him move swiftly down the corridor. Then she moved back to where Bunkie and Pappas were waiting.

"We're wasting time," she said.

XIII

In the labyrinthine underground corridors of the Capitol there are about fifty private suites reserved for the use of Senators. Allocation of these suites is based on seniority. Fiona's father had one. Once the Senator invited a group of her friends to celebrate her birthday in his. Her father claimed that he used it more for "thinking things out" than anything else.

Later, when she grew more sophisticated, she learned that they had other, more varied uses.

The suites are, in fact, one of the most sought-after of all Senatorial perks, private hideaways complete with kitchen facilities, showers and bathrooms. Many of them are arranged as living room/dining room combinations. Some are elaborately decorated. Most are equipped with some form of sleeping accommodations, although their prime intention is not for use as an overnight facility.

Over the years Senators have used these suites for entertaining constituents or colleagues at private cocktail parties, buffet lunches or sit-down dinners. Others have used them as retreats from the rigid and often exhausting legislative routine. Some Senators have used them for afternoon naps, or to cater to some dark and dangerous addiction far from the public eye, like alcohol, for example. Some have used them solely for recreation, like playing poker or gin rummy, or listening to their favorite soap opera or ballgame. One Senator, Fiona's father once told her, was known to set up his easel in one of these suites, strip to the buff, and blithely paint canvases of serene landscapes.

At times they were used for sexual trysts. That went without saying. It had its dangers, of course. Access could be monitored by those with sinister purposes. It was not the place for more serious sexual encounters, but it did function as a place for, as they say, sport fucking between Senators and the more round-heeled members of his or her staff.

These suites were, of course, not well publicized, and, Fiona suspected, there seemed to be a general truce between Senators and media to leave the subject in limbo unless their use was so compelling or scandalous that nothing could stop the revelation.

Bunkie had ducked into another empty committee room to use the phone.

"A real hardhead," Monte said when he had gone. "But a human shield."

"Fanatics make me queasy," Fiona said.

"But it does look as if you can put your suspicions to rest."

"Not yet," Fiona said. Far from it, she thought, but she did not wish to alarm him. The connections these people had with the dead woman were too involved to be dismissed so cavalierly.

Monte moved toward her, held her by the shoulders then drew her closer.

"Thanks for this," he said, kissing her. "Trust is a rare commodity."

"Very," she agreed. Although she was trained to be wary, Monte's presence and character did not disturb her comfort level. She allowed their kiss to linger. Finally she pushed him away, offering the light humor of a time-honored cliché. "I'm on duty, Monte."

They parted just as Bunkie strode through the door. She could tell that he had seen, but he said nothing.

"He's less than happy," Bunkie said.

Fiona said nothing and followed him again through the corridors. At the end of one corridor they came to an elevator, got in and went to a lower level. They traversed more corridors. Sometimes Bunkie or Monte waved to people along the way. She remembered these labyrinthine corridors from her childhood. It had always seemed so self-contained, a world unto itself.

The corridors grew more deserted as they continued, and finally, after a series of turns, they stopped in front of a large polished door. Bunkie knocked three times, then waited. They heard a buzz.

"Go in," Bunkie said. "We'll get a cup of coffee and meet you in an hour."

"Good luck," Monte said.

"You'll see," Bunkie added. "There won't be any reason for you to be suspicious. We're not without our faults. But we don't do murder."

Sam Langford was sitting in his shirtsleeves on a large easy chair, his feet on a hassock. A standing lamp threw light on a pile of papers that he was reading. He put them aside and stood up, showing a broad dimpled smile. His wavy, prematurely greying hair fell carelessly over his forehead. When he got closer she could see his blue eyes, clear and remarkably untroubled, considering all the angst that had to be endured for her to get here.

"Very happy to see you again . . . is it Fiona?"

She nodded, responding to his outstretched hand. He took hers gently. At first it felt soft, devoid of pressure. Then it firmed. His touch was insinuating, enveloping. He did have an aura, Fiona thought. She remembered how she had felt held in his arms, dancing.

There was no denying it. The man had sex appeal. Worse, he knew it.

In a sweeping gaze, she took in the room. It looked much like the living room of a well-appointed home. It was filled with what appeared to be antiques or repros. There was a polished mahogany dining table on one side of the room and eight side chairs. In front of the upholstered chair in which the Senator sat was a couch. Also in the conversational setting around a large, highly polished, dark wood cocktail table were two deep leather wing chairs.

A large secretary covered the bulk of one wall, also a tall clock that she was sure tolled the hour and half hour. On another wall was a bookcase filled with books. A number of paintings were hung about the place. One depicted a naval engagement, another scenes of colonial soldiers resting after battle. There were two pictures of dour men with powdered wigs.

The place had a distinctively historical flavor. In it the Senator looked, aside from the sex appeal, well . . . Senatorial. Perhaps even Presidential.

"Can I get you anything, Fiona?" he asked, sweeping his arm around the room. "Everything is here. This is where we get away from the madding crowd." He smiled again and out came his dimples. "Well, then make yourself comfortable," he said, pointing to one of the wing chairs. "I'm so glad we can have this little chat." He went back to his chair and sat down to study her.

She felt him pouring it on, skewering reality, bringing up the big guns of his charm and charisma. His clear blue eyes were x-rays undressing her. Dammit, she berated herself, feeling, despite all caveats, the thrill of his masculine aggression.

"I know you've already heard about Helga Kessel."

"I can't believe it." He shook his head and his eyes glinted briefly. Was it the hint of a tear? She couldn't say, but he seemed to be moved. "We were great friends."

"Yes, great friends," Fiona repeated. It was a remark meant to be sarcastic, but it seemed almost benign. She had been momentarily awed into a kind of submission, which deeply interfered with her normally creative interrogation. Stop this, woman! she rebuked herself.

"Bunkie told me about your conversation the other night." Midway into the sentence he had to clear his throat as if the words had stuck. She nodded.

"You must think I'm pretty bad. Or stupid."

"On that issue I won't make judgments."

"He also said you're a great friend of Monte's and that you're not here to hurt us." He continued to study her.

"Yes on both scores."

"My first instinct was to duck," he said with boyish candor, showing the dimples again. "Wait a bit until the smoke clears. I'm sure you know the drill from your father. I remember reading about him. I would have loved to have met him. But I came here after he had retired."

"He didn't retire. He was defeated," Fiona said. The reference to her father restored her equilibrium. "Anyway, that's not why I'm here."

"I just wanted you to know that I feel comfortable here with you, that I trust you, that my first instinct was wrong. Sometimes politics can get in the way of good sense."

"Always," Fiona said, back on track now. She watched him bear down on her, his eyes searchlights, inspecting her.

"I don't deny it," he said. "Helga and I were lovers. We cared a great deal for each other. Unfortunately, I had to make a choice in my self-interest. The thing about this business . . . you become institutionalized, like a corporation. Large numbers of people depend on you. A deeply private life can no longer exist." Suddenly he stopped himself. "Why am I flogging the obvious, telling you what you already know?"

To control the agenda, Sam, she thought, but did not give voice to it.

"Why didn't you tell her yourself?" Fiona asked. Subjectively, it was this act, or nonact, of his that she resented most.

"Pure cowardice," he admitted, lowering his eyes in some clichéd rendition of "shame." Will the real Sam Langford please stand up? Perhaps he no longer knew who that was?

She watched him, but did not comment. Worse than cowardice, she told herself.

"The thing is I can't bear to see people hurt." He paused, waiting for a reaction. When it didn't come he said, "So I'm not a paragon of virtue. Anyway, I felt relieved when Bunkie reported that she had taken it like a good soldier. Hell, she knew from the beginning that this could lead nowhere. We both knew the score." He sighed wistfully. "However you cut it, though, it was beautiful between us while it lasted. I'm sure she felt the same way."

"Did you know that Ambassador Kessel was aware of the affair?"

"That's another thing I didn't bank on. When she told me, I was in shock. Theirs was, as you already know, a most unusual relationship."

"And you accepted it?"

"Accept it? No, I didn't accept it. I lived with it."

"Did Mrs. Langford also know?"

"Don't be ridiculous. Of course not."

"Suspect? Did she suspect?"

"How can I know that?" he replied testily. "We have two young children. She's quite a busy woman. It's not easy being the wife of a Senator."

"How would she react if it came out?"

"Not good, I'm afraid."

"You think it would jeopardize your family as well as your career?"

"Is the Pope Catholic? Nell is a proud woman. Nothing would ever be the same, that's for sure."

"So why risk it?"

"Good question, Fiona. You wouldn't be here if that wasn't the case. It's cheating, pure and simple. Call it a weakness. So I'm an incurable romantic." He lifted his hand in a traffic cop's gesture. "I know it's a rationalization. Ten years of therapy might get to the bottom of it. But, for whatever reason, there it is."

His gaze had drifted. Now he raised his eyes again and met hers. "It doesn't make me any less of a political leader. In fact, it is a rather common characteristic, considering what we now know about Jack Kennedy, Franklin Roosevelt, Dwight Eisenhower and Lyndon Johnson, to name just a few." His eyes bore down. "I love women, Fiona. And I love being in love with women. Believe it or not, this has nothing to do with my family. My wife or kids. It's both a personal problem and a political liability to have such a propensity. I'm also less than courageous about breaking things off when it becomes politically necessary. That, I'm afraid, is the full extent of my venality. I also understand your role as investigator. Indeed, in your place I would consider myself a suspect, even though, knowing myself as

I do, I would never, ever . . . I am constitutionally unable to murder . . . indeed, to physically hurt . . . anyone."

He was utterly disarming and passionate in his candor. You could
fool me, she told herself with self-deprecating sarcasm.

"Then you realize why I have to be here, have to probe this," she
said, trying to match his self-effacement, but losing badly.

"Of course."

It was then that she launched into the technical aspects of her
questioning. His answers corroborated what Bunkie had told him,
which relieved her. Her instincts told her that this charming rogue
was only a lady killer in a symbolic sense.

"Are you satisfied, Senator, that Farrington's report on Helga's
reaction to their tête-à-tête is completely accurate?"

Sam Langford rubbed his chin, then tapped his teeth with
his fingers.

"The man has been with me ever since I came here, first as a
Congressman, he was just out of Yale. He can be overbearing at times,
overprotective, hyperdedicated, probably loyal to a fault. He will
deliberately keep me uninformed, especially, like now, if he believes
something will upset me. He will edit out. He will be oblique. Yet,
we have our shorthand. Every successful politician has his Bunkie. He
did this thing with Helga because I trusted him to do it."

"He called it damage-control," Fiona said, noting how cleverly he
had surgically removed himself from Bunkie's excesses.

"Indeed, it is. And I am completely satisfied. Poor Helga's death
had to be the result of circumstances far outside our orbit, Fiona.
Sure, I'd like to keep out of the clutches of the media on this. We
both know it could wipe me out, certainly politically. I've been
lucky so far. I'll admit that. I'm no Gary Hart challenging the media
to follow me. In their eyes, I would be guilty as hell. But I'm"—he
smiled, telescoping the humor that was to come—"off the stuff now.
Scared off by my advisors. This episode with Helga makes it official.
No more. It's my latest slogan. Just say no." He swung his arms in

a gesture of rejection. "Finis. Nada. Verboten." He dimpled his face again. "Anything you can do to help will, of course, be greatly appreciated. I'm not sure it's possible to keep the media wolf from the door. I hope it can be done and I won't blame you if you can't. I happen also to trust Monte's judgement completely. He is the best political strategist in the business, and that takes the ability to know people and what makes them tick."

He had the entertainer's ability to hold one's interest. She quickly cast aside his effusive thank-yous and pressed on. There was more to test, more to learn.

"Did she talk about what went on, as you say, outside your orbit?" Fiona asked. Postcoital pillow talk, she meant.

He nodded his head as if he both understood and appreciated the subtlety.

"She was an enormously positive person. She loved being the chatelaine of the Embassy, loved the parties, the political discussions, loved to dress up, loved jewelry. She was highly educated, and very serious about many things. She also respected her husband enormously. Like me, though, she was a romantic and was able to conjure up a rich fantasy life." He stopped his narrative and looked at her playfully, flashing a thin but still-dimpled smile. "It was good sex, too, and we both enjoyed it."

Fiona felt herself flush and knew she had turned red. He was obviously selling her a picture of total honesty and she was probably buying it. Although flustered, Fiona managed to fire off a related question.

"Anything that dissatisfied her?" she asked.

"Yes, there was," he said swiftly, emphasizing his openness. "She resented not being able to legally hold a job. That was frustrating to her. She had been in business in Europe. She would have preferred working at something productive instead of the endless round of events she attended during the day with only women present. In a way, I suppose, our little meetings gave her a respite from that. Perhaps, at first, she consented merely to relieve the boredom." He raised a finger in the air. "At first, I said. Let's say it started out as a small flame and moved into a conflagration. I think we were both turned on by the danger of it. Can you understand that, Fiona?"

She knew what he meant. Hadn't she been there herself? She had seen it, felt it, knew its power. A sudden image invaded her mind. Herself naked, spread-eagled on the couch on which he sat. He, naked and aroused, moving to embrace her. She felt her heartbeat accelerate and other, more personal physical reactions. *My God,* she cried inwardly, forcing herself to erase the image. Did it show?

"I'm not trying to justify my philandering, Fiona," he continued. Or had there really been a pause in his explanation while he observed her, read her thoughts? Again, she felt a burning hot flush color her face. "I'm only trying to provide some insight into my motives."

And so you have, Fiona told him silently, finally picking up the thread of her interrogation.

"Do you believe that you and the Ambassador were the only men in Helga's life?"

"I never let myself ask that question," he said.

"Do you believe she was capable of having multiple affairs?"

He had to mull that over.

"Probably. She was a passionate woman. Sensuality was important to her."

"And to you."

"Yes. To me as well."

"Did she ever hint to you that she was having another affair?"

He shook his head. "That would have been the end."

"A jealous lover, are you?"

"Color it cautious, both physically and emotionally. I may be reckless, but that could border on self-destruction. Bad enough that the husband knew."

"And you?"

He lifted his eyes, then narrowed them, as he watched her. A brief flash of anger roared across his face, then disappeared, like someone passing through the shadow.

"Actually, you could say I was faithful to her." He paused, then smiled as if he had suddenly thought of some hilarious joke. "A married man must always be faithful to his mistress," he said. This bit of wisdom was delivered as a clever bon mot. She did not react except to shift her focus to another essential subject.

"And you're certain your wife did not know, know for certain?"

She knew she was going over old ground. Jealousy, after all, was primarily a woman's motive. Crime statistics backed that up. She tried to recall Nell Langford's expression as she observed her husband dancing with Helga Kessel. Did she know? she had asked Monte. Did she really know?

"I'm not an angel, Fiona. But I love my family. Nell knows that. She is a very traditional woman. The fact is that, despite my . . . my unfaithfulness, I avoid . . . in the way I conduct my family life, giving her the slightest cause for insecurity."

Translated, this self-deluding explanation equated with something Bunkie had said about Sam Langford having enough to go around.

"Frankly," the Senator snapped, "I resent your bringing Mrs. Langford into it."

"Just doing my job," Fiona said. She felt herself breaking out from his control. "Motive is everything in my business."

"Jesus, Fiona," the Senator erupted. "Not Nell."

"Sometimes men are damned fools," she pressed. "You don't expect that I'd believe that she never suspected, never questioned you, never even raised the issue. Surely there were signs."

"I did my homework," he snapped, raising the curtain slightly on his cynicism. He was a past master at deception, an expert at dissimulation, a practitioner of the sugar-coated lie.

"Senator, up to now, I've been grateful for your candor," she said pointedly, watching him squirm.

"No way," he said. "Not Nell."

"It has its logic. The jealous wife . . . ?"

"She did not know," he said emphatically. "We saw each other only during the day. We were discreet to a fault."

"Farrington saw to that."

"Impeccably."

"Are you saying that Mrs. Langford never questioned you?"

"Only in a general way," he admitted, apparently not willing to defend the obvious.

"Because she knew the kind of man she had married," Fiona pressed.

"My marriage is sacrosanct. It is my oasis and Nell is fully aware of it."

"The deal was never to bring it home."

"I don't like this," the Senator said. He stood up and paced the room. "I definitely do not like this." He stopped suddenly and turned. "You've got to keep her out of it." He was trying to appear firm, but she could tell he was pleading. "We can't do this to her. She's an innocent party. I know her. She's not capable of anything like that."

"Like what?" Fiona asked, waiting for some inadvertent revelation.

"Like murder."

She had been careful not to mention the method by which Helga had been killed. Often murderers have confessed based on being tripped up by information that only they could have known. If the Senator had mentioned strangulation, the ball game would have been over.

"You'd be surprised how many unlikely candidates have risen to the occasion."

"I really should resent that," he said angrily.

Figuratively, she pointed both barrels at him now. It was time to spin a familiar scenario.

"Senator," she began. "A woman marries a philanderer, she worries, looks for signs, observes. Betrayal is a very powerful force. You told me yourself she was . . . traditional. Therefore, she had to be . . .

finessed. Lied to, if you will. Surely there are signs, material clues. A scent. A makeup stain." She paused as if taking aim. "Sexual fatigue."

He stood rooted to a spot in the center of the room, obviously trying to find a role that would fit the circumstances. Observing him in full view, she noted he was a well-made man, slender, graceful. He wore pants well and she could not resist imagining what women sometimes imagine when they study a man's lower body. Again, she slapped her figurative hand. Stop that.

Suddenly he shook his head.

"Frankly, I hadn't expected all this psychobabble." She watched him cross the room and fall heavily into his chair again. "You can overanalyze a thing to death. My wife, Fiona, accepts me as I am. I suppose you might say there is a compact between us. If she suspected, she never made it an issue. Our home life is tranquil. Nell is not . . . well . . . not like my first wife, who drove me crazy with her suspicions. But then, I was a little more blatant in those days. Who could blame her? We had a perfectly civilized divorce after years of a childless marriage."

Again, he was trying to shift the subject.

"Do you know where Nell was that night?"

"You're still on that, are you?" No longer master of the agenda, he was exceedingly uncomfortable. "I presume she was home with the kids. As Bunkie must have told you, I was out with him and others." He became reflective for a moment. "You have to talk with her, don't you?" He looked as if he were in pain.

"It's a base that has to be touched," she told him. Now that she had the upper hand, she supposed she could be magnanimous. "Everything is in the execution."

"Nell couldn't," he said, pleading.

"Believe me, Senator, there are ways to be circumspect. I promise you . . ." She trailed off, not willing to commit in words. Of course, she would avoid revealing his dirty little secrets. Unless it was absolutely necessary. Which she hoped it wouldn't be.

"All right," he said suddenly. "I can understand your asking about
Nell. Frankly, I have to admit I was a bit nonplussed to learn that
the Ambassador knew of the affair. But that implies that he might
have had a fling himself with some lady who might have had her
own reasons for eliminating Helga."

He seemed to want to continue, but stopped abruptly, perhaps
regretting his outburst. But it did reveal the cutting edge of his des-
peration, which lay just beneath the surface. Surely, it was a possibility that had already been gone over with Bunkie in the first flush
of damage-control. It was, of course, a lot weaker than the Nell scenario. And far less volatile.

"In this business, Senator, we peek under every rock," she said.

"Look," he shrugged. "It hasn't been easy. Telling you all this.
Fact is . . . it's a gamble. I admit I'm guilty of something, but not
that—not murder. And I doubt that the others, Bunkie, Nell, even
Monte, could ever . . ." He paused. ". . . Ever. These are good people. We are talking here of taking a human life." He seemed to be
slipping into morbidity. "To destroy our lives on nothing more than
the flimsiest of evidence . . ." His voice trailed off.

"I told you, Senator. I fully understand the consequences for you.
I'll do my best. Keep the circle as small as possible."

"Sure," he said, with obvious hesitation.

She stood up. More than an hour had passed.

"I may have more questions," she said.

"I'm sure you will." He stood up, took her hand, held it. "In a way,
you might say we're innocent victims." He smiled, dimples popping.

"Innocent is a loaded word, Senator."

"You know what I mean."

He continued to hold her hand, and she made no effort to
remove hers.

"We're political people," he said. Up close his blue eyes shone
bright, penetrating. For a moment, they monopolized her and she
felt the strange thrill of his total attention. "Be gentle."

He had continued to hold her hand. Then, lifting his other one,
he enveloped hers. His flesh felt warm as he applied a light pressure.
He knew his power over women.

Then he said something that confounded her, offering a crude but
compelling image that seemed to reach for a level she was not prepared to confront.

"You have my balls in your hands, Fiona."

Only then did he release her as she turned and, hot-faced and
ashamed, strode toward the door.

XIV

There was no avoiding it. She and Cates would have to be prepared to face the eggplant. He would insist on being "apprahzed" and what he was being "apprahzed" about had better pass muster, which meant that if they were planning any editing it had better be constructed with great care.

By the time she got back to the squad room, the Helga story was in orbit. The radio stations were playing it big, complete with inflammatory words like "beauty," "nude body," and "disgorged from a shallow grave." There was also some hint of foreign intrigue. Ambassador Kessel was described as a "potentially important Austrian leader with a brilliant political future," and she assumed that he, too, would be scrambling to protect his public image.

The eggplant was liberally quoted in the initial stories. He would be loving it and looking forward to his appearances on national and international television. To his credit, he was extremely articulate and clever when facing the media. Wisely, and accurately, he had pointed out that "so far" no motive for the murder had been uncovered. Tomorrow's *Washington Post* and surely major newspapers throughout the world would carry the story on their front pages.

So far Senator Langford was not mentioned in any of the radio stories, nor was there any hint of a romantic attachment, a "secret affair" between him and the deceased. It was, in fact, too early for such a report to emerge. One could be assured, however, that the members of the Fourth Estate were on the case, scrambling for scraps to give the story more "spin."

Cates had said he would be back in a couple of hours. She looked at her watch. A couple of hours had already passed.

Her interview with Langford had left her unsettled for reasons
beyond the case itself. It would not be easy to sort it out in her mind.
Confronting one's own vulnerability was always a shock, but the fact
was that she had been moved by the Senator. Alone in her thoughts,
she challenged the euphemism and, after finally surrendering,
defined it for what it was . . . a sexual turn-on. All the physical signs
were present and it annoyed her.

Was it something self-motivating, emanating from deep inside of
herself? Or a deliberate act of subtle manipulation on his part? She
wondered. The man knew he had that ability. It had, apparently,
been validated again and again. He had as much as admitted it. And
if he did have that power, he had no right to use it on her, a professional homicide detective in pursuit of a criminal. It was, of course,
an absurd concept on her part, like blaming the bartender for giving
the drink to the alcoholic. Cease and desist, she begged herself, gathering her concentration, flogging herself forward into the maze of
investigatory details concerning Helga Kessel.

Calling Dr. Benton, she got a confirmation of how the woman had
died. Strangulation, garroted by a soft object of textile construction.
Bits of thread discovered around the victim's neck had been sent to
the lab. From the marks on her flesh, Dr. Benton had indicated that
she had been taken from behind.

"No other signs of violence?" she asked.

"None," he replied. "She was an excellent specimen, in good
health. No pregnancy. No evidence of rape. No trace of sperm. A
simple case of strangulation."

"What about time frame?" She had been making assumptions
based more on experience than science.

"From the contents of the stomach, I'd say she died in midmorn-
ing, before lunch." She never questioned Dr. Benton's accuracy. Only
when there were doubts in his own mind did he offer multiple possibilities. She trusted him implicitly. It was a relief to know that she
had not been far off. Killed in the morning. Buried at dark.

"Were there any signs that she might have been killed elsewhere, then transported to the scene of her burial?"

"I can offer an educated guess," Dr. Benton said, and when she did not respond, he continued. "The killer would have had to be extremely careful in his method of transportation. I'd say she was killed very close to where she was buried. Stripped at the site."

It occurred to her suddenly that she might have been too cursory in her eyeball inspection of the body. She remembered that she had observed Helga's jewelry at Mount Vernon the other evening. The emerald necklace and large diamond bracelet and rings. This was, she speculated, a woman with a European's appreciation for jewelry, the real thing. She thought suddenly of Betty Taylor's barely visible ankle bracelet, a wide leap, to be sure. But the comparison was inescapable. She let it simmer for the moment.

"Nothing foreign on the body? No adornments? Jewelry? Gold geegaws?"

"Only the gold crowns on her teeth. Two of those. She did have pierced ears, but no earrings."

As he spoke, another detail leaped into her mind.

"What about a marriage ring?" she asked.

She waited through a long pause.

"Fiona, my dear, I must be slipping. She wasn't wearing any. Nor any rings."

She was assailed suddenly by new scenarios, like new tributaries branching out from a river's strong flow.

"Forensically speaking," Fiona said. It was her usual qualifier when delving into the nether-nether world of the nagging hunch. She knew he would be bracing himself mentally. "Does it read like the other—the old bones?"

"Both strangled. A similar method. But there's no way of telling for sure what material was employed on the older victim. Could have been something made of textile. Could have been a rope. Or bare hands."

"I was looking for a signature."

"I know."

"They were both buried in backyards."

"We were talking forensics," Dr. Benton said with some amusement, "and death by strangulation is a rather common method
employed to murder females."

"True . . . nevertheless . . ."

"Thirteen years is a long time between murders," Dr. Benton cautioned in a fatherly way. Often, he played the devil's advocate when
Fiona put her imagination into play.

"Murders that we know of," Fiona countered.

"A serial killer?"

"With either a long delayed fuse or we have merely uncovered two
bodies in the sequence."

"A theory not to be overlooked," Dr. Benton lectured. "I'd give it
middling priority as a viable possibility. The signature, method of
causing death and body disposal, is more circumstantial than scientific. Fill in the sequence and your theory would rush to the top of
the list."

"Calls for a coffee klatch," Fiona said. Often, they spent long hours
together in Dr. Benton's living room, amid the memorial mementos
of his beloved, long-departed wife, theorizing, exploring possibilities,
unraveling mysteries, challenging each other in an affectionate and
loving game of cat and mouse. It was always an exhilarating experience. Dr. Benton's scientific mind bore witness as a surrogate for the
victim. "I speak for the dead, who cannot speak for themselves," he
said often.

Her conversation with Dr. Benton, aside from opening up a random serial-killer theory, had also sparked another idea, triggered by
her memory of Helga's obvious fondness for expensive jewelry. She
had to talk with Ambassador Kessel, but when she picked up the
phone, she hung up quickly. No telephones.

Odd, she thought, how quickly she was falling into the mind-set of Washington's movers and shakers in the age of high-tech. Telephone paranoia was now an endemic political disease. She understood the logic, of course, but it had never loomed so menacing in her mind. Was it a given that all embassies, friend or foe, were under surveillance by our intelligence services? She thought of the opportunities for blackmail if, for example, a foreign power or even a domestic intelligence service had the goods on a powerful American politician or even a sitting President. The idea was chilling. She decided to see Ambassador Kessel in person.

She found him in the study of the official residence. His mood was somber. She had had difficulty getting through the barrier of an officious young aide apparently assigned by the Ambassador to screen all calls and prevent all visitations.

"I'm sorry," he said when she came in. "I'm afraid it's shaken me up very badly." He appeared to be genuinely grieving and upset. "She mattered a great deal to me." His superior air of containment seemed to have disintegrated. Everything about him seemed to have changed. His usually impeccable grooming had given way to sloppiness. His clothes were badly creased and he sat slumped in a chair, as if his bones had turned to jelly. His face was red and puffy and he had undoubtedly been crying.

"Why would anyone have killed my beauty?" he said, his voice breaking. Beside him was a brandy bottle and a half-filled glass of amber liquid. He reached for it, lifted it to his lips and sipped. "Devastating. Absolutely devastating."

His reaction struck her as incongruous. His stated value system in connection with his marriage could not foreshadow his present condition. Not to Fiona, who, despite her occupation and experiences, still cherished the idea of the old verities.

"Everything hinges on motivation," she said, taking a seat on the couch opposite. "I need to know something."

He lifted his head and studied her, waiting for her to continue.

"Did she wear a marriage ring?" she asked.

He looked at her strangely, his head cocked in a pose of curiosity. Apparently an open marriage did not mean that the traditional symbols and rituals of the institution had been totally abandoned.

"Of course," he said. His gaze roamed the room. There were numerous pictures displayed of him and his wife with prominent celebrities. She noted that where Helga's left hand showed, the engagement and wedding rings were quite visible. Also other pieces of jewelry, depending on whether the pictures were taken during the day or evening.

Reaching out, he picked up one from a forest of pictures on the table beside him and held it close to Fiona. It showed him and Helga with the Vice-President, a more-or-less candid shot taken at a luncheon. Helga looked particularly lovely, but then her high cheekbones and lean graceful body, always exquisitely groomed, made her exceedingly photogenic. He pointed to the finger of her left hand and explained, "Note that her engagement ring is worn above her marriage ring. Her wedding ring was diamonds and platinum and the engagement ring is a flawless diamond stone of five carats."

Again she could not shake the comparison to the Betty Taylor case. Mrs. Taylor had also reached over to show her a picture of the victim, had also failed to relinquish it, as if somehow such an act would make the picture disappear.

"I'm sure they were quite expensive."

"Expensive?" He offered a wan smile. "Everything about Helga was expensive. We are very comfortable, Detective FitzGerald. I enjoyed buying her exquisite things."

He replaced the picture, but not before Fiona had also noted Helga's earrings. They also appeared to be made of precious stones. She remembered the matching emerald earrings that Helga had worn at Mount Vernon. And the diamond bracelet.

"Did she wear the wedding and engagement rings every day?"

"Of course. Doesn't a married woman always wear her wedding and engagement rings every day?" He seemed affronted and his eyes drifted down to Fiona's hands.

"I'm not married," Fiona said defensively. She repressed a brief tremor of anger. "As you might have guessed, Mr. Ambassador, her body was stripped of everything, including jewelry."

He was learning this for the first time, although he surely surmised what she had been getting at. Often, next of kin did not ask or inquire about the victim's effects at the time of identification. He was aware, though, that she had been buried naked. He shook his head in disgust.

"But to kill for that? Confronted with the danger, Helga would have handed them over."

"Perhaps she did. And saw the robber."

"Still," the Ambassador said, "to kill?"

"People kill for less," Fiona said with a sigh.

The Ambassador lowered his eyes and clasped his hands and she allowed him his moment of grieving silence.

"Would she have worn other jewelry during the day as well?" she asked when she felt it appropriate.

"Undoubtedly."

"Would you know what that might normally be?"

"Certainly a bracelet, necklace, earrings, even another ring. Helga adorned herself liberally. She was, as you saw, a woman of great style. I purchased many of the pieces as gifts. Often, she would buy something herself. It had to be the real thing. She was very European in that regard."

"Where did she keep them?"

"We have a wall safe in the bedroom."

"Is there an inventory?"

"I believe so. We did not insure all the pieces."

"Would you mind checking the inventory for me?"

"If it will help find Helga's murderer, I'll do anything."

"It would be enormously helpful. We know her valuable rings are missing. Might be other pieces as well. Tracing these items is very difficult, but it would be something to hang our hat on. A clue, if you will. Certainly it gives us a credible motive."

She studied his reaction to this carefully. A robbery motive would get them all off the hook, the Senator and his inner circle, including Nell. The Ambassador, too, would be free from suspicion.

He nodded his agreement, but his mind seemed to be drifting back to his grief, which seemed quite genuine. She stood up and observed him for a long moment. There was another issue that had begun to nag at her earlier, but she had filed it away. It surfaced again and she confronted it.

"I know this might seem rather crass and unfeeling, Mr. Ambassador, but I must address another issue that you might think out of line."

"Out of line?" The idea seemed to confuse him, but Fiona continued to press on.

"Apparently you are an important political figure in Austria."

He raised his eyes to meet hers. They were suddenly alert, on guard. The political animal was stirring, even beyond the grief.

"I am," he replied. "Although this is a professional assignment, and I have to be totally objective and, as far as I am able, politically neutral. The answer, however, is yes. I have a political agenda for the future." He was approaching it with a politician's caution.

She hesitated, trying to find an inoffensive way of dealing with the question.

"Obviously no one can possibly expect a tragedy like this to occur . . ." she began. "But why would you put up with such political risk-taking? Your marriage . . . well, it seemed to open you up to scandal. Given that Austria is a deeply religious, traditional country."

He averted his eyes, looking everywhere but in Fiona's direction. Although he had confided in her earlier, he seemed to be wrestling with a sense of personal embarrassment. His confidence had considerably eroded since they had pondered the problem of Helga's disappearance, and he seemed to be working through layers of repressed emotion.

Like many men in the diplomatic and political business, he had clearly learned the process of inner control. At the moment he was having difficulty with that process. After an obviously long wrestling match with himself, he stopped his eyes from roaming and met her gaze.

"I've been less than forthright, Madam Detective," he said, assuming a distinctively formal continental tone. "I have been absolutely faithful to my wife during our ten-year marriage."

He paused for a moment, presumably to allow Fiona to fully absorb the statement. Earlier he had hinted that he, too, was involved in affairs outside the marriage contract, that theirs had been a truly open marriage . . .

"Everyone bears a cross, Madam Detective," he continued. "Helga needed the romanticism of an outside affair and all the attendant excitement. My hope has always been that this need would diminish with time." Again he averted his eyes, then struggled out of his chair and paced the room. "Our only compact was honesty and discretion. I have absolute faith that she observed both criteria. Despite everything, she was a woman of extraordinary integrity. Since, in this case, the Senator was equally at risk, I felt that she had satisfied the compact. It hurt, of course. I had to subjugate my ego. Put up with it, if you will. I hated the idea. But I loved her."

"Why take the pain, Mr. Ambassador?" Fiona asked gently, wondering if such a question really had relevance to the case.

"We make compromises," he shrugged. "It gave her pleasure and, in fact, it did not distract from our own relationship, hard as that is to imagine." He stopped in the center of the room. "I was elated when the Senator broke off the affair. Even Helga seemed relieved, although she adored him in a romantic and, I suppose, sexual way. I detected, as I told you before, no sign of depression. That very evening"—his ashen skin took on a slight coloring—"you understand. It was better than ever."

"Yes." Again he was silent for a long time, standing like a statue in the center of the room, a man lost, unable to decide whether to move or sit. He lifted an arm and swept it across his chest. "Now see? I have nothing. I have lost her completely." His voice broke and tears rolled down his cheeks. Genuine tears, Fiona decided. He was sincerely bereft.

"You'll call me on the inventory, won't you?"

He nodded, then turned his face from her as she left the room.

XV

Often when she needed to think, Fiona would squirrel herself away in some out-of-the-way spot. Among her favorites was "Holloways," a neighborhood bar on upper Wisconsin Avenue, in a block of buildings from another era, still untrammelled by the gentrification of Georgetown and the trendiness of upper Chevy Chase.

Which is exactly what she did when she left Ambassador Kessel. Although she was a curiosity to the regular bartender, she avoided any familiarity. He knew what she drank, a dry martini straight up, rarely more than one. She always chose a booth in the rear.

She felt the first rush of alcohol stimulation, triggering a kind of movie reel in her mind. A cast of characters paraded themselves one-by-one across the mental screen.

There was the Senator—ambitious, articulate, driven by power and sex and willing to take risks to achieve both. Then Bunkie, whose future was in lockstep with the Senator's—ruthless, dissimulating, sly and mean-spirited if faced with something that might thwart ambition.

And poor Monte, like the others, obsessively ambitious, which, despite his protestations and her own feelings, gave some weight to moral ambiguity. And the Ambassador, like Monte, an unlikely suspect. But she had often learned that some people had awesome powers of creating a new persona out of their real selves, undetectable to even the most practiced observer of human nature. Yet he had seemed completely sincere and believable as the bereft and grieving husband.

And little Nell, who might have acted out of jealousy, which created in susceptible individuals a blind, overpowering and often fatal rage.

The political motives were obvious on the part of both the Senator and the Ambassador. Too obvious.

139

Then there was robbery. A simple, but always compelling motive. The leap from robbery to murder was easy. A robbery is committed. The perpetrator is at risk. He or she can be identified. A quick garroting removes the risk. Burial in the backyard of an empty house, on the edge of a lot unlikely to be tampered with, was a gamble, but it could be justified. The house then represented the central core of a clue. Cates was following that lead.

By the time she had finished her martini, she felt that she had adequately worked through the puzzle. Robbery. By a person or persons somehow connected to that house.

She felt better. The alcohol had masked the fatigue, but she knew it would return as soon as the effects wore off. She left the bar, stopped at an Italian restaurant on Connecticut Avenue, ate a small plate of pasta and grilled sole washed down with white wine and drove home.

She caught Monte Pappas in her headlights. He was standing in her driveway, shielding his eyes from the glare as she drove up. Stopping her car, she pulled up beside him and lowered her window.

"You are one elusive lady," he said, ducking down and poking his head into the window. In the shadowy light, his face, framed by the window, looked bearlike. He bent forward and planted a noisy kiss on her cheek.

"Your affection will wake the neighbors," she said, patting his cheek. He backed away and she got out of the car. "Did I miss something?" she asked.

"I hope me," he replied, smiling broadly, obviously feeling good. He held her shoulders and pulled her to him, enveloping her in his arms. She let him hug her, but his mood was confusing. When she had last seen him he was anxious, tense.

He released her to unlock the door and followed her inside.

"Waiting for you, I was growing jealouser and jealouser," he said as he came in.

"There were secret lovers to be satisfied," she joked, leading him into the den. Her hand swept in the direction of the bar. "Help yourself."

She went to the bathroom, freshened her makeup and came back to the den. She was puzzled by his high spirits, of course, but glad that he had come. She had not relished coming back to an empty house.

He had taken off his jacket and was just popping a champagne cork as she came back into the den. The bottle's neck was foaming as he carefully poured the sparkling liquid into two flute-shaped glasses.

"We mustn't let the moment go to waste," he said, handing her the glass.

"So you found the good stuff," she laughed.

"I have a nose for that," he said, kissing her lightly on the lips. With her free hand, she reached up and stroked his face. He needed a shave and his skin felt like sandpaper, but she liked its feel against her palm. They clinked glasses and drank.

"He'll never be the same," Monte said.

"Who?"

"The Senator. The great Sam. Mr. Hot Rocks." He began to roam the room and for a moment she wondered if his high spirits were actually hysteria. She watched, rooted to the spot near the bar, as he circled the room. "It was wonderful, Fi. Wonderful. He was shaken, really shaken. For the first time, I really believe now that he has taken the pledge."

She remembered her own reactions during her interview with the Senator. Doubtful, she told herself.

"Even sobered up the Bunkie-flunkie," he continued. "They were two little boys caught beating each other's bishops in the barn. I loved it."

"Loved what?"

"Their contrition," Monte said. His roamings took him back to the bar, where he poured more into his glass. She covered her glass with her palm and he put the bottle back on the bar. "I now feel," he went on, "that this campaign truly has a Chinaman's chance. The sword of Damocles seems to have fallen . . . and missed."

It was only then that his conduct and words lost their sense of joy and became bizarre.

"What the hell are you jabbering about, Monte? I'm confused."

He had begun to roam again, but her remarks had brought him up short.

"You're kidding." He looked at her with confusion, then, frowning, he walked over to the couch where he had tossed his jacket and removed a folded newspaper jutting out of a side pocket.

"This," he said, handing it to her. "*The Washington Post* bulldog edition. I got it direct from the *Post*. The ink isn't dry."

Fiona opened the paper to the front page. In the lower left-hand corner was a picture of Helga Kessel. Over it was the headline: AMBASSADOR'S WIFE PROBABLE ROBBERY VICTIM.

"How could they know?" she asked.

"Read on," Monte urged.

"Helga Kessel, the wife of the Austrian Ambassador, whose nude body was found in a shallow grave behind a house in Cleveland Park two days ago, was apparently the victim of robbery.

"According to the Ambassador, Mrs. Kessel's expensive jewelry worn that day was not found with her body, leading police to theorize that she was probably the victim of a robbery attempt.

"While police were not available for comment on this aspect of the case, the Ambassador revealed that Mrs. Kessel, whose passion for expensive jewelry was well known, left her home the day of her murder wearing her diamond engagement and wedding rings, and a necklace and bracelet containing gold and precious stones.

"The Ambassador estimated that these items represented a value of 'probably close to one hundred thousand dollars.'

"The Ambassador also indicated that he was told by the police that Mrs. Kessel might have been murdered to prevent identification of her assailant. He told the *Post* that the police were pursuing all leads based on this theory."

What followed was the so-called back story, a rehash of the body's discovery and the eggplant's press conference.

She looked up and saw him smiling.

"We truly appreciate this, Fi. It simply refocuses everything. Takes the heat off. Nipped in the bud, as we say."

"I didn't give this to the *Washington Post.*"

"No, you didn't. As you can see, the Ambassador did."

She was dumbfounded, and he was obviously confused by her reaction.

"When the stakes are this high, you don't pass up opportunities like this."

"This is your idea?"

"It's not a question of taking credit, it's a joint campaign management decision." Lines formed on his forehead and he cocked his head in a gesture of puzzlement. "Hell, is there something wrong, something inaccurate in the robbery theory? It looked cut and dried to us."

It was beginning to dawn on her. As soon as she'd left him, Ambassador Kessel contacted the Senator or Bunkie. A hurried, cautious telephone meeting. They wouldn't have taken the time to meet personally. It was apparently essential that they move to forestall any mud being thrown in their direction. She looked at Monte, confused and hurt at the same time.

"What you implied to the Ambassador was the logical, wasn't it?" Monte asked with obvious agitation. When she didn't answer quickly, he said, his voice rising, "Hell, Fi, we didn't blow anything, did we?"

He looked pathetic and she wasn't certain whether to curse him or pity him. Them.

"Good thinking. Great damage-control thinking. Take the heat off. Did it ever occur to you to tell me? Poor little me, who was trying to get at the truth and, if you were all innocent, hold off the mudslide. Don't you think I should have been consulted?"

"We thought . . ." He hesitated, then stopped abruptly.

"It was in still in the theory stage," she sighed. She knew the mechanics of the act. An anonymous tip. A call for confirmation, and voilà: the Ambassador is available for comment. A bull's-eye in PR management. Just in time for the deadline pressure of the bull-dog edition.

"Will it get you into trouble?" Monte asked sheepishly.

"Trouble?" She thought better of explaining. The eggplant would be furious that he was not "apprahzed," livid that the media was getting privileged information and—she would definitely not tell Monte this—be predisposed to look beyond the robbery theory out of sheer pique and orneriness. Especially if she told him exactly how and why all this had transpired in the first place. Besides his having her ass, perhaps even ruining her career, she would have to contend with the political ramifications.

"Trouble?" she repeated, a wave of nausea rolling through her. "You don't know what trouble *is.*" She paused to let that salvo sink in. From his expression and his pallor she knew that the message had been received. With her knowledge, she could blow them out of the water.

"You wouldn't," he whispered. She had the impression that he might have wanted to speak louder, but had lost wind by her implication.

"Why not?"

"Please, Fi," Monte said, genuinely panicked. "You are not a vindictive person. All right, we might have made an error in judgement. Maybe we should have checked with you. It had to get out fast. But surely you would have agreed with our intentions, considering the stakes here."

She shook her head, feeling suddenly ashamed for him, for his fear and his weakness. And for herself for going soft inside.

"I would have been opposed, totally. Aside from my official responsibilities, I consider it manipulative and cynical. That part disgusts me, if you want to know."

"I'm really sorry, Fiona. I had no idea you'd react this way." He looked helpless and forlorn and his large brown puppy-dog eyes

grew misty. He was a bear all right, a big teddy. Just another frightened flunky who danced around the flame of power.

"A common affliction. A lack of perception about other people."

"The point is . . ." he began, then searched her face for some reaction. She forced herself into a stony deadpan. "It does make sense.
She was stupid enough to go out loaded with jewelry. Somebody
spotted it, or knew she did this, robbed and killed her. The other,
this business with the Senator, has no relevance to her murder. None
whatsoever. Why should we all be penalized for something so obviously not of our making?" He drew in a deep breath, expelled it and
watched her face.

"That's the difference between your business and mine, Monte,"
she said pointedly. "We dig under the surface bullshit. You scrape it
up and package it as the real McCoy. Saying it in print does not
mean it's the truth."

"You don't think it's true?"

"Shit, Monte, we never make judgements on the obvious. We call
that circumstantial. We've got a real conflict of agendas here. We're
looking for a killer."

"Are you saying that you still think . . . ?"

"What I think is now none of your damned business," Fiona
exploded.

He lowered his eyes and fidgeted with his fingers. Her sudden
outburst seemed to flatten him like a hurricane gust. Finally he
looked up. "Listen, I'm sorry. But the milk is spilled. What can we
do now?"

"Still in damage-control," she said with contempt. "I'll tell you
what you can do."

He lifted his two hands.

"I know. I'm just leaving."

He walked across the room and picked up his jacket.

"I hope you don't hurt them—hurt all of us," he said.

"My business is catching killers. I shouldn't have taken any detours."

He looked genuinely whipped and uncertain. Contempt was
quickly turning to pity in her mind and she cursed her vulnerability. If only he wasn't so . . . so cuddly. The thought made her smile.
"We meant well," he said. "We may be assholes, but we're not
murderers."
She shook her head.
"The fact is that it does look like robbery. But we'll never know
until we find the person that did it. That's the bottom line."
He paused, studying her face for any signs of forgiveness. Perhaps
he saw some.
"It's a viable theory then, Fi? That's what counts at this stage,
doesn't it?"
"Yes," she admitted, her anger softening. "A viable theory."
"Then maybe it will all come out right."
"Maybe," she shrugged.
"And you won't . . . not deliberately . . . hurt us?"
"No, I won't, Monte." She hesitated for a moment. No, she decid-
ed, unwilling to let him off the hook. "Not if you're all innocent."
He seemed confused, on the verge of protesting. Then she saw
him surrender.
"I still want you to know—" he began.
"Never mind," she said, cutting him off with a wave of her hand.
He started toward the door.
"And you and I?" he asked when he got there.
"Not even for fun and games," she heard herself say. Next time
she'd buy a pet.
Still he did not leave, his eyes roaming the room as if taking a
farewell look. She was even disappointed in assessing that gesture.
He saw the *Washington Post* and picked it up. Then, without anoth-
er word, he left.
Her instinct, she knew, was to overreact. A cool head must pre-
vail, she badgered herself. They had betrayed her. No question
about that. But, she argued, it had not been a malicious betrayal,

an act designed deliberately to injure her, although it could have that effect.

Reason, you gullible vulnerable bitch, she admonished herself, heading up the stairs to her bedroom. Shower time. She decided a real hot-and-cold treatment was called for. She was out of her clothes in seconds, striding across the bedroom to the adjoining bathroom. Only then did she see the flashing light on her answering machine. Its placement was a quirk of hers, since often, out of sheer exhaustion, she headed first for the bedroom to flop into bed and oblivion.

She hit the rewind, then the play, and listened.

"Got something significant Fiona. Cates at home. Eight P.M."

There were two other messages, also from Cates.

"Heavy date, you sly fox," Cates' voice blared in his stunted version of black street talk. The last message, an hour ago.

"Don't want to interfere with your love life, lady, but when you come up for air, call me."

She pulled the comforter from her bed, wrapped it around her naked body, then punched in Cates' home number. He answered before the second ring.

"You saw it," she said.

"Saw what?" he asked.

"The *Post,* Cates. The *Washington Post* . . ." It occurred to her that the reiteration was not necessary. Also the question. He was obviously on a different tack.

"I get mine in the morning, Fiona," Cates said, his voice reflecting his confusion.

"It goes like this," she began, sucking in a deep breath, pulling the comforter tighter. "First let me take my shower. I'm standing here balls-ass naked and shivering."

"I won't ask why," he snickered.

"You'd be wrong. Its the furthest thing from my mind, body and spirit. I'm going into an imaginary nunnery." But she could not shake off her own curiosity. "So what's so urgent?"

"Remember that lady I talked to at the Judiciary Committee about our old bones?"

Her mind clicked into his mental rhythm, alert now. A surge of adrenaline warmed her body. Betty Taylor, she thought.

"The lady messengered over the Congressional Directory for that year. Feeling obliged, I flicked through it."

"For chrissakes, Cates."

He was doing it too often these days, building the suspense for greater impact.

"He was on the committee for which the lady worked."

"Say it, Cates. Stop this shit."

"Langford. Representative Samuel Langford." Cates said.

Despite her body's apparent warmth, she began to shiver again.

XVI

The Eggplant was just winding down his tantrum, but the adrenaline was still pumping up his anger.

"Thickness of the fucking skull," he shouted, jabbing a dark finger at his temple. "It *is* a disease, an affliction that impinges on the brain, the thinking processes, creates terminal stupidity. And here"—he pointed at both of them for the umpteenth time—"are two prime examples of the condition. What has to be said for the message to sink in? Never, never, *never* talk to the press, not through tenth parties, third parties, any parties. Zip the mouth." He motioned with his finger across the mouth. "Zip. Zip. Zip. We are in the killer-catching business. Leave the public relations to the eggplant. *Heah.* Do you get this message or am I pissing into the wind?"

Since they had expected it and, as best they could, had prepared for it, she and Cates wore their masks of contrition and waited for the flumes of verbal venom to subside.

Since it was the eggplant who had opened up the attack, they had little chance to fill him in on the facts of the case. The story in the *Washington Post,* as they knew, would set him off. It had little to do with substance. To the eggplant, nothing was worse than an invasion of his turf, which is the way he perceived the *Post* article. It was, of course, irrational, egotistical, perhaps even verging on the maniacal, but, as she had often concluded, it was the nature of the beast, an aberration to be accepted. The beast had a good side, as well, which often outweighed the bad.

Apparently, a reporter had made appropriate inquiries the night before, but there was no one around with any authority to answer them. Eventually, the eggplant had gotten wind of it, preferring to duck the call until he could gather all the facts at their morning meeting, not realizing how fast the story was moving. He was a man that liked to set agendas in dealing with the media, not be manipulated by them. What riled him most was that one of his own staff had put the first spin on the story without his knowledge and against his caveats. To him that constituted usurpation of power and bordered on betrayal. While he was in this state, there was no room for protest.

As he spoke, his frustration accelerated. Veins stood out in his neck and forehead and bits of spittle caught at the sides of his mouth. It was not a pretty sight. Fortunately, the dark gloom of the dreary rain days had lifted and the sun shone through the dust-caked windows, making the scene, if not cheerful, bearable.

Finally spent, the eggplant ended his ranting and looked out of the window, one arm leaning against a wall, his broad back offered as a sign of immediate dismissal. Fiona glanced at Cates, her look an obvious solicitation of support.

"We think the motive might not be robbery, Chief," Fiona said, reaching for a conciliatory tone. He did not respond and she spoke again. "We think the motive might be more"—she hesitated, groping for a word that would arrest him—"controversial."

He turned slowly like a heavy door on a rusty hinge.

"I believe the newspaper story was premature, maybe even misleading," she pressed. "Even though it stemmed from my meeting with the Ambassador." He had, she was certain, already surmised that Fiona was the source of the story. His version had her cast as the deliberate "leaker," who passed it along to a reporter to embarrass him. He hadn't yet given them a chance to fill him in on all the details.

"You mean the jewelry is not missing?" he asked, malevolence still resonating in his voice.

"I didn't say that. The Ambassador had promised to take an inventory. Yes, the jewelry is probably missing."

"So where is it misleading?" He walked back to his desk and poked a finger into the newspaper lying there.

"I'm trying to 'apprahze' you," she said, using his pronunciation. His lips curled and his eyes narrowed. Then he sat down at his desk and glared at her. "Show me, bitch," his attitude said.

She and Cates had determined that a bit of deft editing was in order, although she feared that the eggplant's paranoic antenna might pick up the nuances. A woman, in his world, acting out of friendship with a man was always suspect. To him, female vulnerability was endemic, an inherent weakness in the gender. The fact was, it shamed her to acknowledge that such a conclusion in this instance was not far from the truth.

She began her explanation from the beginning, trying to pre-screen her every utterance. She took him through the events of the investigation, her various meetings with the cast of characters, cataloguing their fears, motivations and proclivities. She included her earlier meeting with Monte, Bunkie and the Ambassador when they first learned that Helga was missing.

His reaction to her admission that she had merely been doing a favor for a friend brought a slight tic to his cheek and a barely perceptible denigrating twist to his lips. Naturally, she left out any hint of a quid pro quo with Monte on the matter of keeping their interrogation of the Senator and his staff under wraps, but she foresaw that a satisfactory explanation had to be attempted, and she provided one. Her reference to Monte as a "friend" was transparent enough for him to get the message. She knew he took it for the confession it was, hoping that was the end of it. She needed to get through that before she threw in the clincher, the part about the old bones.

"Blame me, Chief," she said bravely. Of course, he already had. "I made a fine-line judgement. We had every intention of keeping you 'apprahzed,' but the opportunity to interrogate the Senator presented itself and we had to take it as it came. Also, frankly, I did not yet want to open a Pandora's box that could involve the Department in a political donnybrook, especially if the Senator and his staff were blameless in the woman's death, which is still a possibility." She watched for his reaction. She was being deliberately oblique, talking in the kind of shorthand she knew he would understand, but before he could make an overt conclusion she proceeded: "You've drummed it into us . . . this sensitivity to cases involving politicians, especially a Senator about to announce his campaign for the Presidency. We didn't 'apprahze' you of it yesterday, pending this meeting, because we wanted to have a more complete story to present for your judgement."

Toadying it was, but she preferred to mentally refer to it as "defusing." She watched the eggplant's face for the desired effect and actually saw it happen. He nodded, not quite a nod, but close enough. And she knew why. She had struck a chord of accommodation. He had finally seen the personal benefit to himself, always his prime motivation.

Through the eggplant's good offices, he undoubtedly reasoned, the Mayor would have another chit to collect from a politician, an important factor considering that the District of Columbia Government was still beholden to the Congress for its funding. More important, the eggplant, if he chose, could hold the chit for his own purposes. Not corruption, really. Perhaps a form of blackmail. But part and parcel of the political process, which, like most endeavors, was dependent on trade-offs, favors and, ultimately, the power to manipulate.

"So they decided among themselves that robbery gets them all off the hook," the eggplant said. He was calmer now, sopping it up like a sponge. He was, she knew, a quick learner when his mind was freed from his emotions.

"And that's the genesis of the *Post* story," she said. "They engineered it for their own political purposes."

Except for his tight-lipped interpolation, he had barely moved a muscle in his face, his bloodshot eyes fixed into a stare from which she did not flinch.

"But you did say that the woman's jewelry was probably taken. I can see premature. But misleading?"

Again she shot Cates a glance and nodded. It was his turn to carry the relay stick.

" 'Could be diversion' would be a better description," Cates said. She watched the eggplant's stare move from her face to Cates'. "Technically speaking, it was accurate. No question about it. The woman was robbed."

Before the eggplant could show his dissatisfaction with the explanation, Cates plunged ahead. She watched as the eggplant moved his upper body forward, planting his elbows on the desk.

"It has to do with those old bones," Cates said. "Betty Taylor." He paused for a moment, perhaps waiting for an expected groan from the eggplant that did not come.

"Could be just a presumption. But certain connections are inescapable. Connection one: Betty Taylor was believed to be having an affair with someone who wished to keep his identity secret. The Senator, then a representative, a philanderer of the first rank, is on the Committee that Betty Taylor had worked for. Connection two: In the instance of Mrs. Kessel we know that she was having this affair with the Senator. Both women were killed by strangulation. Both were buried in the yards of houses that were then unlived in, on the sales block."

Cates had, Fiona learned earlier, managed to track down the status of the Woodland Drive property on which Betty Taylor was buried at the time of her death. Like the property in Cleveland Park in which Helga had been buried, it, too, had been empty at the approximate time of the murder. In fact, it had been empty for nearly a year.

"Helluva theory," the eggplant said. He did not smile, but his eyes were dancing his approval. Fiona sighed with relief.

"And there might have been more," Fiona said. "We only know of these two."

"You really think the Senator . . ." the eggplant began, his voice trailing off.

"If the logic holds," Fiona said cautiously, "the more likely perpetrator is the Senator's flunkie. Bunkie-Flunkie." In her explanation
earlier, she had already mentioned him, without fleshing him out,
which she did now. "Farrington. You know him. A stock character
in political theater. Overzealous, overidentified with his fearless
leader. He takes care of everything. Chief pimp and bottle washer.
You know the type."

"Gets rid of anything that gets in the way," Cates said.

"He becomes the alter ego," Fiona added. "Most politicians have
one. Stays in the background. Pulls strings on his own sometimes.
Takes the fall, if necessary. Depending on his commitment."

"And this guy's commitment?" the eggplant asked.

"Total," Fiona said. Cates nodded.

The eggplant straightened and stood up. There were no traces of
anger now. He was playing to his strength, doing his job, pacing the
room, as he did when deeply immersed in attempting to crack a
homicide puzzle.

"We trace Farrington to the jewelry, he's on the ropes," the eggplant said. It was rhetorical. He was thinking out loud. Then he
turned to them. "Get the ice descriptions out as soon as possible.
Maybe a search warrant."

"With respect, Chief," Fiona interjected. The eggplant turned
toward her. "My impression is that the jewelry, any personal material gain, is out of it for him. He's got other fish to fry. He'd have
dumped the jewelry, maybe buried it elsewhere, thrown it into the
Potomac. If he's our man his purpose would have been to put the
lady—ladies—away forever, with no identifying possibilities."

"Hoping that the beautiful Helga would become, like the other
lady, old bones." Cates interjected.

"I'll buy it. No search warrant then," the eggplant said, still pacing, shaking his head in agreement. "Besides, we stick too many fingers in the mix we blow the Senator out of the water. Better if he
thinks we're protecting him."

"Unless he's the one," Cates said.

"Or the one behind the one," Fiona added.

"Remains to be seen. Meanwhile why deep-six the poor bastard?" He looked at Fiona. "If having sex was murder, half the politicians would be in prison." She had expected him to chuckle. He didn't. He was dead serious.

She was locked into his thought pattern now. What's in it for the eggplant? Easy, she decided. Two possibilities. Chits or glory. Either one had value for him.

If Bunkie were an innocent and none of this slopped over into the media, the eggplant would have his chit. On the other hand, if Bunkie was the perpetrator, the Senator gets blown out of the water, not just out of the Presidential race, but out of Washington, far out. Breaking a case like this becomes an international incident, a sure-fire name identifier, grist for the media and the supermarket tabloids. New worlds opening for Chief Luther Greene.

"We handle this gingerly," he warned, stopping his pacing, pointing his finger like a weapon. "No surprises."

"No surprises," Fiona agreed.

"Let's get us Mr. Bunkie," the eggplant said. He looked around the office. "Sweat him up. But best we keep him out of here." He looked up and, for the first time that morning, showed a genuine smile. This was his meat. "Your place, FitzGerald?"

"I thought you'd never ask."

XVII

He had come without a hassle, willingly. Nor did it surprise him that she had asked him to her house.

"We want to keep this out of channels," she had assured him on the phone, knowing that he would accept the conspiratorial nature of the request. That was all the shorthand he needed.

Even when he was introduced to the eggplant, he showed no signs of irritation.

"We want to keep the Senator out of it, is all," the eggplant told him. He had placed himself on the leather wing chair. Fiona and Cates had taken the two upholstered chairs on the other side of the cocktail table and they had maneuvered Bunkie to the center of the couch. Nothing but space on either side of him. He was alone.

He had crossed his legs, showing his red socks with the polo symbols coming out of his tasseled loafers. To illustrate, or feign, his lack of concern, he had stretched both arms along the rim of the couch's back, a casual gesture. He had found a way to keep his smile fixed, although his wary, feral eyes roamed their faces in an effort to discover what they had in mind.

She had made a pot of coffee and placed coffee cups and Oreo cookies in a dish beside them. Only the eggplant and Cates took the coffee. Bunkie declined.

"Makes me jumpy," he said cheerily, his polka-dot bow tie dancing on his Adam's apple. He wore a blue striped shirt and a blazer with gold buttons.

He was, of course, no pushover. Fourteen years in the political arena surely had honed a great many useful skills. Fiona figured that hair-trigger alarm bells were set to go off in his mind at the first faint sign of danger.

157

"There was no way we could keep our commanding officer out of this, Bunkie," Fiona explained.

"I understand." Bunkie nodded toward the eggplant, who waved two ebony fingers in acknowledgment.

"Nothing is cut and dried," Fiona said. "No question that the woman's jewelry is missing." The Ambassador had, indeed, taken an inventory and acknowledged that to her in a phone call.

"Seems pretty obvious where the motive lies. She was always a walking jewelry store."

"Even when she met the Senator at your place?" Fiona asked.

"Always. I often told her that it was damned dangerous in this city."

"She wouldn't listen?" Fiona asked.

"Apparently not. It finally killed her."

"You're absolutely certain about that?" the eggplant asked. It was the opening salvo. Bunkie's guard went up. His smile stayed but his eyes gave him away. He also had another habit, Fiona observed. She had not seen it before. He swallowed nervously and the bow tie bobbed on his Adam's apple.

"Is there any doubt?" Bunkie said, adopting a slight tone of bemused arrogance. "You've just confirmed that she was robbed."

"That's the way it looks," the eggplant said calmly.

"How can you possibly say otherwise?" Bunkie asked, bow tie bobbing.

"You saw her on the Senator's behalf one day before she was killed?" the eggplant asked, his voice calmly modulated, unthreatening.

"That again." He turned toward Fiona. "I'm sure you've filled the Captain in on that."

"Such an assignment was part of your job?" the eggplant asked, his tone unchanged.

His eyes speeded up their inspection of each face in turn. In his mind, Fiona decided, he had begun to sound retreat, get back into the castle, lift the drawbridge.

"Yes," he acknowledged, "The political ramifications are obvious. Senator Langford is about to become a candidate for President of the United States. I'm not, as Detective FitzGerald knows, trying to hide anything. Helga Kessel was the Senator's mistress. It was decided that the affair, which was clandestine, had to be ended. To avoid a scene, I was designated to make it known to the lady that all was over."

"Forever or for the time being?" the eggplant asked.

"I offered no time frame. She was quite understanding of the realities. Her husband, too, is a politician." He uncrossed his legs, shifted his position, removed one arm from along the back of the couch, then recrossed his legs in the opposite direction. He was, Fiona observed, getting antsy. "Why are we going over this ground?"

"Have you ever carried out such an assignment before?"

"Unfortunately, I have had to," Bunkie said. "They tell me that years ago the media would have kept those secrets out of the public eye. There's lots of screwing around in this business. It's become fair game when you're running for office. Do I have to cite chapter and verse?" His eyes flitted from face to face. When he got no response, he continued. "The fact that the woman was murdered, frankly, scared the living shit out of us." He looked toward Fiona. *No,* she cried within herself. She could see it coming. He was poised to put a psychic knife between her shoulder blades. "Thank God for Detective FitzGerald and her ah . . . friendship . . . with Monte Pappas, our chief campaign consultant. She led us through the mine fields."

To his credit, the eggplant kept his eyes fixed on Bunkie's face. Fiona felt her cheeks grow hot. She knew she had reddened. But she was thankful that her instincts had opted for confession.

"Mr. Farrington," the eggplant said, tugging at his ear, his eyes deliberately hooded and seemingly indifferent. "Did you know a Betty Taylor?" In the clinches, Fiona thought, he was beautiful.

Bunkie's reaction was merely to look at the ceiling as if the shard of memory was embedded there. It did not strike Fiona as an untoward or guilty reaction.

"Betty Taylor." His glance roamed the ceiling, then moved to his hands. "Betty Taylor." He shook his head, bit his lip.

"Go back say fourteen years. The Senator is a Representative. He serves on the Judiciary Committee."

"Betty Taylor. Jesus." His face brightened although his bow tie continued to bob. "A real beauty." He looked toward the eggplant and his gaze lingered. "It's so damned long ago. I think I was with Langford no more than six months." He laughed. "Betty Taylor."

"You and she had one of your little talks."

"Had to. He was planning for the Senate."

He appeared totally without guile, showing amusement.

"And he was married," Fiona added.

"That was unraveling," Bunkie said. "The downside for him was . . ." It had obviously occurred to him that he had better be careful about the racial angle. "Florida is a southern state. In some parts of the state it wouldn't be taken kindly. The Senator hasn't got a bone of prejudice in him." He seemed confident, unwavering. "She was gorgeous, what they call high yellow. She had actually passed as white . . . until we checked." He backtracked, turned his eyes away from the eggplant. "It wasn't easy for me. It was my first time at this. I hated to do it."

"You told her it was all over."

"Yes I did."

"And what was her reaction?"

"You're making me go back fourteen years. Christ." He studied the faces surrounding him. The space on either side of him must have appeared to expand. Undoubtedly, he was beginning to feel totally alone and certainly suspicious. When they did not respond, he uncrossed his legs again and took the other arm from the back of the couch. "I think she bawled like hell. She was just a kid. He really liked her, treated her very well. He always treats them well." Suddenly, arrogance surfaced again. "Hell, they got value received."

"Did she go quietly?" the eggplant asked. "Like Mrs. Kessel?" His bow tie bounced on his throat.

"I can't remember. She might have called once or twice. But the Senator never took the calls. Soon she got the message and was gone with the wind."

"You never heard about her or saw her again?" the eggplant asked.

"Never."

The eggplant let silence take over for a while. Fiona and Cates knew the drill. Force him to break the silence, show his nervousness.

"You think I like doing this? It's the pissant part of the job. The Senator likes girls. He can't keep his zipper closed. It's a problem and he's the first to acknowledge it. Maybe he needs some kind of therapy for it. Problem is how does a politician with Presidential aspirations get therapy without the world finding out someday? It's another no-no. So we hang on and hope for the best. It's an addiction, but somehow he manages to keep things under control around election time. So far he's been lucky . . . and he's had me."

"You've done this often?"

"Not often," Bunkie sighed. "Only when it gets out of hand."

"He falls for the lady?" the eggplant asked.

"Gets involved. I wouldn't say falls for. Hell, they're all over him." His eyes met Fiona's. Remembering the Senator's effect on her, she turned away in embarrassment.

"To keep all of them at bay would require a full-time staff of dozens. Sometimes he got hooked. Only then did I have to get involved."

"How many others?" the eggplant asked. "Not counting Betty Taylor or Helga Kessel." Something had changed in the calibration of his question. He was starting to push.

"Maybe two," Bunkie said, his comfort level falling rapidly. "Not bad in fourteen years."

"I don't want maybes," the eggplant thundered. His manner caught Bunkie by surprise. He blanched.

"I know of two others, okay?" Bunkie said after a long pause. He was genuinely alarmed, getting testy. His hands began to shake. "What the hell is going on?"

"What were their names?"

"How can I remember—"

"Remember," the eggplant intoned. The color drained from Bunkie's face.

"I do remember Harriet Farley. She was on our publicity staff during the Senator's first campaign. He spent a week with her in the Bahamas. I had to do that one quick."

"No repercussions?"

"Got a little messy. She got so involved she left her husband. The Senator was actually single then, but the husband was getting antsy."

"What does antsy mean?" the eggplant pressed.

"He kept calling. You know how it is. She had this jiboni that she had married in college. He was a salesman somewhere. Then she got a taste of the Senator, thought there was more to it and had to be set straight. It all cooled off pretty soon."

"How so?"

"The husband stopped calling and we never heard from Harriet again."

"And the other?"

"Judy something," Bunkie said. "She wrote speeches for us. I can get her last name. She was really bright. Suddenly he was spending lots of time writing speeches. He had married Nell by then, had their first kid."

"Same pattern?" the eggplant asked.

"Not really. It was getting hot and heavy. I could see that the time had come. Then before I could act she came to me. Said good-bye and upped and left. Just like that."

"How did the Senator react?"

"The thing is," Bunkie said with a smile, "I told him I had sent her away."

"That satisfied him?" Fiona asked.

"Look at it this way. I spared him the rejection." He shook his head. "Sounds awful, doesn't it?"

"Did Nell know?" Fiona repeated, cutting a quick glance at the eggplant, who nodded his approval.

"I would doubt that."

"Why do you think Judy something left so abruptly?"

"I told you. She was smart as hell. Knew it wouldn't work, I suppose. Jumped the gun."

Whatever her feelings about him, which were highly negative, Fiona felt he had been forthcoming, almost too forthcoming. Indeed, he seemed to go out of his way to leave that impression.

They gave him another treatment of extended silence. Finally he said:

"I've answered all your questions. I've been a good boy. Now tell me what the fuck is going on."

"You don't know?" It was Cates who asked. He had been silent throughout the entire interrogation.

"Haven't got a clue," Bunkie said.

Suddenly, the eggplant took an envelope from the table beside him and handed it to Bunkie. Fingers fluttering clumsily, he opened the envelope. He looked at the pictures, his eyes squinting.

"Looks like a skeleton," he said hoarsely.

It was the pictures that had been taken at the site where Betty Taylor had been buried.

"Betty Taylor, Bunkie," the eggplant said. They were all watching his face. The color disappeared from it. His lips trembled.

"Betty Taylor?" He could barely say her name.

"Strangled," the eggplant pressed. "Not long after you gave her the word. Buried in the backyard of an abandoned house. Same MO as Helga Kessel. What do you make of this, Bunkie?"

"I . . . I . . . I'm speechless."

"So I see," the eggplant said.

"I can't believe it," Bunkie said, faltering, gasping for air.

"Have we been leaving something out?" the eggplant said gently.

"Leaving something out?"

"Still think it's robbery?" Fiona asked.

"I don't know what to think."

"It's over now, Bunkie," the eggplant said gently. "It'll take some work on our part, but we'll get it right, Bunkie. Why go through all that pain? It's all over now."

"What the hell is happening here?" Bunkie exploded. He looked into their deliberately expressionless faces. "You really believe it. You think that I did this." He waved the pictures in front of him, then dropped them onto the coffee table.

"Gotta admit," the eggplant said. "It's an idea with legs."

Bunkie seemed to have collapsed from the inside out. All the bravado had disappeared and beads of sweat had broken out on his upper lip.

"Sam know this?" he whispered.

"We thought you'd like to be the first," Fiona said.

"He'll go crazy," Bunkie said. "He'll think I fucked everything up. All that we've been working for."

"Maybe you tried too hard," the eggplant said.

Bunkie's nostrils quivered as he sucked in a deep breath. All the Ivy League arrogance had run out of him like air from a punctured tire.

"I didn't do these things," he whispered. "I couldn't." His eyes welled with tears and he wiped what spilled over with the cuffs of his jacket. "The question here is, how will this impact on . . ." He moved his hands in a way that suggested that he was too choked up to continue. It was hard, Fiona decided, to generate any sympathy for the man. The craft of acting was part and parcel of a politician's arsenal, extending to his staff and sycophants.

"Make it easy, Bunkie," Fiona said gently, falling into the good-cop role, knowing that the eggplant would take off the gloves now. He got up from the leather wing chair and moved toward Bunkie.

"You're a fucking killer, man," the eggplant said. He stooped down and grabbed Bunkie's jacket, half-lifting him from the couch. "We're going to fry your ass one way or another. Hard or easy, you're finished."

The eggplant's face butted close to Bunkie's. His bloodshot eyes were popping and he was blowing sour breath in his face. The eggplant was doing his "physical intimidation" act now. She had seen it work before. Bunkie's body hung limply above the couch, like a puppet whose strings had suddenly been cut. He made no effort to resist.

"I'm no killer," he insisted.

"Fucking liar," the eggplant sneered, pushing him back on the couch. He paced the room like a caged animal, then came back and pointed a finger at Bunkie's nose.

"We'll squeeze you like a grapefruit. We'll be on your ass day or night, Farrington. One day other bodies will turn up."

Up to then he had been accepting the intimidation with only the mildest protest. Now he seemed to have pulled some strength from a hidden resource.

"Destroy for the sake of destroying, would you?" Bunkie said. His voice seemed stronger, and his confidence level had risen considerably. She could not understand why. "That would be damned shitty. Least you could do is give us the benefit of the doubt. We're not killers."

"Sure. The jails are full of innocent guys. We just put people away for fun."

But the fire was burning out in the eggplant as well. None of the strategies was working. Innocent or guilty? She wasn't sure. None of them could be sure.

There was something else troubling her. Bunkie was certainly the logical suspect. He had openly admitted his connection. But something was awry and she felt a troubling barrier between the obvious and the real truth.

The fact was that all the evidence presented was circumstantial. No confession. No case. Not yet. They'd have to keep digging.

They'd have to check out Harriet Farley and Judy Something. Were they, too, buried in someone's backyard?

"I'm no angel," Bunkie managed to croak, sensing that the tension had eased. "But I didn't kill anybody."

"We'll see, won't we?" the eggplant said. He had stopped his pacing and now leaned against a wall. He looked toward Fiona, widened his eyes and gazed toward the ceiling. His message was obvious. No point in pursuing the interrogation any longer. The parameters had been set. They'd need more evidence before Bunkie would break. He was either acting, stonewalling or truly innocent. One thing was certain. No confession was forthcoming. If guilty, he had opted to play out the string and there was nothing they could do to force the issue.

Bunkie uncrossed his legs and folded his hands around them. His knuckles were white, yet he seemed to have finally taken command of himself again, although he was emerging as someone else. He was, Fiona knew, exercising the chameleon option, the politician's last resort, changing colors in mid-campaign.

"You can destroy us politically with this," he said. "You know it and I know it and soon Sam will know it. Even if we're innocent, which we are. Neither Sam nor I is guilty of any of this. I don't know how or why these terrible things occurred. Could be coincidence. I don't know. But the least you can do, without any other corroborating evidence, is to protect us. Is that too much to ask?"

"Might be," the eggplant said, leaving open the possibility. If, indeed, they were innocent, he would not want to lose the chit he had earned. "Hard to keep these things from the media."

"I wish Sam were here," Bunkie said. Obviously, he had realized that he had gone as far as he could go by himself.

"You're welcome to use the phone," the eggplant said.

No way, Fiona thought, and he made no move to look for a telephone.

"May I go now?" he asked, standing up, straightening his jacket. A flash of arrogance had returned, which was puzzling to Fiona.

"For the moment," the eggplant muttered.

"I know you'll want to speak with the Senator," Bunkie said, shooting a glance at Fiona. "And you can bank on his cooperation." He started to walk, then stopped. "We have nothing to do with this. Once more can I prevail on you to keep this quiet? I mean as far as the media is concerned."

"We'll do our best," the eggplant said, pausing. "Up to a point."

"What point is that, Captain?"

"The point that heads in your direction, Farrington," the eggplant said. It was intended as a threat, but for some reason it seemed to lack teeth, as if even the eggplant was losing conviction. Again Bunkie started to move, but there was something contrived in the way he was doing it, the cadence, perhaps, as if all along he was preparing to turn and confront them. Her observation proved correct. As he exited the den, he turned.

"Judy something," he said. "I remember her name. Peters. Judy Peters." He stood there watching them, making no move to leave. "I said I haven't heard from her since my conversation. I haven't. But she's very much alive. I just saw her picture on the cover of a cookbook."

XVIII

Judy Peters lived in a townhouse on P Street, renovated to take advantage of every architectural strategy to make the house seem more light, airy and spacious than it really was. Floor-to-ceiling windows, a mirrored wall, a painting with a long-distance perspective, hanging plants, exposed blonde wood beams and bookcases snaking everywhere screamed out the pretense of the intellectual and superior taste level of the occupant.

From her vantage in the living room, Fiona could see the professional-size kitchen with its array of butcher block surfaces, hanging pots and up-to-date cooking devices, including a gold-plated cappucino machine, the obvious signature of a woman who writes cookbooks. On the coffee table in front of the couch where Fiona and Cates were seated were an array of these books, all by Ms. Peters, dealing with gourmet cooking sans such ingredients as salt, sugar, eggs and red meat. One was titled, *Cuisine Without Pesticides*. Ms. Peters, Fiona decided, had indeed found her *ouvre*.

The woman herself was tall and slender, with a high-cheek-boned esthetic face that went well with the house. She wore a long belted sweater and an expensive-looking, egg-shaped clock hanging from a beaded necklace. Her wrists were festooned with lines of gold bracelets.

Ms. Peters reeked with feminine militancy. Miss would simply not fit the subject. Her brown eyes peeking out from long lashes, despite an effort to appear serene, seemed wary, guarded. She had agreed to see them on the usual grounds of confidentiality, although from her initial questions on the telephone Fiona detected an inordinate curiosity. They had, of course, concocted a subterfuge, deliberately vague, something merely hinted at, about a scheme to blackmail Senator Langford. They were, of course, careful not to use the word blackmail.

"I'm not part of it?" she had asked with a dollop of expectation.

"Not yet," Fiona had answered, her voice pregnant with warning.

Fiona attributed Judy Peters' consent to the side-effects of what she called the "star-fucker syndrome." In Washington this was usually the affliction of women who interpreted participation in the political process as a sexual connection with an important politician or other powerful figure. Although most of those who were victims of the syndrome were the first to deny it in themselves, they were an accepted part of the fabric of the Capitol. Nor could Fiona deny to herself that there was some special excitement in it, a tantalizing temptation despite all the caveats and pitfalls.

Which was not to say that Ms. Peters was a typical example. But Fiona had found that after years had gone by, women who had "starfucked" were not reluctant to discuss it. Jack Kennedy's women, for example, had been blabbing all over town for years.

Both Cates and Fiona had accepted her offer for, what else, cappucino, which they sipped from cream white cups.

After their abortive interrogation of Bunkie Farrington they had all agreed that if this was, as it had originally appeared, a kind of serial crime, they had better discover what had gone wrong with the serial and, consequently, their logic. All were also agreed, however, that there was a direct relationship between the murders of Helga Kessel and Betty Taylor.

"Yes, I did," Judy Peters acknowledged, after Fiona had finally posed the question. The initial opening had been the usual small-talk of ingratiation and the eliciting of biographical details. Judy Peters had been a legislative aide on the Hill until she had discovered cookbook-writing. She had actually been a legislative assistant to another Senator at the time of her meeting with Senator Langford. Not long after, she had joined the Senator's staff as a speechwriter.

She showed no embarrassment at the revelation.

"I came of sexual age in the sixties," she explained. "I was as much to blame as him."

Fiona figured Ms. Peters for a couple of years older than herself, but of the same mind-set when it came to men. Sitting beside her, Cates fidgeted. Being younger and having grown up under the strict supervision of a stern mother, Cates rarely alighted conversationally on the subject of sex and, in the course of business, would deal with it in rigid, clinical terms. When he made an effort to loosen up on the subject, his comments were always forced and hollow.

"It was ages ago, of course," Judy Peters clarified. She closed her eyes to dramatize her calculation. "Eight years."

"And how long did it last?"

"Oh, no more than six months."

"How was it conducted?"

"Ah yes, the modus operandi," Ms. Peters said, smiling. "Sweet impulsive youth. He was gorgeous. Still is. I adored him. We met a couple of times a week at a house on the Hill."

"Bunkie Farrington's?"

"Now there is a first-class prick," Judy Peters said.

Fiona wanted to acknowledge agreement, but kept quiet. She cut a glance at Cates, who smiled.

"You met at his townhouse?"

"I must say, Officer FitzGerald, you know a great deal."

"There were others," Fiona acknowledged.

"Oh, I'm sure of that. The man was irresistible." She laughed. "And insatiable." She showed not the slightest embarrassment. "He also brought out the tigress in a girl."

"Did you rate it as a real romantic attachment?" Fiona asked.

"A love affair, you mean," Ms. Peters said.

Fiona nodded

"Most definitely that. A glorious, romantic love affair."

"Were the feelings mutual?"

"Very much so. It took a great effort for us to keep our hands off each other. I would often find excuses to get to his office." She paused. "God, we were like rutting pigs."

"People noticed?"

"Only those who weren't blind. That probably led to our undoing. He had been married less than six months. Can you imagine? Six months. She found out." Ms. Peters shook her head. Fiona and Cates exchanged glances. "I felt awful." She straightened in her chair and caught Fiona in her gaze. "One thing I'm not is a home-wrecker."

"How did she find out?" Cates asked. By their immutable law of unseen signals, it became his turn to ask the questions. Judy Peters shifted her attention seamlessly. She seemed to enjoy talking about it.

"Someone told her."

"How do you know?" Cates asked.

She sucked in a deep breath, and for a moment her eyes lost their sparkle, glazing over.

"She told me."

Fiona's heart lurched. Cates pressed on.

"In person?"

"On the telephone. Called me at the office. She said she had heard that I was having an affair with her husband. I was shocked. I lost the power of speech. What was I supposed to say? I was also ashamed. Oh, I thought of the possibility of being the third Mrs. Langford. To his credit, he never hinted at that as a possibility. Wouldn't have worked anyhow. I like my freedom."

She was drifting and Cates pulled her back.

"Did you tell her it was true?"

"I'm one of those people who are constitutionally unable to tell a lie. I said yes. I was." She shook her head. "I remember there was a long silence. Then she said, 'Can you see your way clear to end it? You see, I'm pregnant.' Christ, I felt *that* small." She made the appropriate gesture, then fell silent.

"What did you do?"

"I said I was sorry that she had found out, that I never meant to hurt her."

"And the ending of it?"

"There and then. I went in and saw Farrington. That was his department. I said bye-bye as of that moment."

"Not to the Senator."

"I was too embarrassed. And I didn't want to face him. Cut it clean. That's what I was after. To get the hell out of there."

"And what did Bunkie say?" Cates asked.

"Best all around or somesuch. He sounded relieved. In a way I was, too. It was getting out of hand."

"Did you tell him about the call from Mrs. Langford?"

"I didn't want to. But, for Sam's sake, I thought it wise."

"Did you ever call Mrs. Langford and ask her how she found out?" Cates asked.

"No, I didn't."

"Who do you think told her?"

"God knows. The fact was that our affair was so blatant that anyone with malicious intent might have done it."

"Are you sure it was Mrs. Langford who called?" Fiona asked.

Judy Peters' eyes opened wide.

"No, I wasn't." She paused, bit her lip. "Maybe it wouldn't have mattered. Brought me to my senses. It was time to go. I wasn't a damned fool. I had a great time. He was the best . . ." Her voice trailed off but her smile remained.

"Did Mrs. Langford, the voice on the phone, imply any dire consequences if you kept up the affair?" Fiona asked cautiously.

"Dire consequences?"

"Like cut it out . . . or else." Cates said.

"Or else? Sounds ominous." She thought about it for a moment. "No, she didn't. That would have ticked me off. Made me stick with it. The fact is I knew I couldn't compete with her, not in the real world."

"The real world?" Fiona pressed.

"The lady was loaded. Family in real estate, oil, precious metals. All those goodies. She was right out of central casting. Perfect mate for an ambitious young Senator. No contest." She lowered her eyes, reflected a moment, then said: "I went on into the sunset like a good little girl. Went off to Europe actually . . . the very next day."

"Is that what Farrington suggested?"

"I wouldn't listen to that prick. Fact is I understood why I had to go, even as a kind of plaything. Sam had little choice. A very rich and very pregnant wife. His political career. You know what it means. You have to pretend to be someone you're not. The great unwashed wants you to be a saint. What could I do? I was up there on the Hill. I knew the score."

"Do you think Sam, while you and he . . . do you believe he was unfaithful to you?" Fiona asked. It was, she was certain, a question that only a woman might ask another woman and get the correct answer. Judy Peters looked past her into the mirror that was behind the couch, studying herself. After a while, she said,

"I don't think so. Maybe, but I don't think so."

She did not elaborate. It was an answer with many layers of meaning. Sam was, after all, unfaithful by virtue of his marriage. An old story, Fiona knew. A mistress rarely counted the wife as "the other woman." Judy Peters' revelation, Fiona noted, stopped at that point. What she held back was hers—deeply personal and hers alone. In that moment, Fiona could tell that this was more than a lady who had just wanted to put a scalp of a powerful man on her belt. Despite her telling it now, there had been more to it. She had been, Fiona was certain, deeply hurt. She had loved the man.

"And that was that?" Fiona asked.

"Best thing that ever happened. Going cold turkey." She snapped her fingers. "Stayed in France for a year. Went to the Cordon Bleu cooking school in Gay Paree. As you can see"—her hand swept the room—"it changed my life."

"Have you seen him since you've been back?" Fiona asked.

"Sam?" She smiled and her gaze seemed to turn inward. "From a distance sometimes. Once we exchanged a look or two . . . as the song says . . . across a crowded room. Oh yes. My heart still goes pitter-patter." She snapped back to reality. "I wouldn't want to see Sam hurt in any way. That's why I'm telling you this. Politics is a sick business. Lots of people standing around ready to take potshots, especially now that he's moving up."

"Did it occur to you that it might have been someone other than Mrs. Langford who had called?" Fiona asked gently.

She grew silent, turning over a private thought. "That would be a laugh. Someone put up to do that. Never know with these bastards. I wouldn't put it past Bunkie Farrington." Fiona noted that she hadn't accused the Senator of such conduct.

"Or some scorned woman?" Fiona asked.

"Could be. Every woman that ever got caught in his aura might be suspect then." Her eyes locked into Fiona's. "Sounds incredible, doesn't it?" Her nostrils quivered as she drew in a deep breath. "You have no idea about this man's attraction."

Oh, yes I do, Fiona thought. *Oh, yes I do.*

XIX

It never failed to amaze Fiona how an important case mobilized her inner resources as well as that of those around her, especially the eggplant. Professionalism took precedence to pettiness. Even the masses of hidden agendas that gnawed at the eggplant's innards like maggots were repressed. Even his paranoia subsided and he no longer feared that he would not be fully "apprahzed" as the investigation progressed. Everything was put at the service of "the case."

They were, at this moment, plugged into a single wavelength. There was also tacit agreement between them that they would protect the Senator as long as it was feasible, meaning as long as it did not impinge upon the investigation or bend police ethics beyond what was acceptable, legal or promotion-friendly.

There was, however, one point about which all were in agreement. At the next interview with the Senator the eggplant would have to be present. The agreement might be subject to misinterpretation on the grounds of appeasing the eggplant's hidden agenda for collecting future chits, which it certainly did, but more important was the fact that the matter was now too nationally sensitive to be pursued without the top rung of the police establishment represented. The eggplant, whatever his strengths and weaknesses, was able to short-circuit the Commissioner. He was plugged directly into his own power source, the Mayor, who, in turn, had his own constituency and favor bank among the political elite. As public servants, Fiona knew, they were vulnerable without some political protection.

Bunkie Farrington was still suspect number one, despite his protestations. But beyond gut instinct there was nothing to validate him as the perpetrator.

177

They had, Fiona knew, individual murder scenarios spinning in their minds, but it was too early for them to trade revelations. All agreed that the connection between the murders of Betty Taylor and Helga Kessel was inescapable, although a serial pattern had not totally emerged. Another body killed and disposed of in the same manner would quickly have confirmed the theory. That had not yet occurred.

The next morning the *Post* carried a follow-up story on the Kessel murder, quoting the eggplant as saying that "the police were still pursuing the robbery theory," which cut both ways and carefully signaled to the Senator and the Ambassador that they were not yet off the hook.

But the first surprise of the day was a call from Bunkie Farrington, who requested that they meet him at his townhouse "as soon as possible." Fiona and Cates were there within an hour.

They followed him into his kitchen, a jungle of unwashed dishes and general chaos. He appeared in the same physical state as the kitchen. His eyes were puffy, his skin pasty, his hair matted. A sour effluvium rose from his body. He poured oily coffee, which literally tasted fried, into chipped mugs.

He also appeared to have suddenly, as of a few hours ago, taken up smoking, which periodically sent him doubling-up into coughing fits.

"You people are making me a nervous wreck," he said.

He indicated that they should sit down at the table. They reluctantly accepted the invitation.

"Sorry for the mess." Bunkie said.

He shook his head and lit another cigarette, managing to get through a puff without coughing.

"Damndest thing," he said. They waited through a long pause. He squinted into the smoke, then looked up at them. "I found out what happened to Harriet Farley."

Fiona and Cates exchanged glances. They had planned, of course, to check it out themselves.

"Saves us the trouble," Cates said.

"Dead," he said flatly. "Killed in an automobile accident. I called Herb Frank in Florida. He had hired Harriet for the first Senatorial campaign. She was a beauty, six foot tall, one of those athletic, perfectly proportioned amazons. Sam went nuts for her. Right in the middle of the campaign. Three years ago. She had to go. Our opponent was gathering dirt and there she was, bigger than life, a perfect target. It didn't take a genius to see that Sam had reserved that for himself. And she was getting real hooked."

"So you gave her your best Dear-John," Fiona said.

"You make it sound like it's a crime. I did the best I could. Gave her a month's severance." He shook his head. "You may not believe this, but I felt real bad about Harriet. I really liked her, big blue-eyed baby."

"Boss got first dibs," Fiona said with a sneer.

Bunkie shrugged, but his silence told her she had hit a raw nerve.

"She was killed on a secondary road in the Middleburg area."

"Was she drunk?"

"No evidence. I got the report from the Loudon County Police. She was into horses, rode with the Hunts in Middleburg when she got a chance. Anyway, this was one of those winding country roads."

"When was it?"

"Did you have to ask? Three days after I spoke to her. Not a word in the Washington papers. Happened in broad daylight, too. Bang into a tree. Police could find no reason for it. She wasn't drunk, wasn't drugged. No sign of foul play. They simply shipped the body back to Oklahoma, where she was from. We never know how the end comes. Damned shame. She was something."

"We'll check it, you know," Cates said.

"I hope so." He punched out a half-smoked cigarette, then lighted another with a match, and puffed in a drag. He blew it out without inhaling.

Fiona studied him. In this business nothing was ever as it seemed. Could the killer have deliberately thrown them off the scent? Serial killers were crafty devils who, for the most part, understood their aberration. It was Bunkie, after all, who had identified Harriet and Judy. They could have been merely two among many, two whose history belied the serial pattern. This did not rule out others who became entangled in the Senator's amorous escapades. A twinge of curiosity invaded her. Involuntary sexual images surfaced in her mind. With an admonishment to herself, she brushed them away and came back to Bunkie.

Indeed, if one were to carry suspicion to the outer limits, she reasoned that Bunkie could be covering for the Senator himself. It was the kind of thought one filed away for future reference.

"By my count," Fiona said, "you administered three Dear-Johns." She didn't count Judy Peters.

"All dead ladies," Cates snapped.

"Christ. Sounds awful," Bunkie muttered. "Remember, though, Harriet had an accident."

"Maybe," Cates said.

"Come on, guys. That's a big leap of faith," Bunkie countered. "And Judy Peters gave Sam the boot."

"You would have gotten around to her, Farrington," Fiona said.

"I guess so," Bunkie mumbled.

"Were there any others?" Cates pushed.

He took the question with resignation.

"That again?" he sighed.

"And again," Fiona said.

"I'm not counting the transients," Bunkie said. "You'd need a computer. I've only considered serious threats to his career."

"Just four?" Fiona asked.

"I don't have eyes in back of my head." He lit another cigarette, inhaled, hacked then said, "He's a bull loose in a cow pasture. What can I say?"

"Ever recommend a psychiatrist?" Fiona asked.

"In this business?" he shot back.

Cates looked at her, not understanding.

"It's a public antishrink prejudice," Fiona explained. "Shows a politician's clay feet."

"You've got to admit, Farrington," Cates said, "the evidence is compelling. They get serious, then they die. Except for Judy Peters."

"It wasn't me," Bunkie said. "And certainly not Sam. He may be a terror in the sack, but at heart he's a pussycat."

"Okay then. We're open to suggestions," Fiona said.

"I haven't any. It's too weird," Bunkie said. "I can't figure it out. Why?"

"Easy enough for us," Fiona said. "Had to be someone who had a great deal to lose, personally or careerwise, by these continuing affairs." She suddenly remembered Judy Peters, the one who had gotten away. "Maybe Mrs. Langford." It was a stab in the dark, she knew.

"Nell? No way."

"Why not?"

"She's on the team is why. But Sam is a good family man. Loves the kids. Nell never rocks the boat."

"You mean all's well on the home front?" Fiona asked.

"Believe it or not."

"She doesn't bug him, threaten to leave?"

"He keeps the other separate."

"With your help?"

"I try," Bunkie said with self-deprecating sarcasm. "It seems I fucked it up."

They left him with that idea hanging in the air.

"We've talked to Judy," Fiona said.

"I figured," Bunkie said. "Proof positive. She corroborated what I told you."

"More or less," Cates said.

"Jeez. Give me the benefit of the doubt. I'm trying to help you, help clear the air." He puffed deeply, coughed, then, catching his breath, spoke again. "What do you mean 'more or less'?"

"Who told Mrs. Langford about the Senator and Judy?"

"Beats the shit out of me," Bunkie said. He puffed again, coughed, bringing a fist up to his mouth.

"You never asked?"

Bunkie looked at them. His tongue flicked along his lips, moistening them.

"I stayed out of that one. I didn't even tell Sam about it."

"What *did* you tell him?" Fiona pressed.

"She cut out. Had enough. Good riddance."

"How did he take it?"

"Like all of them. He really liked the kid, but he got over it."

"You think Mrs. Langford brought it up to him?" Fiona asked.

"Probably not. I told you. She doesn't rock the boat. The fact is we don't discuss his family life. I told you. The woman doesn't exactly care for me."

"Maybe she's the one? That ever occur to you?" Cates asked cautiously.

"Nell. A killer. You crazy."

"Why crazy? She could have set it all up herself," Fiona suggested. Such an idea had both precedent and logic. A rich jealous wife had the means and motive to put a private dick on the Senator's tail. And worse. Hiring someone to ice the offending ladies was not unknown in the annals of crime.

"Never." Bunkie said. She could tell that the thought might have crossed his mind. Even if he was the perpetrator the idea had good possibilities in terms of shifting suspicion away from himself. She pressed him further.

"Never say never," Fiona said.

He blew a gust of breath through his lips, making an obscene sound.

"Cops always ask the question, 'Who profits?' " Cates said.

"Bimbos killed, career saved," Fiona added.

"That goes for all of us," he acknowledged. "He goes down. We go down."

If he had any admirable qualities at all, it was absolute loyalty to the cause.

"So you don't really know if Mrs. Langford ever brought up the matter of Judy Peters?"

"And I didn't ask," Bunkie reiterated.

"You expect us to believe that bullshit?" Cates snapped.

"I deal in the irregular. Not the regular. Problem with Sam, he only goes wrong when he gives pussy an identity, recognizes the whole woman."

Odd, Fiona thought, how being a cop made her sometimes appear asexual at times, especially to macho assholes like Bunkie. Worse, he was so insensitive, he couldn't even acknowledge his statement as a gaffe. The man had a real problem with the gender. Not so the great swordsman Senator. He knew the way to a woman's heart, all right. And apparently every other part, as well, including what went on in their collective heads.

"So you say Nell Langford is innocent?" Fiona asked. They were going round and round now, getting nowhere.

"I do."

"And the Senator?"

"No way."

"Monte Pappas?"

"You're kidding. Not a chance."

"Ambassador Kessel?"

He shook his head.

"Leaves you," Fiona said, watching as he attempted to inhale a cloud of smoke. They left him in the kitchen, hacking away.

XX

Nell Langford sat in the sunny living room of her spacious Spring Valley home showing all the confidence that was not apparent when Fiona saw her last at the dance. Through large floor-to-ceiling windows, they could see brightly colored swings, a seesaw and sliding pond planted on the grass. A high cedar fence surrounded the yard and a large dog lay sleeping under a tree.

The neat living room was expensively decorated with lush fabrics. Framed Currier and Ives prints, obviously of collectible quality, hung on the walls. There were also nests of family portraits intermingled with silver-framed political photographs on every available flat surface.

True or not, the ambience offered the feel of deep family roots, symbols of what modern politicians were now calling "values." Dropped from the sky without a historical context for the Senator, one might infer from his home that he was a faithful and devoted family man, a loving husband and father. Knowing what she knew, Fiona felt offended by the hypocrisy. Even Sam's little Nell could not escape responsibility for the charade.

Nell Langford was wearing black slacks and a white turtleneck sweater, which showed the lines of a well-endowed female body. The gown she wore at the Mount Vernon dance had muted those lines.

Fiona and Cates had, by design, imposed themselves on her, flashing their badges. If Nell recognized Fiona from the Mount Vernon dance, she gave no sign. It was clear that she had not expected them, had not been forewarned by Bunkie or the Senator. This was good. They had been counting on the element of surprise.

"It's that important, Mrs. Langford," Fiona had pressed, much like a door-to-door salesman about to put his foot in the door. Nell had hesitated, her eyes searching their faces. Her instincts, Fiona

185

observed, from the flash of anxiety that passed across her face, were certainly correct. An enemy was at the door.

"Just routine," Cates said pleasantly, in a poor version of a dissimulating movie cop. She could tell that Nell Langford was not fooled.

It had to be done, of course. There was no avoiding it. If Nell refused, they would have to threaten. She seemed to be weighing the alternatives. Nor could Fiona detect any signs of guilt or innocence, only the palpable fear of the unexpected. The wife of a potential Presidential candidate had to be cautious. In that context anything remotely controversial was to be avoided. Nell chose to speak with them.

Leading them into the living room, Nell was cautious and not unpleasant. Also not hospitable. Her consent had been strictly business and no frills were to be expected.

"You have a lovely house, Mrs. Langford," Fiona said with sincere admiration.

"Thank you," Nell replied coldly.

"Like an oasis," Fiona pressed.

"We worked quite hard to create it," Nell said with an air of haughty dismissal. "Now what can I do for you?" She was, Fiona felt, being deliberately patronizing, but she could not completely hide her wariness.

"It's about the murder of Helga Kessel," Fiona began. No small-talk now, she had decided. Plunge right in. Despite a desire to be objective, she could not chase a feeling of irritation based on Nell's not remembering her from the Mount Vernon party. So she wasn't important enough to remember, was she?

Fiona, her expression deliberately stern, focused hostile eyes in Nell's direction. She wanted her to feel under scrutiny, intimidated. It was quite clear that Nell, for her part, had marshaled all her forces to resist them.

It struck her suddenly that this same attitude marked all the others. Like turtles, they had ducked their heads into a protective crust.

Kessel, Bunkie, the Senator. Now Nell. And although there were elements of a conspiracy, they all seemed to be holding back pieces of the puzzle for their own purposes.

"Poor woman," Nell said. "But she had no business walking around wearing all that expensive jewelry."

"Did you know her well?" Fiona asked.

"Does anyone in Washington really know anyone well? She was on the circuit. I was at a dance with her just a few days ago. At Mount Vernon."

Still, she showed no recognition that she had ever met Fiona. Nor was Fiona moved to remind her.

"How well did the Senator know her?" Fiona asked. The question was direct, with no attempt to deflect its real meaning.

Nell caught the message. Her eyes unlocked themselves from Fiona's and turned to look through the windows. The grass's sudden reflection turned her hazel eyes a luminous green. Her recovery took place in a flicker as she turned toward Fiona again.

"No more than I did," Nell said with a feeble attempt at a smile. A frown line broke on her forehead, giving away an increasing anxiety. She didn't know about the affair, Fiona decided. Not for sure. Behind the facade, she is steeling herself for the blow. It might have occurred to her, of course. Fiona had seen the suspicion in her eyes the night of the dance, when the Senator and Helga cavorted on the dance floor together.

Satisfied that the message had been received, Fiona was ready for a combination punch.

"Is the name Judith Peters familiar to you, Mrs. Langford?"

Nell's eyes narrowed as she appeared to search her memory for a recollection.

"Go back eight years," Fiona urged, knowing it was a gamble, that Nell might not have made the call after all.

Part of the reality of the political life was the "play dumb" role assigned to wives and children of politicians. Nothing was to be revealed about a politician's private life without first passing through an image-making screening process. Was Nell playing this role with flawless precision? Fiona studied her intensely, waiting for the dice to fall.

"I'm sorry," she replied. "It escapes me."

"Shall I refresh your memory?" Fiona asked cautiously. She glanced at Cates, who gave her a quick supportive blink. In for a penny, in for a pound, she thought.

"You called this woman . . ." Fiona began, halting deliberately to check the impression she was making. Nell's face was expressionless.

"Did I?"

Never volunteer. That was the axiom of the stonewaller. Apparently Nell was quite good at it. Okay, lady, you asked for it, Fiona decided.

"She was having an affair with your husband, Mrs. Langford. You called her and told her to back off."

Only the slightest tremor in her cheek gave her away. But it was there. Loud and clear.

"Why are you asking me these questions?"

"I could explain it better if you cooperated," Fiona rebuked. At that moment, Nell's mind had to be filled with options. She could throw them out. She could call her husband for his immediate advice. Or she could tough it out, hoping that whatever was happening would not spill over to hurt her husband's, and her, aspirations.

The question behind the question, of course, was her culpability, if any. With undoubtedly a great effort of will, Nell managed to keep her features composed, although the little nerve in her cheek offered a tiny betrayal.

"If I remember correctly I merely responded to a rumor. I was a newlywed. I had not yet learned that a public figure was a prime target for any crazy with the price of a telephone call."

Well put, Fiona thought. A half-confession.

"So you did call this woman?"

"For which I was soundly admonished," Nell said, offering a tight smile.

"I take it your husband denied it."

"We were married six months and I was pregnant. It was an ugly rumor and I overreacted. My husband, as you can see, is a very attractive man, an easy prey for designing females." Her hand went up to her single strand of pearls and the tiny tremor in her cheek subsided.

"So he did deny it?"

"I would not ever put him in such a position. I have since learned to discount such rumors."

"Have there been others?"

"Countless." She smiled, still playing with her pearls. "We are, you see, a very close family. A political family must expect those things." She turned her eyes full-glare on Fiona, telescoping that she was determined to show her superior credentials. "You have to be there to fully understand. Families of major figures in the political world are subject to these stresses. We grow used to them. It is very difficult to transfer this experience to others." She meant Fiona, of course. As for Cates, he might have been a piece of furniture for all the attention she paid to him.

It was time to throw the bomb, Fiona thought. The woman's attitude made it easy to do.

"Then I take it you did not suspect that your husband was having an affair with Helga Kessel."

Her eyes went into a repetitive nervous blink and her fingers, instead of caressing the pearls, began to pull on them.

"That is quite absurd," she managed to say. But she was having some difficulty keeping her cool.

"Not only is it not absurd. It is a fact. The Ambassador knew. Farrington knew. I know. My partner here knows. The point to be made is that Helga Kessel was murdered by someone, person or persons unknown. We do not believe robbery was the motive."

"What, then?" she asked, her voice quivering.

She apparently had chosen to skirt the issue. Obviously she was still denying it to herself. But the turmoil within her was apparent.

"Jealousy, perhaps," Fiona said pointedly.

"There, you see? Even you suspect another crazy. Now do you get my point?"

It was a valiant effort to take a mental detour.

"We make no conclusions," Fiona said. "Helga was strangled in the same fashion as another woman, years earlier."

"Now you're losing me," Nell said, reaching for a haughty air. But her nervous tension kept her from achieving it.

"This was fourteen years ago."

"I hadn't even met him then," Nell interjected.

"We know that."

Since the serial aspect had been discounted, they could speculate that the two murders were unconnected, although it stretched credulity. The present murderer could have simply come up with the same modus operandi by coincidence.

"The point here is that both women were having affairs with your husband."

"He was somebody else's husband fourteen years ago," Nell protested. She was lashing out now. A slight flush broke out on the cheeks of her well-scrubbed skin.

"But you do see the connection. Why we have to ask you these questions. Believe me, Mrs. Langford, we are not here to harass you."

"This is a very good imitation of it," she said testily. "My husband, I can assure you, will be quite upset about this confrontation."

True to form for these types, Fiona thought. She had expected the threat earlier.

"Mrs. Langford," Fiona said, adopting a deliberately weary tone. "We are trying to protect your husband's reputation and career. But the inescapable fact is that we cannot turn away from the obvious. There are only a few motives that make any sense. One of them is jealousy."

"Are you suggesting . . ." Nell began. She shook her head, trying hard to control any display of anger.

"We're investigating. Not suggesting. We're doing what needs to be done. If you knew about this affair you had every reason to get rid of this woman."

"This could be actionable, you know," Nell said frostily, still stonewalling. Again, Fiona ignored the threat.

"Neither your husband, yourself, Ambassador Kessel nor Bunkie Farrington is off the hook. You all had your reasons."

"How utterly despicable of you . . ." She could not go on. Her voice broke. To her credit, the anger never quite got the best of her. When she got control of her voice again she said, "Are you accusing me of murdering this woman?"

"Did you?" Fiona asked.

"You're not serious?"

"Dead serious," Fiona said from between clenched teeth.

"My husband will be appalled."

Off the high-horse, lady, Fiona thought.

"You're not getting this message, Mrs. Langford," Cates said suddenly. He had been patient. Perhaps he was tired of being ignored, treated as if he weren't there. The woman turned to face him.

"What message, Officer?" she asked coyly, as if she were poised to intimidate him.

"A woman your husband was seeing has just been murdered. You can't ignore either fact. Would it be better if we invited your husband to attend this interrogation and put the question to him directly?"

"He has already admitted it and Bunkie Farrington has confirmed," Fiona added.

"Bunkie." she said coldly. "That man makes my skin crawl."

"Well, we all agree on something," Fiona said. The hint of alliance was not appreciated by Nell.

"That mutual feeling changes nothing," Cates said, clearly assuming the role of bad cop. In this case, badder cop. "Can you account for your time on Tuesday, day and night?"

She started to protest, obviously thought better of it, then paused as if to recall the time frame. Then she nodded.

"Of course I can. And you will find it can easily be confirmed." They assumed as much, but did not pursue it. Time for that later. The psychological aspects seemed more to the point at the moment. It was time to increase the pressure.

"I'll ask you again, Mrs. Langford. Did you know about your husband and Helga Kessel?" Fiona pressed. Surprisingly, she was beginning to show some admiration for Nell. She was fighting it all the way, refusing to be drawn in, although defeat in this regard was inevitable.

"I never asked," she said after a long pause.

"Why not? Didn't it matter?"

"There would be only one way to be sure," she said. "To observe for myself. Everything else would be hearsay."

"Photographs, too?"

"They could be altered."

"And if your husband admitted it, would you believe it then?"

"Not necessarily," she said, defying all logic. "He might have his reasons."

It was exasperating. Nell Langford had the great facility of skewering reality, bending it to her will. She remembered Bunkie's words. "Not Nell." He was dead wrong. Nell could easily hire a hit man to eliminate Helga or anyone else, then cavalierly dismiss it from her mind.

"All right then," Fiona said, as if it were an announcement of a changing tack. Ready about. "Were there any other women rumored to be having an affair with your husband?" The use of the word "rumor" was an obvious placebo. Nell grabbed for it like a life preserver.

"There were always these rumors," she replied with some eagerness, as if the question had been some sort of a cue. "I put no credence in them."

"What about names?"

"If I heard them, I put them out of my mind. The Senator is a good and faithful husband and father. I resent these rumors, not for myself, but for my children. I have explained to them that they will hear them. Children will bring them to school. And I have instructed them to pay no attention. Like me. These rumors are manufactured by his enemies and those that are jealous of his success. He is a national political figure. We are conditioned to expect such things."

She delivered this speech flawlessly, as if it were by rote, to be trotted out for just such occasions. It was, unquestionably, a summation and signaled that she was on the verge of dismissing them. Not so fast, lady, Fiona thought.

"Did you think the Helga thing was a rumor?" Fiona asked, determined not to be deflected.

"I never heard it. If I did, I would have dismissed it as such. Yes."

Fiona's level of exasperation was rising. The woman had an enormous talent for obfuscation.

"You're not helping your husband, Mrs. Langford," Fiona said. In her mind, she decided, she would give the woman the presumption of innocence. At least for the moment. Nell listened silently. "This case stinks of scandal. The media would have a field day and in their environment rumor becomes truth. So let's stop all this bullshit and get to the point."

Still stonewalling, Nell glared at her.

"I have nothing to say," she said haughtily.

"Next thing you'll be calling for your lawyer," Cates interjected.

"Better believe it."

"More people to tell," Fiona sighed. "Keep spreading the word until you destroy your husband's career. He's in real political trouble, Mrs. Langford. Somebody, for reasons that are directly related to your husband, killed those women."

"So you say," Nell said, as if to further prove her resilience. "But it is obvious that you haven't got an iota of evidence to back up that contention." She stood up, pulling back her shoulders, illustrating what Fiona supposed was her sense of aristocratic authority.

"You realize, of course, that you're forcing us to widen the circle."

The threat could not be made any clearer. In fact, the potential demise of Senator Langford's career might be considered the theme of the meeting. It apparently had not fazed Nell, which, for Fiona, was the heart of the puzzle. Why not?

The answer came after they followed her out of the room. They passed through the living room, festooned with sunlight flowing from window walls that faced out to lush greenery, enriched by the recent rains.

But in the tiled vestibule, Fiona hesitated, waiting for Nell Langford to turn. She did not wish the interview to end. Something was awry here. The woman did not fear the detonation of her husband's career.

Perhaps she hated him with such intensity that she was hoping for it to happen. On the other hand, she might be guilty of the killing of Helga, and valued her own skin above all else. A cool number either way, Fiona decided. Once again the social scene was a poor arena for psychological evaluation. People wore masks in that setting. For this visit, Nell Langford had simply changed masks.

"One might say that it was you who are pulling the trigger." Fiona had chosen the metaphor carefully.

Nell's face, instead of the expected anger, registered a confusing serenity.

"You know," she said, "I admire your tenacity, but you're coming from the wrong place. I'd be quite happy if my husband abandoned his career. Public life is a treacherous jungle. And if his aspirations are scuttled by this affair, I'd be the first to stand up and applaud. I love my husband dearly, and, if you must know, I hate being a political wife. Politics destroys marriages. Yes, he is ambitious. Yes, he is also enormously attractive to women. The important thing for me is that I'm the mother of his children. I'm the woman he takes home at night and I'm the woman he sleeps with. He is also not a person who hurts other people, certainly not intentionally. As for being a killer, that is preposterous. The fact is that, if my family were in danger, I am a more likely candidate for murderer than my husband." By then, her expression had become sweet, benign. A clever act or the soul of sincerity. The latter judgement was terribly convincing. "Do whatever you have to do," she said after a brief pause. "But I'd suggest you look elsewhere for your culprit."

"That"—Fiona said, holding onto a brief shred of purpose—"is why we are here."

"I can't help you," Nell said, opening the door to let them out.

"Won't," Fiona said as she went through the door, carrying with her the uneasy feeling that Nell, despite her apparent indifference, had more than an idea of who the killer might be.

XXI

"Ghouls," Mr. Haber said. "We had two contracts on the house by noon."

His pink cheeks creased into a broad smile, showing a row of perfect white, but obviously false, teeth. With the exception of thick rimless glasses, he was pink from his chin to the back of his bald head where grey hair formed a natural ridge line.

"It has cachet now. A landmark of sorts. Here's where the body of the Austrian Ambassador's wife was buried. They'll probably frame the clippings and put it in the den."

They were getting this lesson in real estate sales from the President of Haber and Weston, a man of obvious self-importance. His office was filled with plaques, framed certificates and photographs that attested to his energetic pursuit of ego-fulfilling honors and sales-motivational ploys.

Real estate sales was Washington's second-oldest profession and the number-one topic of conversation wherever Washingtonians gathered from Georgetown to Capitol Hill. Fiona was not immune to the subject. She was, after all, a property owner herself and the astounding rise in Washington real estate values did not leave her unaffected.

Fiona had inherited the house in the Forest Hills section, which her father had bought in 1953 for $32,000. When last she checked, it was worth $750,000 and rising, and not a week went by without some real estate person soliciting her interest in a sale. Although she was inherently practical, her sentimental attachment to the house remained stronger than the potential monetary gain.

Cates, who rented his apartment, listened with a student's interest.

"You'd think the house would be less attractive," he said with some surprise.

197

"Houses are a reflection of our need for identity. They represent our deepest yearnings. The people who expressed their desire to buy were bringing a yearning for celebrity into their lives." Haber unraveled his spiel, honed down by obvious repetition, to appear as if it were coming from Mount Sinai.

"You said ghouls," Fiona reminded him.

He leaned over his desk and lowered his voice.

"Ghouls buy houses, too, Officer FitzGerald. We have only one interest in life here." He raised his arm in a gesture to encompass the universe. "Move 'em out. Stroke 'em. Feed the fantasy. Bring 'em to settlement and take our commission. Name of the game."

It struck Fiona that he was "relating," playing the cynic. Somewhere out there in TV land he had been shown cynical cops.

"How many people," Cates asked, "would have some knowledge that this house was empty?"

"For one thing, everyone in our offices." He moved his hand across his chin, exhibiting a huge star sapphire on his right pinky.

"How many people?"

"Counting part-timers, nearly eight hundred."

Cates cut a glance at Fiona. He had not expected the answer. Seeing this, Haber pressed forward with obvious enjoyment.

"We have twenty offices, all hooked in by computers. Then, of course, there are the people that drive by and see our sign. Be surprised how many people buy that way. We also do a big trade promotion. Hold an open house for agents from different companies. We give them a walk-through. Then, of course, there's Multiple Listing, a computer network plugged into most of the real estate people in the area."

"Brings the access to how many people?" Fiona asked, mostly for Cates' benefit.

"Thousands. Multiple Listing is a data base showing the bulk of the inventory in this area. Every sales agent worth his or her salt knows what's on it. They match a prospect with a house, then make a connection with the listing broker to see the property. It's a salami business." He chuckled at his comparison.

"Salami?" Cates asked.

"Everybody gets their cut. The person that gets the listing splits with the broker and they in turn split with the agent that makes the deal, whether it's from our company or not. Everybody's happy."

"Any other way people learn about the house?"

"Advertising," Haber said. "After a while it's no secret."

"Was the house in Cleveland Park advertised?"

He opened a file on his desk and studied it.

"Not for a while."

"How long ago?" Fiona asked.

"Three months ago. Price was too high. We brought it down some. Then pow. The Kessel murder. Front-page advertising in the *Washington Post*. None of the customers brought to contract quibbled over price. Actually we could have gotten more. That's the way it goes in this business."

"And the people who lived in the house?"

"They moved out two weeks ago. An elderly couple. Lived there for twenty-five years."

"Do you make a list of everyone who visited the property?" Fiona asked. An idea, still in embryo, was trying to bubble to the surface of her consciousness.

"It's a cockamamie system. We try to save the salesman's cards, but more often than not, we blow it. The point is, if they do make a deal, they have to come through us anyhow."

A presumption was growing in her mind. The perpetrator had to be somewhat familiar with the property. He would need to pick a site that might remain untouched for years. The chances were it would not be a compulsive decision. Something well planned, requiring a passing knowledge of the property. A friend of the family, perhaps? A relative? A neighbor? A friend of a neighbor? A relative of a neighbor? All possibilities. More than likely, Fiona decided, someone who had already made a decision to kill, someone who wanted a sure-fire body-disposal system, someone who could research the site without fear of discovery and someone who knew the site would be empty when it was needed.

"Would Multiple Listing indicate that the house was empty?" Fiona asked.

"Not necessarily. But there would be lots of ways to find out. In the first place, there aren't many houses in Cleveland Park that come up for sale. In the second place, this is a network business. People find out. A house is harder to sell when it's empty."

With all their psychological meanderings into the motives of the Senator, Bunkie, Kessel and Nell, they had missed an essential ingredient. They had not connected the four in any way with the house in Cleveland Park or its occupants. As for the case of Betty Taylor, two of the suspects were not even in the picture at that time. Thinking about Betty Taylor suggested an idea.

"I know there are records of property transfers," Fiona said. "But is it possible for your records to tell me when a house was actually being offered for sale?"

"I think I just explained that," Haber said, somewhat confused.

"I mean fourteen years ago," Fiona explained.

Haber thought for a moment, then nodded his head.

"Take some doing, but I think we might find it."

She found the Woodland Avenue address in her notebook, then transferred it along with the probable dates to another piece of paper and gave it to Haber.

"Anything to help the defenders of the civic peace," he said, showing the full set of his perfect white false teeth.

"Now tell us about the elderly couple that lived in the Cleveland Park house," Cates said. He looked toward Fiona. It was certainly a reasonable tack to take.

Haber consulted his file.

"A recent retiree from the Justice Department," he said, looking at them over half-reading glasses.

"What did he do there?" Cates asked.

"He was with the Congressional Liaison Office," Haber said, consulting the file again.

"A lobbyist!" Fiona exclaimed.

"More than that," Cates shot back, turning to Fiona. "What committee would concern him?" She saw Haber searching their faces, obviously confused, trying to pick up their shorthand.

"Judiciary," Fiona said.

"Bingo!" Cates exclaimed.

"No prizes until all the numbers are confirmed," Fiona said.

They thanked Haber, who offered his hand in a "sincere" salesman's shake, and left the office.

XXII

"More holes in this case than Swiss cheese," the eggplant said, biting into a sticky jelly doughnut. A drop of jelly squirted on his tie. "Shit." He fussed with a napkin and made it worse.

Fiona had come to the same conclusion after a sleepless night. They were sitting in the eggplant's office. Apparently the windows had been cleaned. With the removal of layers of dust the spring sun bathed them in light. Despite the light, no one made a move to lower the blinds. It felt good to have clean, warm sunlight in the otherwise drab office. It filled the room with an air of optimism that had long been absent. Even the eggplant seemed infected by the mood created by the changed light.

"At least we're off the front page," the eggplant said, stabbing an ebony finger into the *Washington Post* spread out on his desk. A bland one-column headline in an inside page read: PURSUE KESSELUPDATE. The story was a rehash. Thankfully, the reporter was not an eager beaver and he was still flacking the robbery theory. He had not written that "an arrest is imminent."

Both Cates and Fiona had been meticulous in their reporting to the eggplant, who sensed that he was getting the full picture, which, indeed, he was. For his part, the eggplant had reported that nothing had turned up about the jewelry.

"Coincidence or connection," the eggplant had mused when they reported what they had learned about the occupation of the owner of the Cleveland Park house.

The former occupants were on safari in Kenya, Cates had discovered, and currently out of touch. But the euphoria of the revelation had dissipated. At best, the circumstantial thread had little currency without witnesses, and, so far, a canvass of the neighborhood had yielded little and no one had stepped forward to offer any further information. Nor could Cates' informant at the Committee provide any connecting links.

In an effort to accelerate action on the case, they had gone the psychological route with Bunkie and Nell. Spin a web of circumstances that threatened suspects into believing either they were trapped or triggering deep guilt responses, forcing them into confession. So far it hadn't worked.

What was even more troubling to Fiona was that neither Bunkie nor Nell had given her any intuitive sense of their guilt. Not that such feelings were a foolproof barometer. She had often overreacted to these inner signals, only to find that they had guided her in the wrong direction.

"We've got to talk to the man," the eggplant sighed. "I was hoping for more, before we got to him." He shrugged and licked the jelly and sugar off his fingers. "Something really concrete to open him up."

"And then?" Fiona asked. It was the kind of innocent question that often riled others. It had been inadvertent and she moved to quickly correct the situation. She had no desire to change the mood in the room. "What I mean is . . . suppose he does open up. Maybe after all this he knows no more than we do."

The eggplant pondered the idea, stood up and moved toward the window, transforming himself into a silhouette.

"Still," the eggplant mused, "we have the power to blow him to hell and back."

"Or save him," Fiona argued, forcing the issue back into the area of self-aggrandizement. To catch a killer, she could be single-minded and ruthless. But something about the Senator left her with a soft center. No politician is ever truly innocent, she knew. And a womanizer like Sam Langford was not deserving of compassion. And yet . . .

"We're missing something," Cates interjected. He was, after all, the only really neutral force in the group. "I wish I knew what it was."

For some reason, Fiona's mind had jumped to focus on Helga Kessel. Had she really, as Bunkie and Kessel had alleged, "gone quietly"? And if not, how strong was her capacity to disrupt the Senator's career? In effect, she would be destroying two careers. Her husband's as well as the Senator's. Would that be the rational act of a sophisticated woman of the world? Fiona thought not.

Her mind fastened on the Betty Taylor connection. Nell was absolutely correct. That was before her time. Also Ambassador Kessel's, which considerably diluted the possibility of their committing what on the surface seemed like a serial crime.

But the young Betty Taylor, in the throes of a passionate love affair with an older man, offered a troubling prospect, especially for Bunkie and/or the Senator. She might have been quite capable of making waves, tempting fate. Ambition, especially in Washington, had a force beyond measure. To stand in its way was like deliberately planting oneself in the middle of a track in the face of an oncoming train.

And the power of love, since time immemorial, was capable of making people, both men and women, commit all sorts of acts contrary to their own self-interest. History and literature were filled with examples of such destructive behavior.

"I keep thinking cover-up," Fiona said.

"Has all the earmarks," the eggplant said.

"They could all be in it together," Cates said. "Including the Senator and his wife."

"Which still leaves how Betty Taylor fits," Fiona said.

"Or doesn't," Cates said.

"She fits," Fiona insisted. "I know she does." Intuition again, she cautioned herself. In the game of random selection she played with herself she allowed one intuitive thought to outweigh another.

"Have to go with that," the eggplant said.

At that point the phone rang. The eggplant picked it up.

"For you," he said, handing the phone to Fiona. It was Haber.

"Found what you wanted, Officer FitzGerald," Haber said as if he were pitching a prospect.

"Great," Fiona acknowledged. She covered the mouthpiece with her hand. "The real estate man," she said. The eggplant nodded.

"House was empty for six months fourteen years ago. Couldn't move the damned thing for $300,000. Goes for one million one now. Imagine that. Only fourteen years."

"Who was the listing broker?"

"Another company. Heller and Smith."

"Was it on Multiple Listing?"

"Sure was."

"Thanks, Mr. Haber."

"Ever ready to oblige," he said. But he did not hang up. "Say, Officer. I understand you have a prime piece of property in Forest Hills. I think I can get you close to eight if you want to move."

"How the hell did you know that?" Fiona snapped.

"Ve haf our methods." He chuckled. "You look for killers. I look for real estate. You got a real hot and easy one, Officer. At least eight. Maybe more."

"Thanks and no thanks," Fiona said, hanging up. She shook her head and looked at the phone. "Says he can get me $800,000 for my house."

"Was me, I'd take the money and run," the eggplant said. She was instantly sorry she had mentioned that. The class issue was always a silent irritant in her police relationships, more so than the matter of race. It fed her own paranoia as well, since she truly believed that many of her colleagues secretly believed that her serving in the police was a form of slumming, and, therefore, her reaction to them was always patronizing. No matter how much respect she had won, how many psychic medals were strung across her chest, how many cases she had broken, there always lingered the fear in herself that she was still an alien, still arrogantly superior, still the hated lily-white cunt.

"Run to where?" Fiona replied, pausing. The idea that had been bubbling in her subconscious suddenly broke to the surface. "He did sell me one thing, though."

"What's that?" the eggplant asked.

"Ten to one our murderer is a real estate salesman," she said, bells of intuition clanging in her head.

XXIII

It was Sam Langford's choice, a Vietnamese cocktail lounge and restaurant in a strip shopping center a few miles south of Roslyn on that stretch of Lee Highway now known as Little Vietnam. A reincarnated Robert E. Lee, for whom the road was named, would have rubbed his eyes in disbelief. Even in the darkened interior of the lounge there wasn't a single anglo or black face.

"This your idea of low-profile, Senator?" the eggplant asked. Langford had gone to elaborate lengths to keep their meeting secret. He had returned Fiona's call from a pay phone, providing cloak and dagger instructions. He would meet them at a Giant Supermarket parking lot off Lee Highway.

The car, they noticed, had no Senatorial license plates.

"Man's a paranoid," the eggplant had remarked.

"You'd be too, running for President."

"With his zipper open?"

The Senator was aghast when he saw the black face in the driver's seat. She had switched to the back seat to put the Senator next to the eggplant.

"My boss," Fiona had told him. "Captain Greene, Homicide Division, Senator Sam Langford."

"Call you Captain?"

"Your choice." The eggplant shrugged.

"I'm Sam," the Senator said, offering his most ingratiating political smile and shaking the eggplant's hand as he got in beside him. "I know it's a spy novel," he grunted. "It's also a nightmare."

Except for giving directions, he grew silent, while Fiona made comments about the changes in the area.

"Crazy wars," she said. "They came over without a dime. Now they're buying real estate." Odd, she thought, how her mind focused on real estate.

"Wasn't on a slave ship, though," the eggplant grunted. She dropped the subject.

They sat in a darkened corner of the restaurant, far from the nearest customer. The dinner hour was over but a few stragglers were lingering over tea. The eggplant ordered a beer and Sam and Fiona ordered Diet Cokes.

"Hungry?" the eggplant asked.

"No. But I recommend we order *Bo Xao.*"

"For appearances?" Fiona asked. The Senator turned to look at her, his face tight, his mouth set firmly. He was definitely not happy. Yet, in the half-light, his sad, handsome face looked mysterious and vulnerable. Even in these circumstances, he sent out vibrations. In fact, the vulnerability and sense of fear it implied made him even more desirable. Ashamed, she pushed the idea from her thoughts. Not too successfully, however. Do your job, Fiona, she berated herself.

"I did not appreciate your visit to my wife," Sam said to Fiona.

"She didn't either, Senator," Fiona replied.

"It upset her," he muttered.

"She gave as much as she got," Fiona acknowledged.

"Public life is getting to be a pain in the ass," Sam sighed. "Makes you wonder if it's worth all the trouble."

"Lots are standing in line to get in," the eggplant said.

"Too much of a strain, I'll tell you. Problem is none of us are perfect people. We're all flawed. Has been that way from the beginning. Public servants should be judged on the way they handle their jobs, not on extraneous matters."

"They say a man's personal life is a reflection of his character," the eggplant lectured, shooting her a glance.

He shook his head.

"Well, you all know my problem."

"And we're trying to keep it out of the public arena," Fiona said.

"Fat chance," the Senator said. The waitress brought them their drinks.

"The *Bo Xao* will be coming shortly," the woman, a delicate Vietnamese, said, gliding away from their table. There was a certain indifference in her expression that explained why the Senator had chosen this place and this area. Like all recently arrived minorities, the Vietnamese conspired to silence. She knew he had been here before, probably with one or another of his girls. It occurred to her suddenly that this was undoubtedly a place and an area also kept secret from the ubiquitous Bunkie. A second hidden private life, she snickered to herself.

"You do remember Betty Taylor?" Fiona asked.

"Of course I do."

"You know what happened to her?"

"Bunkie told me." He expelled air, his lips puffing. "It's beyond belief."

"We would never have found her, Senator, if it wasn't for that little slave bracelet you gave her. It was still wrapped around the bone of her ankle."

"That poor kid," the Senator said.

"'My Bet' was engraved into the gold."

"My Bet," he whispered. "How awful. She loved that little gift." His voice broke and his throat worked to swallow deeply.

"Did she, like Helga, go quietly?" the eggplant asked with a touch more sarcasm than was needed. Sam's gaze washed over both of them.

"I know you must feel that I've been a real shit about this. Sending a surrogate to do my dirty work."

"It had crossed our minds," Fiona said.

"I'm not too proud of it myself," he muttered. "I have a tendency to want to avoid confrontations—"

"With ex-mistresses," Fiona interjected.

"It's morally repulsive but politically expedient." He reached for his glass, raised it and sipped. Then he said, "The fact is that they did go quietly."

"That's a helluva criterion," the eggplant said.

"I know," Sam replied. "Looks awful. But you see, that's the way this game is handled. Everyone knows the rules."

"Not necessarily the young ones," Fiona countered.

"They learn fast," he snapped. His gaze drifted inward. "It's a trade-off, really. I've discovered a real urge out there for young ladies to be star-fuckers. I'm giving it to you straight. Doesn't speak well for me, but if the truth were known it's one of the perks of public celebrity. A regular pas de deux. As they say, it enhances the flavor, especially for the girls." He shook his head. "Not exactly a character reference. It's opportunistic and contemptible. But I've always treated the ladies with the utmost respect. Never like dirt." He became reflective. They waited through his silence. "Okay, it's repugnant by most standards. You'll find far more integrity in my political life. But as to killing—my God. Besides—this may strain your credulity—I adored those girls." He looked pointedly at Fiona, who turned her eyes away first.

"I assume you've been informed about what happened to three of them," the eggplant said. "Three that got the word from Farrington."

"Yes," the Senator acknowledged, lowering his eyes.

"It's beyond my understanding," Sam whispered. "Shakes me up." He looked into his drink. "If you want to know, it makes me feel like shit."

"And them," the eggplant said. "Think about how they might feel—if they could."

"None of them ever tried to contact you . . . after?" Fiona asked.

"You mean before," the eggplant corrected, meaning before they died.

"There was a time gap," Fiona explained pleasantly, not wishing to show the Senator any cracks in their solid front.

"The answer to that is no. Not Betty. Not Harriet. Not Helga. I'm sure they did not think very kindly of me. I wouldn't if I were them."

"Two of them were definitely murdered, Senator," the eggplant snapped. "Were there others we don't know about?"

It was one of those outbursts designed to inflame the person being asked. But the Senator remained calm.

"Others?" Sam asked, frowning.

"Judy Peters, for example," Fiona said.

"Judy? Is she also . . . ?"

"No," Fiona said. "She is, apparently, the one that got away."

"Gave *me* the heave-ho, that one," Sam said, smiling wryly.

"Yes," Fiona said. "We've talked to her."

"I guess you might call her lucky," the eggplant said.

"Am I the kiss of death?" Sam wondered aloud. He paused and shook his head. "All right, I made love to them. I cared for them. As for killing them?" He shook his head.

"Bunkie then?" the eggplant asked. The waitress glided quietly to their table and put down a large plate of *Bo Xao*.

"Thank you," the Senator said. "It's really quite good."

"Bunkie?" the eggplant repeated.

"Not Bunkie," the Senator said, biting his lip. "Hard to accept. He is loyal to a fault. Ambitious as hell. Sometimes he thinks he's the tail that wags the tiger. A killer? In a figurative sense, yes. If it could hurt me, watch out. But in a literal sense, a murderer . . . ?" His voice trailed off. Despite his denial, he seemed tentative, unsure.

"But he did demonstrate that he was capable of a kind of cruelty," Fiona prodded. "He was willing, perhaps eager, to take on chores that hurt others."

"A far cry from murder," the Senator repeated, but his defense seemed less certain. After a long pause, he looked up at them. "Are you seriously considering such a possibility?"

"Yes, we are," the eggplant said.

"And me as well?" the Senator asked. "The man behind the man."

"In our business, anything is possible," Fiona said, cutting a quick glance at the eggplant.

"I'll say this," the Senator said. "In our tight little circle poor Bunkie gets no defense. Except from me. He does come over as an arrogant bastard. He plays the hatchet man, the bad guy. He does the shit detail. But he's a trusted lieutenant and confidant. You know how valuable that is to a politician." He shook his head. "Bet Nell gave you an earful on that."

"She led me to believe that he was not one of her favorites," Fiona said, picking at the *Bo Xao*. It was too spicy and she took a deep gulp of her coke.

"Only natural. She hates him. Both my wives hated him. Fact is, being a politician's wife is a bad rap from the go."

"Your first wife, Senator . . ." Fiona began. For some reason, she had hardly focused on that. She suddenly remembered that she had seen her at the Mount Vernon dance. Seemed ages ago. A tall blonde, regal-looking woman, bigger than life, amply endowed. They had politely exchanged smiles across the dance floor. Fiona had noted that she had stolen glances at him all evening. ". . . Did she know about your . . ."

"Peccadillos," the Senator said. He offered a small laugh between clenched teeth. "Afraid so."

"Only natural, you said," the eggplant said. "They wouldn't have been too happy with Bunkie. Not the pimp part."

"He was never that," the Senator snapped in a sudden burst of anger. No way, Fiona thought. Of all things, this man could find his own ladies to park their shoes under his bed.

"They were jealous of the relationship," Fiona said, as if it were an explanation for the eggplant.

"Couldn't be helped," Sam muttered. Obviously this was a sore spot.

"How come you broke up with Frances?"

"We were college sweethearts. Florida State. She was the campus queen. I was the BMOC. Remember that expression? A good soldier she was, and I was a good boy—until we got to Washington."

"And then?" the eggplant pressed.

He looked into his drink and smiled.

"Opportunity presented itself," he muttered.

"She caught you?" the eggplant asked.

He looked up at them.

"You're really digging," he said, shrugging. "Anyway, it's history. We've been divorced for eons."

"What was the trigger?" Fiona asked, working to keep her excitement under control.

"The trigger?" the Senator asked, frowning.

"Did any one thing set her off?" Fiona pressed.

He took his time mulling it over.

"It's been a long time," the Senator sighed.

"It's important," Fiona said, cutting a glance at the eggplant, who leaned closer toward the Senator from across the table. She sensed a crackle of excitement. Even the Senator, eyes shifting from one face to the other, seemed to pick up the electricity.

"Frances?" he asked.

"Just tell me," Fiona said.

His eyebrows rose in surprise. Then his eyes grew vague, as if he were plumbing his memory.

"She suspected I was playing around. She was right, of course. Maybe she smelled it. I tried to be discreet. She actually began to follow me. Saw me with women in my car. Naturally she wasn't happy about it."

"She had fits of jealousy and rage?" the eggplant asked.

"I don't know about rage. She wasn't one for demonstrations. She was a pouter. Wouldn't talk to me for days. Just looked at me with those liquid brown eyes of hers, full of contempt. Our marriage was falling apart by then. Finally she did catch me."

"In flagrante delicto?" Fiona asked with a touch of sarcasm.

"Afraid so," he sighed.

"Who was the woman?" Fiona asked.

"Betty Taylor."

He frowned, suddenly appalled by the connection.

"Of all people," the eggplant said.

"She was following me. She found out that Betty was living in this apartment on the Hill. Just walked in on us. Found us in the sack."

"She make a scene?" Fiona asked.

"Hell no. Not Frances. She just stood there for a moment while we scrambled for cover. I must tell you, it's a very tacky situation to be in." He paused and shook his head, obviously pained by the memory.

"And then?" the eggplant asked.

"Downhill all the way. Aside from her own indignation, she did bring up the career aspects. Hell, the Senatorial campaign was only a few weeks away."

"So you called in Bunkie," Fiona said.

"You make it sound like a crime."

"In a way it is," Fiona snapped.

"But not THE crime," the Senator rejoined. "Not *murder*. Cowardly. Objectionable. Repugnant. But not murder."

"And Frances' reaction to all this?" Fiona asked.

"A good sport, actually. We both knew it was over. I told her the fire was out and I assumed the feeling was mutual. We played at marriage through the campaign, then, when it was over, we quietly split. No scenes. No wild confrontations. We split what we owned and parted amicably."

"It just ended?" Fiona asked, snapping her fingers. "Like that?"

"More or less. I see her around. She's quite cordial. We had no children. Nobody really got hurt."

"You don't think she did?" Fiona asked.

"The thing about Frances is her . . . well, her pragmatism. By the time we split, I felt nothing for her."

"And she? Did she feel anything for you?" Fiona pressed.

"It wouldn't have mattered," Sam said. For a politician, he seemed utterly without guile, which confused her.

"Did you ever see Betty Taylor again? After Bunkie's conversation?"

His mood changed suddenly, but it was too dark to see if the color had changed in his face. He shook his head.

"No, I didn't," he whispered.

"Or inquire about her welfare?" Fiona asked.

"I told you. I'm a flawed man."

"Did Bunkie report to you about her reaction to his . . . surrogate Dear-John?" Fiona asked.

He nodded.

"He said she cried. She was very young, you know."

"And you believed him?"

"Of course I did. Why should I doubt it?"

"Maybe she didn't go quietly," the eggplant said. "Maybe she told him she was going to stand and fight. Blow your Senatorial chances out of the water."

"Hell, she was just a kid," the Senator said defensively.

"But she could have caused you trouble," the eggplant said, tapping one finger on the table.

"I suppose," the Senator mused.

"And Bunkie could have foreclosed on that," the eggplant snapped.

"Your premise is wrong, Captain. You'd have to know Betty."

"I'm afraid I'll never have that chance. None of us will."

The Senator shook his head and bit his lip.

"Damn, that hurts to hear," he said.

"I'll bet," the eggplant rejoined.

"Listen, I felt like hell about Betty. Going through this thing with Frances and then Bunkie. I felt like hell. Frankly, it's a bit unbearable to know that she was murdered . . . in that way. God, how awful."

Lowering his eyes, he looked at his hands with an air of helplessness. It was apparent that he took his self-effacement seriously.

"With Betty you went further than with the others. Set her up in her own place. Why?"

Sam shrugged.

"I guess I cared."

"Because she was black," Fiona said. "You wanted some method of isolation."

"That was part of it, of course."

"There could be political consequences beyond just womanizing."

"Everything has political consequences."

"And Farrington took care of the political end of things," the eggplant said.

"I've told you all that."

"There were other women as well, Senator?" the eggplant said. His quick change of mood was startling, like a whip cracking, although he did not raise his voice.

"I won't deny it."

"Quickies?"

"More or less."

"Only the quickies were your business. Bunkie didn't know about those," the eggplant shot back.

"They weren't political," the Senator said.

"Meaning that the ladies didn't take them seriously," the eggplant pressed.

"Or you," Fiona said, completing the idea. They were speaking in shorthand and all three understood. To the Senator and his handlers, only emotional involvement posed a political threat.

With the exception of the one bite she had of the *Bo Xao*, no one touched it. The restaurant emptied out, but the waitress, perhaps understanding the gravity of their discussion, did not intrude or ask that they leave.

"You say the breakup with your first wife was amicable?" the eggplant asked.

"Considering."

"Considering what?"

The eggplant's question seemed to confuse the Senator.

"Considering," he began hesitantly. "that she had just found her husband . . ."

"Exactly the point," the eggplant interrupted. "Why go to all the trouble of investigating, following, the confrontation, all that messy business, if it didn't mean something? Something big? Then the lady is a good sport? Come on, Senator."

"She was," he countered. "Still is. Are you suggesting . . . ?"

"Considering you've eliminated Farrington from contention," the eggplant said. He cut a quick glance at Fiona, who knew better than to interrupt the eggplant's onslaught.

"Not Frances, too. Surely not Frances," Sam said with an air of protest. "Way off the mark. First Bunkie. Then Frances."

It was interesting to see his method at work in this interrogation. He knew exactly how hard to push. Every question seemed designed to elicit an oblique piece of information, a nuance. She knew he was observing the Senator carefully, the wheels in his mind turning, taking in every subtlety. What he was doing now was tracking the Frances option, which opened up an entirely different tack. Up to then, she hadn't remotely occurred to them as a suspect.

Despite all Fiona's disagreements with her boss, despite her aggressive dislike of his often self-serving agenda, she loved this special skill of his, especially when the diamond was being diagrammed for the tap that might finally split it.

"Well then, let's go down both routes," the eggplant said. "Two possibilities." Fiona was perfectly tuned in, knowing what to expect. "Bunkie did her because she would not go quietly. Or"—he paused, his eyes dancing with alertness—"Frances, burning on the inside, acted out her own version of revenge."

They both watched Sam react. He tapped his fingers on the table and shook his head. Then he picked up his glass with shaking fingers, but did not drink from it, putting it down instead.

"I'm sorry. I can't reconcile the possibility . . ." He choked up and seemed too overwhelmed to continue. The eggplant exchanged a glance with Fiona. Your turn, he seemed to say.

"Let's concentrate on Frances. She's a big woman," Fiona said. "Did she have the strength to use a scarf to yoke and strangle another woman? Then dig her grave, carry her to it, cover it up?"

The Senator appeared genuinely shaken. When he finally responded, his voice was reedy.

"That's scary. But yes, she is a strong woman. Very athletic—on the girl's volleyball team at college. Frances was very physical. But really . . ."

"So she could do it," Fiona pressed.

"Physically . . . I suppose," the Senator said. "But . . ." He hesitated, shook his head in disbelief, then spoke again. ". . . It seems so out of character. At the beginning she was a big, happy, gentle girl, a knockout. Six feet tall in her stocking feet and perfectly proportioned. Even at the end, she showed no sign . . . I admit she became increasingly, well, private. She did keep things in. But *murder* . . . for what reason?"

"Revenge," Fiona said. "Powerful stuff in a scorned woman. Powerful stuff."

"I won't argue with that. But I never saw that in her character."

"I'll admit we're theorizing," Fiona said. "Carrying it further, perhaps she did Helga as well. Same modus operandi. We are talking here of someone with a psychological aberration . . ."

"I can't buy that," the Senator said. "No way. After all these years to still harbor a desire for vengeance. That's crazy."

"You got it," Fiona said, shooting the eggplant a look. His eyes blinked with approval.

Again Sam shook his head in disbelief.

"Then how do you explain Nell?" he asked with a tremor of relief, as if he had just come across this new argument. "We courted. We loved each other. That, too, could be said to begin as a . . . a meaningful affair."

This new theory was taking shape in Fiona's mind and she had no doubt that the eggplant was coming up with a similar scenario.

"Maybe she never counted Nell as extracurricular. We are dealing, after all, with bizarre reasoning," Fiona said.

"But how would she be able to determine . . . ?" Sam began.

"The wheat from the chaff?" Fiona said.

"That's a quaint way to put it."

"She could have made it her business to find out. She spied before. Who knows? You may think you were being discreet." Fiona paused, watching his reaction. "But if someone truly wanted to know, they could find out."

"I rarely saw her," Sam said.

"Because you weren't looking for her," Fiona pointed out. "But it could be that she was always there, watching, waiting."

"Pure fantasy," Sam muttered.

"It happens," she said.

Fiona could tell that Sam was absorbing the information, although he appeared to be continuing to resist it.

"But there's no real evidence," Sam protested.

"Right, Senator. Only theories," the eggplant interjected suddenly. He paused quickly, nodding, his signal for Fiona to press on.

"If it wasn't for the rain no one would be the wiser," Fiona said.

"Gives me the creeps," Sam said. "Unfortunately, I can't reconcile the idea with what I know about Frances. I grew up with her. I knew her folks. They were good solid people, lived in Pensacola. Her dad was an ex-Navy pilot. I knew everything about her. She was a big, gentle woman. Happy, too. At least at the beginning. Above all, incapable of such an act."

"How come no kids?" Fiona asked.

"We deliberately postponed. Hell, I was 24 when we got married. So was she. By thirty I was in Congress. We thought we had time. Then it all fell apart." He paused, then spoke again before anyone else had time to respond. "My fault. Same old problem. I'm not a good boy. Here I had a great flavor at home, but I had to try the other varieties. It's a kind of addiction, I suppose." He shook his head vigorously. "But no. Not Frances."

All this self-abnegation seemed sincere, but she had trouble being convinced. A bit too much sackcloth and ashes, she decided.

"You noticed nothing out of the ordinary in her behavior?" Fiona asked. "No changes in her personality or character in the stress of your breakup? And later?"

"Nothing that points to what you suggest. That's why, bottom line, I can't buy it."

Nor did Fiona totally buy his protestations. If the Senator's ex-wife was the murderer it would be the death knell of Sam Langford's Presidential bid, perhaps even the end of his Senatorial career. Of course, he was vastly popular in his state and might be perceived as a victim of circumstances, depending on just how much dirt surfaced. Considering the motive they were postulating, it would take a miracle for him to recover politically.

Surely, he was calculating all this as he wrestled with the information. And yet there was no way that a cover-up was possible. Under all the posing and posturing, she was certain that even a master politician like Sam Langford could not live with the idea of these murders going unpunished, despite the consequences to himself. In every politician, as she had learned from her father, there are latent seeds of nobility and martyrdom. Such thoughts went a long way to temper her cynicism.

The Vietnamese waitress glided toward them. It was obvious now that they wanted to close the restaurant. The bartender had cleaned up and was waiting with his jacket on.

"I'm terribly sorry," she said, handing them a check.

"Of course," Sam said.

The eggplant pulled out a billfold and paid it.

"This one's on the cops," he said.

They got up and left the restaurant. Outside it had gotten chilly.
The streets were deserted now. It was nearly midnight. For a while
they drove in silence, each lost in his own thoughts.

"It's really very upsetting. I think you're both way out in left field.
Bunkie and Frances? Too incredible to take seriously," Sam said.

"Call it thinking out loud," the eggplant said, squinting through
the windshield.

"We're sharing a possibility," Fiona said from the back seat.

"It seems to me that you're fishing for something that may not be
there." Sam mumbled.

"We're fishing. We admit that. And notice how carefully we're
doing it. You know why?" She did not wait for an answer. "Because
you are a significant American political figure," Fiona said, hoping
he would understand the implications without her spelling them
out. She could see the eggplant's head bob in approval. "Certainly a
career worth saving if we can. Again the eggplant's head bobbed in
approval. "And, more important to us and the community is the fact
that someone has been murdering women and getting away with it."
There was, of course, something left out.

"It could be all coincidence," Sam said, offering the last flickering
spark of resistance.

"More remarkable than any miracle going. These were your ladies,
Senator. As much as you may deny it to yourself, these murders are,
in a very significant way, related to you."

"I'm not denying that," Sam said. "But you're asking me to believe
something I can't. Simple as that. Frances, for example, did not give
me the slightest bit of trouble. Hell, she didn't ask for anything, no
alimony, no money, nothing. We split the furniture, the books, everything. She could have given me a bad time. At least there weren't any
financial problems. She was already doing quite well herself."

The Giant Food parking lot loomed before them and they pulled
into it beside the Senator's car. He started to let himself out, but
Fiona stopped him with a question.

"Senator," she asked. "What does Frances do for a living?"

The car had stopped and the Senator had already put his hand on the door handle. He turned to look at her.

"I thought you knew. She's one of the hottest real estate salesmen in town."

XXIV

"It's the only way," Fiona told Monte.

They were walking along the Tidal Basin in the golden glow of a spring sunrise. The cherry blossoms had just begun to pop, but had not yet achieved the full flowering of their display. Aside from its heart-pounding ceremonial rituals and Greco-Roman architectural splendors, the blooming cherry blossoms, a gift to Washington from the Japanese, were Washington's most spectacular, albeit seasonal, wonder.

"You could be wrong," Monte protested lamely.

"Well then, we'll know for sure, won't we?"

Across the basin the heroic statue of Jefferson peeked out between the columns of his marble gazebo. It was a stirring sight to the most jaded heart and, Fiona had decided, an ideal and secure spot to make peace with Monte Pappas. She had told him everything and he had taken it like bad medicine.

"If true, there goes the ballgame," he sighed.

"Depends."

"Finis, Fiona," he chuckled with resignation. "Salivating stuff for the media. Goes to trial we're dead."

"That's the point. We get her dead to rights, you might work some kind of credible denial. You guys are good at that."

A long shot, she knew. They'd have three alternatives. Come clean. Lie. Or make no comment.

"It's a tough one, Fiona," Monte said. "Besides, you've got to do what you've got to do. My favor bank with you is overdrawn anyway."

"That it is," Fiona agreed. "But that doesn't mean he couldn't be politically saved in the Senate," Fiona pointed out. "You could paint him as a victim. People have compassion. Hell, Teddy Kennedy saved his seat."

"He lied."

"Just trying to look at the bright side," Fiona said. The point of
the conversation, which they both knew, was the extent to which
Monte could get the Senator's cooperation on the plan that was ger-
minating in her mind. Without that, they might never be able to
break the case.

She had spent the night wrestling with the problem. They could,
of course, hassle Frances, try to wrest a confession from her. They
could search her home, look for clues. Fiona had to assume that
Helga's jewelry had been, quite literally, trashed. Apparently the
woman had plenty of money, although vanity had a way of convo-
luting self-interest.

But if none of Helga's jewelry was found in Frances' home, nor
any evidence tying her to these murders, they would be back to
square one. And unless the clues found were utterly damning, like a
confessional diary, Helga's prints on suspect surfaces, the burial
shovel, mud in her car trunk, for example, they would have no real
evidence or, at best, purely circumstantial evidence, which was
unlikely to bring a conviction.

Also, they had to assume that Frances, if she was the killer, had
demonstrated extreme craftiness and evasion skills. In the absence of
real clues, they would have to search for eyewitnesses, none of which
had yet been found. Even if they did find a connection between
Helga and Frances in a potential real estate deal, that would still not
constitute any more than circumstantial evidence. There was only
one sure way: Get Frances to repeat the crime. No, she corrected.
Get Frances to attempt to repeat the crime.

"You know her?" Fiona had asked earlier.

"I've met her," he had replied. "She's on the circuit. Goes everywhere. You know these real estate types, always networking, ingratiating, hustling. Part of the game. She and Sam often bumped into
each other. But it was strictly ships that pass in the night. She was
long out of the picture before I came on board."

"So she'd be accessible?" Fiona probed. That was crucial. Everything suggested that Frances was getting her information by clever and sometimes surreptitious observation. "We'd have to get the point across, trigger her modus operandi."

"I still think it's crazy," Monte said.

"Maybe so. But calculate the risks if we don't do something."

"I'm calculating," Monte said. "You're setting yourself up as a target."

"Macho me."

"I don't know if I want to be a party to that," he muttered.

In her heart, she had forgiven Monte. He was driven by his own dreams and priorities, ambitious but not malicious. She berated herself for getting too rigid, too parochial.

"You are a party to it, Monte. There's also the big picture." She watched his face, the big brown eyes looking sad and hangdog as they walked. "Let's say we do nothing. He could be President. Living in the White House, they tell me, makes it easier to screw around. Kennedy and Johnson were no angels."

"Johnson, too?"

"We're the cops. We have files." She hadn't seen them, but had heard rumors. So she was going slightly out on a limb for a good cause.

"Well, they were good Presidents just the same," Monte muttered.

"That's Senator Langford's contention too," Fiona said. "Bottom line is that she can't be on the loose."

"Have you told him your idea?"

"Not yet. You're my test case. I thought it might be nice to have a voice of reason on my side."

"Suppose she catches on?" he asked.

"We'll just have to be convincing, won't we?" Fiona said. She felt a blush begin at the base of her neck.

They stopped to contemplate the view. As the sun rose higher, she had the distinct impression that blossoms were popping by the second. They were whitening the branches like snow. It was a deli-

ciously soothing sight. For a long time they said nothing, then
began to walk again.

"You'd be asking Sam to participate in what could spell his political self-destruction," Monte said. "Won't help me much, either."

She did not respond as they walked on in silence for a long time.
Washington was awakening. She could see a steady stream of cars
snaking across the Potomac bridges.

"What about doing what's right?" she asked finally.

He stopped, turned and looked into her eyes.

"Got me there," he said.

"Then you'll push him?"

"Hard," he said. "Under all the bullshit, I think he'll vote his conscience on this one."

"So do I," Fiona agreed.

They headed back along the path to the parking lot. When they
reached their cars, Monte reached out tentatively with his hand to
grasp hers. She took it, mostly in friendship and affection.

"You're a pal, Monte," she told him, looking into his eyes.

"Now there's a word pregnant with meaning." She could detect a
sigh lurking behind the response.

"Relationships have a life cycle," she said, noting the edge of
pomposity in her tone. Had she said this before to others? she wondered. Perhaps in different ways.

"Typical Washington, I suppose," Monte replied. "We've raised
euphemism to a fine art."

"Less pain in it, I suppose."

"It's okay. We're both old enough to stay cool."

Of course there was sadness in it. And relief. For him as well,
she hoped.

Then he said, "If Sam does go along, I'd make it a point to keep
mylegs crossed."

There was a touch of macho in the remark. But she let it stand
without challenge.

XXV

From where Fiona sat at a round table along the window side of the grand ballroom of the Pan American Building, she could see Frances Langford, looking larger than life in an off-the-shoulder white ballgown that greatly flattered her ample figure.

Frances sat at a table placed along the wall where one entered the ballroom through wide open doorways from the marbled mezzanine, which led to the twin staircases. The magnificent green-domed building was designed and built in the thirties to commemorate hemispheric solidarity.

Sam and Nell exchanged glances often with Fiona, whose designated "cover" was to appear in animated conversation with Monte Pappas. Bunkie had been deliberately eliminated from their group, sent by the Senator to California to talk up a preliminary committee for the Presidential campaign, which was, at that moment, much in doubt.

Peripherally, Fiona had seen Frances look their way, her gaze swiftly moving past them, as if she were merely scanning that side of the room. Was there something proprietary in this glance? Or was it merely idle curiosity? She would soon have that answer.

Fiona sat next to Sam, and Nell sat beside him on his other side. The other chairs around their table for eight were occupied by a Senator from Wisconsin and his wife and a Congressman from Oklahoma and his wife. It was a charity event for the benefit of Juvenile Diabetes.

Frances Langford's ubiquitous social agenda had been simple to track. She was everywhere, a networker of extraordinary energy. The "strategy," as it was referred to by Fiona, did not have the enthusi-

astic support of the Senator and his wife. But Monte had apparently
convinced them that they had little choice.

"You're asking me to torch myself," Sam had told Fiona, after he
had agreed to the plan.

"With your luck you could turn out to be the phoenix, rising from
the ashes," Fiona had replied.

Surprisingly, the eggplant was the most reluctant about Fiona's
participation.

"Unacceptable risk," he had argued. Cates, knowing Fiona's absolute
commitment to the idea, had given it his blessing. "If we're right, we're
dealing here with a brilliant psychopath. She's put away two ladies
without leaving a clue. If she decides to do you, she'll find a way."

"That's my job," Cates said. "I won't let her out of my sight."

"Easier said than done," the eggplant said.

"I've got to do this, Chief," Fiona said firmly.

He had rubbed his chin with ebony fingers. Then he reached for
a panatela and lit it with a match, puffed deeply, and expelled the
smoke through his nostrils like a dragon.

"It's the only way," Fiona pressed. "I'd decline, really I would, let
one of you be the patsy. Unfortunately, the good Senator Love isn't
into guys."

The eggplant's lips formed a rare grin.

Fiona waited for him to make a decision. It was too long in coming and she broke into the silence.

"The hard part will be to convince her that the Senator and I
are . . . well . . . that way about each other. Enough to trigger the
aberration." Again she could not control a blush. "We know the
MO. If she's the one, I'll be ready."

The eggplant took a deep drag on his panatela and spoke.

"People like that come up on you when you least expect it." The
smoke flowed out of his lips on the words.

"I've gone to the police academy. I know how to defend myself."
The benign sarcasm was meant to prod him.

"I don't like my people to take unnecessary risks."

The subject of risk was quite common these days. Cops were fair game. So far this year seven had been blown away—five in uniform, two in plainclothes.

"She doesn't know I'm a cop," Fiona argued, skewering the logic deliberately, wanting to illustrate how lightly she was taking the danger. "What's worse, Chief? Keeping her on the street to do another? Just be a matter of time before someone gets wind that it's the work of a serial psychopath. It happens."

The implied threat was deliberately soft. She had no intention of setting him off. There was also a subtle appeal to his own self-interest. Breaking the case in this way had real media legs and he, of course, would take all the credit for it. He had slumped in his chair. Now he sat up straight and pointed the burning end of the panatela at her.

"You get your white ass in a sling, you're in trouble," he said. Then, turning to Cates, "You stay connected. I want you glued, capish?"

Cates cut a glance at Fiona and grinned.

"Like Siamese twins, Chief," he said.

Cates, dressed in his tux, sitting at a table in a far corner of the room, was watching her at that very moment. He was a slender, handsome man with mostly Caucasian features and skin that looked like he had gotten himself a deep tan. Only his hair, which was cut close, and a nose with a slight Negroid flatness gave him away as black. Not that it was an issue with him. He was proud of his race, despite the occasional slights of his fellow cops, who had made him feel doubly alien, high yellow and Jamaican, British-dipped variety. In his carefully pressed dress clothes, he looked elegant.

Liveried waiters proceeded to serve the dinner, which consisted of roast chicken, asparagus and cheddared potatoes served French style. It had been agreed that Fiona would call the shots.

The band, which had played dance music before dinner, was now playing background music. She had danced with Monte, and the Senator had danced with his wife. Frances took the floor with a distinguished grey-haired man, obviously her date for the evening. As Fiona had observed before at Mount Vernon, Frances greeted both Sam and Nell with a pleasant smile, and they returned the courtesy, a gesture that had surely passed between without incident or second thoughts scores of times.

"Still inconceivable," Sam said when they had returned to the table for dinner.

"She never gave us a spot of trouble," Nell whispered. From the beginning, she had been wary of the idea. Having continued to deny to herself that Sam was having an affair with Helga, she saw little logic in the plan. Nor, apparently, had she confronted her husband for an admission. And he had not volunteered a confession.

"Our theory is based on her perception of events," Fiona had explained diplomatically, "which does not necessarily have anything to do with the truth."

This seemed to satisfy her enough to consent to go along with the plan.

As the waiters completed serving the baked Alaska, Fiona turned to the Senator and moved her head closer to his, nodding to Nell, who directed her attention to her partner.

The Senator put his hand on Fiona's bare arm and stroked her. Her skin broke out in goose bumps.

"How am I doing?" he asked mischievously.

"You're being very realistic," she said, her attention drawn to the table across the room. "I think we're getting her attention."

"Probably your imagination," Sam said. She felt him searching her face.

"You are rather attractive," he said.

"For a cop," she bantered.

"I don't believe this is happening," he said, bending closer. He whispered in her ear.

"Shall I caress your thigh?"

"You're not taking this seriously." She was suddenly alarmed. He moved his hand and put it under the table. She froze, pressing her legs together, but he did not touch her.

He continued to study her, while she concentrated on catching Frances in her peripheral vision. She noted that Frances was no longer panning the room as she had done earlier. She was watching them.

"She's got a bead on us," Fiona whispered.

"Wish-fulfillment," Sam snickered.

"We'll know soon enough."

Beside him Nell was playing her part, talking with animation with the man beside her. Monte was doing the same with his partner on the other side, a shy horse-faced woman wearing a gown that had seen its best days in the fifties.

"In the meantime, what shall we talk about?" Sam asked.

"You're the politician. They're never supposed to be at a loss for words."

"I keep asking myself. Why are we here?"

"You're helping to catch a killer."

He grew silent, his taste for banter obviously fading.

Fiona's eyes darted toward Frances' table, then returned quickly.

"I'd say we have deeply arrested her attention," Fiona said. She looked into Sam Langfond's blue eyes. Despite the tension of the situation, they appeared somewhat bemused.

"When they play dance music, we'll get on the floor," Fiona said.

"I can't wait," the Senator said. He was back to banter now.

"Act, dammit. She's biting."

"I'm a lousy actor," Sam muttered.

"The hell you are," she said.

Leaning closer, he brought his lips close to her ear. But he said nothing. Instead, he kissed her on the earlobe.

Her heart began to pound in her chest and her temperature seemed to have risen. But she knew that Frances had picked up the signals, was watching them with greater and greater interest.

"Did I do all right?" he asked.

"I'd say a trifle indiscreet," she said, as the waiters began to clear the main course. "We'll dance soon."

She had instructed both Monte and Nell to restrain any desire to look toward Frances, and they had cooperated fully. Both of them looked quite interested in the conversation with their dinner partners. They were doing their part. Fiona was quite pleased.

The band struck up a slow dance tune and couples began to head toward the floor.

"Now," Fiona said.

Sam got up, took Fiona's hand and led her to the dance floor. Close dancing in Washington was socially acceptable. People tried hard to be ingratiating, and men and women rarely exhibited scandalous conduct. Image was everything. Sam's image was that of a handsome charmer and target for the ladies. That was a perfectly acceptable persona to exhibit publicly. After all, he was married to an attractive woman and had two delightful children. Stepping out of line with other ladies was assumed for any man of power and clout, but never flaunted. A level of philandering was tolerated just as long as it stayed deeply in the closet. Sam's propensity was outside the parameters of what was considered acceptable. Far outside. That was the real secret to be kept. That was media fodder of the first rank.

Only someone who truly observed with a high level of concentration could detect the real meaning beneath the surface of body language—interpreting what to others might be harmless dance titillation as blatant sexual foreplay instead. That was what Fiona was betting on.

She saw Frances rise and glide onto the floor in the arms of one of her dinner partners, a heavyset man exactly her height.

"Make it authentic," Fiona whispered, her arm creeping upward along Sam's back, a trifle north of mere affection. He pressed his pelvis against hers, his fingers caressing her bare back. In another prearranged detail, Monte and Nell were dancing in a far corner of the room, well away from Sam and Fiona.

Deliberately Fiona closed her eyes, as if to simulate the ecstasy of the proximity to the Senator. She followed Sam's short steps. He was light-footed and graceful. His body ground into her, rhythmic, with a slight gyration. Oh my God, she thought again. Hazardous duty. She felt his erection.

"You wanted convincing," he said. "I'll give you convincing."

"Jesus."

"It's an involuntary reaction," he whispered. "I can't help it. Live with it."

Worse, she felt a complementary reaction in herself and opened her eyes. At that moment, Frances' eyes locked into hers. She was no more than five feet away and there was no misinterpreting the look. Malevolent, hate-drenched, violent.

With hand pressure on his back, she signaled him to move laterally. She had to get away from those eyes, that look.

"I saw her, the real Frances," she whispered. "I'm right. I know I'm right."

Responding, Sam had whirled to get a better look at Frances. She felt him nod, then turn again.

"All I get is a polite smile," he said.

"I see murder," Fiona said.

"I still don't get it." The expelled air from his sigh brushed against her cheek. She felt his erection subside.

"You're doing just fine," Fiona said, somewhat relieved. "Just keep an open mind."

She took him by the hand and led him toward the exit doors of the ballroom. They moved down one of the marble staircases to the lobby level. There, she led him to a darkened spot in the atrium situated between the two staircases. She had carefully staked out the spot in advance. It provided a clear view of them to anyone who looked over the balustrade, yet masked the possibility to anyone watching from the lobby.

She deliberately placed herself so that only she could see any heads that poked themselves over the balustrade. They stood closely together, facing each other, only inches apart. Sam's back faced the balcony. Recognition would be difficult.

Turning slightly, she could see through the glass entrance doors to the building, where uniformed security men and chauffeurs milled about. Not far from where they stood and just out of sight was the hat-check facility. She could hear the women clerks talking softly among themselves.

"Is she watching?" the Senator asked.

"Not yet."

"You could be wrong."

"I'm not," she said with conviction.

Then she saw a head pop up over the balustrade. Cates. He was standing just where the balustrade made its long graceful turn toward its downward descent.

Sam had sensed her tension.

"Her?"

"No."

When she looked again, he was gone. Then suddenly Frances was there, her face visible over the balustrade. She was looking directly down at them.

"Bingo," Fiona whispered. She pressed closer to the Senator. "Please kiss me," she said.

"Always ready to oblige," he whispered, embracing her, pressing his lips against hers. A moment later, he was offering his tongue. Despite her presence of mind and the duty that demanded her attention, she lost the battle to resist. She opened her lips. Act, she begged herself. Don't think.

He rubbed against her, his erection obvious and, it seemed, too determined for comfort. Her pelvis tried to retreat, but he was persistent, grinding against her. Eye on the ball, Fi, she urged herself, fighting to attend to business.

She felt his hands caressing her downward, squeezing her buttocks, then lifting her dress, getting his hands on bare thighs, reaching around to separate them. Despite her official mission, her professional ethics, her sense of duty, she felt a desire to surrender to him. She shook her head.

From that distance, Frances might have assumed her eyes were closed. They weren't. Fiona watched her through tiny slits. The woman stood there, watching, her face pale and expressionless.

Finally, with a wrenching twist of her head, she forced him to disengage from the kiss. It took her a moment more to realize that the front of her dress was waist-high and he was fiddling with his zipper.

"Are you crazy?"

"Just horny."

"No," she said firmly, backing away enough to lower her dress. She looked up. Frances' glance met hers. But only for a moment. Her face quickly pulled back and she was gone.

"You asked for realism," the Senator said. He took out his handkerchief and wiped his lips. She looked up to make sure. Frances had not returned. But Cates was there again, which embarrassed her. Conduct unbecoming, she rebuked herself. But she did respond and that was disturbing.

"She saw it all," Fiona said, straightening her dress, then patting her hair.

"Isn't that what you wanted?" he said.

"Yes," she admitted. "You really got into the part."

"Yes, I did." He studied her for a moment, started to say more then became silent.

"Do you believe me now?" she asked.

"You may be onto something," he admitted. "On the other hand, it might be simple curiosity."

Their eyes met and locked. He shook his head.

"This could be dangerous as hell," he said. "Especially for you."

"I know my job, Senator," she said.

He followed her up the stairs to the grand ballroom again. The dance band blared on and they threaded their way through the dancers to their table.

"She's on the case," Fiona whispered to Monte. She looked toward Nell and nodded. Nell smiled thinly and Fiona could not chase the sudden feeling of guilt. The Senator took his seat. He looked pale, worried.

Frances' observation was no longer surreptitious. It was blatant, knowing. She turned and again their eyes met. She saw it clearly. The jealousy, the danger.

"How can you be sure?" Monte asked.

"I saw it. Blood in her eyes."

Monte paused, studied her face.

"It's your blood, Fiona," he said. "*Your* blood."

XXVI

"Name of the game," Sam said, spreading his cards on the flowered bedspread.

"Got me on a schneid," Fiona said, marking the score on the little white pad imprinted with the words "Ramada Inn."

"It's another of my special skills," Sam said. "The way I figure it you owe me more than a hundred thousand dollars. Now how are we going to work off that debt?"

It was the third of their so-called "trysts" at the Ramada Inn. They had established a pattern, Tuesdays and Thursdays. They were into the second week since it had begun and Frances had taken the bait. Since the dance, she had waited her own vigil and had caught up to them on Thursday, the second time they had checked into the Ramada.

The modus operandi was for the Senator and Fiona to stay exactly two hours. Arrive by noon. Leave by two. It was made to appear as a luncheon rendezvous. Sam would be back in his office before two-thirty.

Fiona had found out that the Senator liked gin rummy and she had brought a deck of cards. It would, she reasoned, keep his mind off what apparently was always on his mind. Maybe hers as well. Not maybe. Her vulnerability was a definite burden.

"I keep telling myself I'm mad to go along with this," he had told her as they sat in one of the Ramada's rooms the first time. "Not that the company isn't outstanding."

"Thanks, Senator," she had replied.

"A good exercise in self-discipline," he had joked, just short of being overly flirtatious. At times he had turned gloomy. "I'll never forgive myself if anything happens to you."

"Nothing will."

Had he forgiven himself for the others? She did not wish to probe
further on that point. In fact, she wished that she might character-
ize him as venal and exploitive, a callous man without feelings or
redeeming qualities. She couldn't. More and more, she thought of
him as the victim, a victim of his own attractiveness.

After the gin game, he had kicked off his shoes and taken off his
jacket and tie, stretching out on the bed, his head resting on his
arms. She sat sideways on the bed, her feet on the floor. She had
taken off her jacket, but not her piece in its shoulder holster. Lifting
his hand, he touched the holster, stroking it.

"Who's to know?" he whispered. It was no secret between them.
There was sexual tension in the room, both of them knew that.

"I would."

"Strike that," he sighed, removing his hand.

"I did."

She picked up the deck and ran a nail down its side. It made a
raspberry sound. He sat up Indian-style while she shuffled the cards.

"I need to know something," he said. She did not respond, watching him, continuing to shuffle. "If the circumstances were different . . ." He stopped, then shrugged.

"They're not," she said. "Besides, such conduct has already gotten
you into lots of hot water."

"I know." He lowered his eyes and sighed. "It's as if all the ladies
are facets of one ideal female. Sometimes I feel like a surfer looking
for the perfect wave."

"Nothing is perfect," she said. She knew what he meant. She was
also a searcher.

"When do you think she'll make her move?" he asked.

"When she's convinced that this is the real thing."

"Then she had better not bug this place."

So far Fiona had been on target. They had apparently tempted
Frances into following them. Now the goal was to convince her that
this was an ardent affair. A pattern had been established for its pur-

suit. There was a difference, of course. In a desire to keep him out of the loop, they were not using Bunkie's townhouse. They hoped that Frances would accept the Ramada as a logical alternative.

They had also established a pattern for getting into the Inn with discretion. The Senator parked in the most deserted section of the parking lot, using a car without Senatorial plates. He then went into the side entrance, where there was a handy pay phone away from public traffic.

Fiona was already in the room, registered under an assumed name. They had been amusingly creative on that point. She had already been Theda Bara and Molly Bloom. Today, dealing with the same clerk as the last time she had checked in, she was Theda Bara again.

The desk clerk, a young man in the early twenties, had not cracked a smile. She told him she had no credit cards and paid him in cash for one night's stay, as she had done the previous week.

"A pleasure to have you again, Miss Bara."

"Why, thank you," she had replied.

"Any baggage?" he had asked.

"I can manage," she said, offering a smile.

Cates had followed Frances, who, in turn, had followed the Senator's car. He reported later that she had stayed patiently in her car, parking it within view of the Ramada's side lot. She did not leave until the Senator came out two hours later. That had been Thursday. Today she was following the same pattern, waiting in her car.

By the very act of following the Senator's movements, literally spying on them, Frances had established the suggestion, if not the fact, of her guilt.

Fiona heard a sound in the corridor, got up and looked through the lens in the door. No one. Then she walked to the drawn blinds and peeked through the slit where one side met the other. A shaft of sunlight twinged her eye.

They had given her a room high up, facing the river. This Ramada was a high rise built on the edge of the Potomac, just beside the

flight path of descending planes at National Airport, a mile down
the Mount Vernon Highway.

The choice of the Virginia side had been deliberate and had been
debated by the eggplant, Cates and herself at length. The idea was
to authenticate the affair in Frances' mind not only as clandestine
and illicit but so intense that chances had to be taken by both participants. They were careful to use the word participants as a euphemism for lovers, too careful, collusively careful. They were being
deferential to her, avoiding anything that might embarrass her.

What Cates had also witnessed from the balcony of the Pan
American Building was a passionate embrace. No question about it.
Under other circumstances, another place, her surrender would have
been inevitable. Hazardous duty. Without exactly saying it, she had
planted the suggestion that it was merely playacting, which was
only partly true.

Cates had asked her how the Senator and she spent their time during their mock tryst and she had taken out the deck of cards from
her pocketbook and shuffled the deck.

"Better than watching the soaps," she had told him.

To his credit, he made no further comment.

"Don't know what's more dangerous. Being holed up in a motel
with that lecher or putting your body in front of that crazy lady."

"I've got the lecher under control," she had replied, resisting turning to meet Cates' gaze. She was certain he had another view of that.

By choosing a hotel on the Virginia side, where the MPD had no
jurisdiction, they were also saying that this was the real thing, that
this was not police business. By now, Frances would know she was a
police officer. She would have made discreet inquiries, checked her
out, found out about her big house in the District.

In the days following the ball at the Pan American Building,
everyone involved had been alerted to "watch their tail" for any signs
of Frances. The eggplant had wanted to put Frances under surveillance by another team of cops, but Fiona had resisted.

"She catches on, the case is blown," Fiona had argued. "There's too many on it as it is."

The eggplant, still insecure about her making herself a target, knew she was right and, once again, reluctantly consented. Secretly, she was certain he still harbored fantasies of the Senator being in his debt. Indeed, the possibility of Langford becoming President was still a lure, albeit a fading one.

It was the Senator himself who had spotted Frances. He had just driven his car out of the Senate garage one evening and had seen her, suddenly illuminated by a streetlight, following him in her car. He made a number of redundant turns to make sure she was, indeed, following him, then he headed for home. It was only when he turned off Nebraska Avenue into the residential streets of Spring Valley that she veered away.

So she was hooked, stalking him now. The trick had been to discover the pattern of her surveillance. Generally, he wanted to be home before the children went to sleep, which was around eight, which meant that he would leave his office most times around seven-thirty, unless there was an event to attend.

They had instructed the Senator to begin to take Nell's car, the one with the unmarked plates, every other day. The logic behind that was that it would send a message to Frances that he was taking his wife's car to appear anonymous. More importantly, it was a green Jaguar, distinctive and easily followed.

Fiona came back to the bed, sat down and began to reshuffle the cards.

"Do you think she'll . . . act today?" Sam asked. He sat up against the bed's backboard, making a headrest from two pillows.

"We'll know soon enough."

"It doesn't bother you?" he asked.

"Sure it bothers me."

"Are you afraid?"

"Yes. But I have confidence in my ability and my partner's to prevent such an occurrence."

"You're very brave," he said sincerely, adding, "It's very tough on Nell, too, All this tension."

"I can imagine."

"And if you do get her to attempt your . . . your demise, what do you really have?"

"Two possibilities. We get her on attempted murder. That's really not what we want. What we want is a confession."

"Juicy stuff either way. Not exactly a good image-builder."

"Afraid not."

"I've been wondering if all this was worth it."

"It is if we can prevent her doing this to others."

"But I can do that," he sighed. "Keep my nose clean. Stop fooling around. Be satisfied." He looked at her and sighed. "You know, I really care about Nell, the kids. Fact is they're beginning to mean more to me than politics."

I've heard that before, she thought, remembering how politics had absorbed her father's entire life.

"Sure," she said with a light touch of sarcasm.

"I keep wondering what my real motives were for getting into it in the first place." He paused, grew reflective.

The Power and the Glory, she thought, but said nothing.

"I told myself," he continued, "that I wanted to make a contribution, help others, give of myself. I was dead certain I was an idealist." He looked at her. She was sitting beside him and he put his hand on hers. She did not pull it away. A brotherly gesture, she decided. They had become friends. Why not? "I'm not sure anymore."

"My father used to say, It's important for your heart to be in the right place."

"Meaning what?"

"He never quite explained it. But what I think he meant was that you had to believe you were helping others, making sure that the pie was shared equitably so that everybody had a running head start. Then showing some compassion for the losers. He said you couldn't be a really good politician or leader unless you had the common touch."

The memory of her father had kindled something deep inside of her. She saw his sweet Irish face, the good smell and feel of him.

Sam was silent for a long time. He continued to hold her hand.

"Sometimes," Sam said, "I feel corrupt." He shot her a glance, and absently picked up her hand and kissed it. "Not material-greed corrupt. Never that. Besides, Nell has plenty of money. Never was my bag anyway. I mean selling-my-soul kind of corrupt. The thing I wrestle with is . . . well . . . I hope you don't mind." Again he kissed her hand. "Not that I'm worthy. Not that I don't have the skills. The thing . . ." He turned and looked into her eyes. She had no doubt about his sincerity. ". . . The thing I have to decide within myself is . . . Am I a good man? Not a perfect man. A *good* man."

"Like my father said, Is your heart in the right place?"

"But politics makes you devious. You have to be devious to get elected. That's corrupting."

"I suppose that's true everywhere. Maybe devious is the wrong word. Maybe you mean finding a strategy that works for you."

"To achieve what?"

"To fulfill your aspirations. To be."

He shook his head and his eyes misted as if he were suddenly caught up in some strong emotion. She sensed the contagion in herself.

"How is it possible to be truly honest?" he whispered.

"It's a dilemma," she admitted, feeling again something move deeply within her.

He gently pulled her hand and her body followed. He put his lips on hers, exploring gently, then opened his mouth. She yield-ed, taking his tongue. He continued to be gentle and unaggressive. But not tentative. When he disengaged his lips, he whispered in her ear.

"You think we can deal with this, Fiona?"

"Only if we do our Dear-Johns and -Janes in advance. When it's over, it's over."

He opened the top button of her blouse. She started to finish the job, reaching to remove her holster.

"Leave it," he whispered.

She did not question the idea. He watched her as she removed her blouse, leaving the holster, then her brassiere. Her breasts fell free. She felt good letting him watch her. He reached out and gently touched her nipples.

"I think women in general are the most wonderful creatures on earth," he said as he removed his shirt.

"I think that's the heart of it, Sam," she whispered. "Women know. They sense how you feel and it attracts them enormously. That's your secret, Sam." And here I am responding to it, she thought, without shame, tapping into it, feeling the joy of it.

Bare from the waist up, they moved toward each other. Slowly they undressed each other, taking off what remained. She studied him in the faint light. He was a fine-looking man, slender and still boyish. His erect penis was as smooth and white as ivory and she bent down to kiss it.

She felt a delicious trembling begin within her. Reaching out, he helped her up and held her tight against him. His kiss was deep, his hands strong, as they lifted her buttocks, placing her body at the edge of a dresser for support. Then he entered her and she gasped as she surrendered to the pleasure.

Later, if he would have asked her, "Did the earth move for you?" she would have answered proudly in the affirmative. Three times it moved. She could not bring herself to ask such a question, but she knew he, too, had transcended some previous barrier. It was something sensed, something sure.

As before, after a much more tender farewell than they had experienced before, he left her. She looked at her watch. They had overstayed by more than a half hour. She showered and dressed in ten minutes, then dashed down to her car.

Through the rearview mirror, she could see Cates' car waiting by the curb. Starting the car, she moved slowly out of the lot. She unlocked the glove compartment and removed the walkie-talkie. But she did not raise it to her mouth.

Another car had begun to follow her. Through the mirror she could see the driver.

Frances was following her now. Only her.

XXVII

Frances' call came early Sunday morning. It seemed so banal a gesture for such a potentially ominous event. Cates had moved into Fiona's house, occupying the room next to the master bedroom, which had been hers when she was growing up. They were connected with an open radio, and there was no way that Fiona could be approached without Cates hearing.

On Friday they had gone to work as usual. Sam had called her early.

In their conversation, the communication between them was less in the words they spoke than in their tone and the pauses between them. The very idea that they were protecting their secret exhilarated her and the sound of his voice was undeniably exciting.

"You have got to be careful," he told her. He had, of course, been informed that Frances had followed her home. Was the message of his concern subject to another, more personal, interpretation? Like he needed her to be careful because he needed her. Dammit, put a lid on that one, she rebuked herself.

Rather than return to headquarters after leaving the hotel, Fiona had chosen to drive home on the theory that, if Frances was to act swiftly, she would hardly make a move in or near police headquarters.

Frances' car stayed at a respectable distance. Cates had pulled in behind her. But when Fiona pulled into her driveway, Frances proceeded past it. Cates had continued to follow her car, which took a series of right turns, then headed back down Wisconsin Avenue to her home in Georgetown.

"She's sniffed the bait and her appetite's up," the eggplant commented after hearing the report.

"Live bait," Fiona replied, like the boy whistling in the cemetery. Am I scared? she asked herself. Bet your ass.

249

"That extra forty minutes had us concerned," Cates pointed out. Fiona repressed the urge to kick his shins. Did he know? she wondered, searching for a logical explanation.

"We thought it might send a tougher message, prod her to believe that this one was really hot, heavy and serious. It cost me another fifty thou in gin losses." She could not suppress a girlish giggle. Liar, liar, she railed at herself. She took a quick reading of their expressions. Nothing untoward. They were either hiding it or buying it.

She felt no guilt. Nor any sense of violation of professional ethics. Time had to be killed anyway. What better way? Dirty lady, she admonished herself. The fact was that the memory of those moments with Sam, both psychic and physical, still lingered deliciously.

She could not remember a more powerful experience. And yet his history mitigated against his being as moved as her. The reality was that she had been one among many. Not, as she might have fantasized, that special one, the perfect one, the searched-for one. Or, perhaps, the unspoken assumption that this would be the one and only time had forced their passion to a penultimate explosion of feeling. In her heart, she longed for more. It was, she knew, a greedy, selfish, stupid idea, unprofessional and risky. And it led to a malevolent wish . . . that Frances would be cautious, string things out, keep the ploy working. Now there was a conflict of interest.

With only limited success, she tried to brush away such thoughts. Next, would she be contemplating the meaning of love? Oh God. Not that.

"Still, she might not act for weeks," the eggplant said. Her heart lurched. Could she handle weeks without slipping over the edge? Edge of what?

"I don't know if the Senator will sit still for that," she had replied.

"Considering the potential downside for him, I doubt it too," the eggplant had pointed out. "He's liable to say, 'Look, I've been a good soldier. I've given my conscience a good ride. Done my duty as an honest citizen. Gimme a break.'"

"I think she'll act fast," Cates interjected. "She's motivated. Nobody unmotivated hangs around hotels. I'd say she's agitated, ready and plotting her move."

"Looks like it," the eggplant said. "Sure you don't need more backup?"

"Either I'm a real target or I'm not," she had managed to say with some authority. "She spots backup, the ballgame is over."

The object had always been to foil her in the act, force her to confess. They were all betting that the confrontation would induce an overwhelming need to tell all. Criminologists were divided on the premise. Human behavior was too complex for slide-rule verisimilitude.

To record such a confession, if it came, they had fit her with a trick brassiere with a mini-tape recorder attached. It was laughable, but practical, Miranda notwithstanding. The woman had to be stopped one way or another.

"Wearing it?" the eggplant asked.

Fiona nodded and the eggplant showed a thin smile.

"No 'talk to my tits' jokes," she warned.

"Would I joke about something so serious?" the eggplant had commented, unable to suppress a broader smile.

Actually such jokes would have lightened the load. It wasn't only the fear of Frances. She had the courage to face that. It was the other that troubled her more, the female trap. Wanting it to be meaningful. There was no solace for it, except to curse her gender.

"I'm going along, but I still don't like it," the eggplant said yet again.

"I'm ready," she told him firmly.

"Talk about macho."

With Cates, she had practiced how to resist a garrote attack from the rear and had polished up her karate. She did not fear a one-on-one physical attack, especially by another female. On the other hand, the woman could use another method, a gun, poison, explosives. Here again, they were betting that the same MO would be used, strangulation by a strong, soft object like a scarf.

Frances' telephone call was a surprise. They had figured on a more surreptitious method, a sneak job. Frances would suddenly appear behind her, flip the garrote around her neck and squeeze. Fiona would overpower her. Cates would come running to her aid. Defeated, the woman would sing her sad song. Finis.

"This is Frances Langford," the voice said after Fiona had identified herself. They had been drinking coffee in the kitchen. Cates had run to the extension in the den.

"Oh yes," Fiona had replied.

"I guess you know who I am?"

"Yes, I do."

"We've met casually," Frances said. For a moment, she seemed tentative, pausing. "We saw each other at the OAS a couple of weeks ago." Her voice was pleasant and chatty. Saw each other indeed, Fiona thought, remembering her face peering above the balustrade.

"We probably did," Fiona said cautiously.

"You know we did."

Now it was Fiona's turn to pause. She was genuinely confused.

"I saw you and Sam. Then you looked up and saw me."

"That was you?" Fiona said, trying to generate surprise, knowing she wasn't convincing.

"I know you must think I'm crazy. I've actually been following Sam and you. I mean, I know where you go."

"Really, Mrs. Langford," Fiona replied, reaching for indignation.

"I have to see you," Frances said. "I just can't wait any longer."

"What for?"

"I don't want to say over the phone. But it's very important. Very."

"When do you suggest?"

"Today. As soon as possible."

"Where?"

"You know the Four Seasons in Georgetown?"

"Yes."

"Noon okay?"

Fiona looked at the digital clock on the microwave.

"I'll be there."

Still, she did not hang up. Fiona could hear her breathing.

"And, Miss FitzGerald."

"Yes."

"Be very careful."

Cates rushed back to the kitchen after the call.

"How do you read this?" he asked.

"Obviously a ploy," Fiona said.

"A public place. Witnesses. She's taking risks she may not have taken with the others. Why?"

Cates shrugged.

"She must know you're a cop."

"I have to assume she knows everything."

They called the eggplant at home and told him what had happened.

"Think she knows we're tailing her? Setting her up?" he asked after they told him about the call.

"No indication," Fiona said crisply. "But we can't be sure. Not yet."

"Sounds weird," the eggplant said.

"Cunning," Fiona corrected. "She has something up her sleeve, that's for sure."

"Cates."

"Yes, Chief."

"Like glue. Understand?"

"Perfectly."

"And you, FitzGerald. Be careful."

He hung up. Funny, Fiona thought. That's what Frances said to me.

XXVIII

The Four Seasons in Georgetown boasted a cocktail lounge that had the look and feel of a huge reception room in a European luxury hotel. Floor-to-ceiling windows opened to gardens that were carefully constructed to give the illusion of a great expanse lying beyond the immediate view. Deep upholstered chairs and couches were strategically placed for both comfort and privacy. The decor was impeccable. A pianist in black tie played popular tunes on a shiny black baby grand.

Frances was already there. She had chosen an out-of-the-way spot in a far corner. She was, Fiona noted, carefully groomed, wearing a beige suit that set off brown eyes flecked with yellow. Blonde hair fell gently to her shoulders, and, while her appearance was very youthful from a distance, closer up tiny nests of smile-wrinkles around her eyes and lips gave hints of an ominously accelerated aging process. Long, tapered fingers played with a double string of what looked like genuine baroque pearls.

She appeared open and friendly, with a real estate salesman's flair for ingratiation. Her handshake was firm, strong as a man's.

Studying her as the waitress poured coffee from a silver urn into delicate cups, Fiona could not detect any sense of the viciousness and evil that motivated those crimes which the woman had allegedly perpetrated. Were they wrong? Fiona wondered. Yet her experience had taught her that the most ruthless murderers often seemed docile and benign.

"I'm so glad you could make it," Frances said. Only then, as she spoke, did the sunny mood conveyed by her appearance change abruptly. When she bent to raise her coffee cup, Fiona did a quick take, catching Cates just as he opened a newspaper at his seat at the other end of the room.

"Your invitation was more like a summons."

"I know. I'm sorry. But I'm deeply troubled."

"You are?"

She took a deep sip and put down her coffee cup.

"I've been following you, Miss FitzGerald," Frances said. "Spying on you. On one level I'm terribly ashamed."

"And on the other?"

Fiona tried to mask her confusion with a show of sarcastic indignation.

"I'm frightened for you," Frances said flatly. "And I only hope I can sell this idea as good as I sell real estate." Her gaze revolved around the room. Was it genuine fear Fiona saw in her eyes?

"What idea?"

Frances continued to play with her pearls.

"I think . . ." Frances hesitated, then sucked in a deep breath, offering an expression that one might make when one is about to ingest some foul-tasting medicine. ". . . I think you're exposing yourself to extreme danger. Someone is going to attempt to kill you."

"There's a happy thought," Fiona said with a deliberate air of skepticism. She would resist the idea, make Frances push harder.

"I know I sound off-the-wall. But hear me out before you make any judgements. The essential point is that you're having an affair with my ex-husband."

Should she stand up? Make some obvious gesture of indignation? No, she decided. She might not be able to pull it off.

"You said it up front. You've been spying on me."

"I had to be sure."

"Sure that we were having an affair?"

"Sure that it was the real thing."

"How in the name of hell could you determine that?"

"I can't really. I'm making an assumption based on experience and intuition."

"And of course, it's none of your business."

"You're right."

"Then why all the interest?"

"I could say it's because I want to see justice done, but that would be corny. Let's call it a sisterly thing then. An alliance of the gender."

There was, after all, something compelling about such a female call to arms. Fiona shrugged and said nothing, her silence an encouragement for Frances to continue.

"Fourteen years ago, he was having an affair with a young black woman, Betty Taylor. She was never heard from again. Ever since then, I've been, well . . . uncomfortable. We were still married then and I found out. Caught them actually in the throes of passion. Quite embarrassing all around. He was up for his first Senate seat. He wasn't exactly contrite, but he was realistic. I made a bargain with him. If he stopped the affair, I would stay with him through the campaign. Oh, the marriage was over. I knew that. And I kept my end of the bargain."

"Did he?"

She remembered Sam's explanation, comparing versions now. So far everything fit with what Sam had told her.

"Perhaps too well," Frances said.

"What do you mean?"

"The woman disappeared."

Fiona's heart lurched.

"How do you know?"

"Because I tried to contact her."

"When?"

"Must have been a couple of weeks after the incident. Sam told me that it was over by then. That was his part of the bargain. But you see, I felt badly about the poor girl. Can you understand that?"

"Yes. I think I can understand," Fiona said, nodding her head.

"She was probably a sweet but very naive young woman and I had embarrassed her. I felt uncomfortable about that. I really felt a sense of compassion for her. More than that."

"The sister thing."

A tiny smile belied any bitterness. Fiona could not detect a single false note.

"Her telephone was disconnected and she had moved out of her apartment. Even the people on the Committee were in the dark about her. She had simply upped and left."

"Disappeared?"

"There's no other explanation," Frances said. "I even called her mother in West Virginia. I told her I was a friend of Betty's from Washington. The poor woman was beside herself. I used to call from time to time, to see if Betty had contacted her, then, what with one thing and another, I stopped calling."

"What do you think happened to her?"

Her whole body seemed to mobilize itself. She lifted her chin, focused her eyes, straightened her back.

"I think she was done away with. Murdered."

"By your ex-husband? By Sam?"

She shook her head.

"Sam couldn't kill anyone. Especially a woman."

"Then who?"

"Let me continue," Frances said. "A few years later, Sam had made it to the Senate. We were long divorced, but I would see him from time to time. Observe him, actually. I know. None of my business. But he had married Nell by then. Anyway, I read in the paper that a woman staffer, Harriet Farley, was killed in an automobile accident."

"What did that mean?"

"I checked it out. A woman driving alone, dead sober, on a lonely road in Virginia suddenly wraps herself around a tree."

"That's pretty circumstantial," Fiona said.

"Who would know better than a homicide detective?" So she does know lots more about me, Fiona thought. Frances plunged ahead with her story. "It just didn't sit well. I couldn't prove it. But I would bet that this Harriet Farley was having an affair with Sam."

"You think foul play did her in?"

Frances nodded.

"I suspected it then. I know it now."

She paused.

"The murder of Helga Kessel has convinced me."

"But the woman was robbed," Fiona said cautiously.

"The papers said that this is the police contention, Miss FitzGerald. I also know that's the way you met Sam." She studied Fiona and smiled. "You are a lovely looking woman, Miss FitzGerald, although, I must say, a very unlikely detective. But I bet you must hear that frequently."

"So you've added all this up in your mind. Three murders."

"I believe it sincerely."

"And no evidence."

"No."

She hesitated, then spoke again. "Believe me. For your sake, I hope I'm wrong. But I've decided to speak out regardless of what you might think of me."

"And who do you think is the culprit?"

"I have nothing to hang it on. No hard facts or evidence to impart. I know in my gut. That's all I can give you."

Fiona knew what was coming and she was busy concocting alternate scenarios.

"Bunkie Farrington," Frances said. "This man is diseased. He is corroded by ambition. He would stop at nothing."

Fiona saw the flash of anger, the effort to keep it under control. It seemed perfectly appropriate to the moment. Was this woman such a superb actress? Was her own theory faltering? Could she be right?

"We are not fools, Mrs. Langford," Fiona said. "We considered all that."

"I've always felt there was more to it," Frances sighed. "More than just protecting Sam's career. I remember this boy when he first came with Sam. A young, pretty boy just out of Yale. He took immediate possession."

"You seem to be implying something beyond ambition," Fiona said.

"Oh, I've always felt that. It's a breed very common in politics, a kind of a homosexual psychopath that hides his real motive under the guise of ambition."

"And Sam?"

"There's a theory that philandering men need to keep proving their manhood to themselves."

Suddenly, she felt Frances' scrutiny become more intense. She knew she was blushing to her hair roots and it was playing havoc with her objectivity.

"Are you saying—" Fiona began.

"Sam and Bunkie? I'd vote no to anything overt. As for Sam knowing and willing to manipulate Bunkie, that's another matter." She had let go of her pearls. Now she took them up again.

"Heavy stuff," Fiona said. She turned it over in her mind, rebuking herself for blocking out the obvious. And yet, hadn't they "rousted" Bunkie, put him through their gauntlet without success?

"I feel better now," Frances said. She signaled for the waiter. "I can use a drink. You?"

The waiter came over.

"A bloody Mary," Frances said, looking at Fiona.

"Same," Fiona said. Again, she stole a glance at Cates, who was watching her peripherally now. Then she looked at Frances, who exuded credibility, a hundred and eighty degrees from where she had been in her mind. Still, Fiona had made no move to test the woman, largely because she had not been able to think of anything that might trip her up.

"Forewarned is forearmed," Frances said. "It's not like you would be out there in the cold. You're police people. You know how to handle these things."

"He couldn't know about Sam and me. No way." This had to be a hard fact. He had been deliberately taken out of the loop. The trap was set for Frances, not for Bunkie. Had they been playing to the wrong gallery?

"I know he's out of town. I checked. I figure that he may not know with who, but he surely knows something is up. There's a real gap in Sam's schedule on Tuesdays and Thursdays in the middle of the day. No way to hide that. He'll find out. Count on it."

There was a test, Fiona thought. A test of something. She had a question ready.

"Did you know that Sam kept some of his business to himself?"

"Maybe that's what he thought. Believe me, Bunkie finds out. He'll find out about you and Sam and put two and two together."

"He might think it's just another roll in the hay. Not worthy of much attention."

"Not Bunkie. Bunkie would know."

"But we've kept him out-of-town," Fiona said, wondering if she had gone too far.

"Out-of-town for Bunkie does not mean out-of-mind. Besides, he'll be back. He'll know. He has his methods."

"Wouldn't he question it. So—soon after Helga?" Fiona asked, then wished she hadn't. Was she asking for herself? Or professionally?

Frances shrugged. "Ask yourself that question."

The message, because Fiona had shrouded it in obfuscation, was reaching her obliquely. In her heart lay the answer to that. But to confront it would mean that she was expecting more from Sam than was given. Jesus, this was getting out of hand.

The drinks came, concoctions containing a large flowering stalk of celery. Frances reached for the stalk and bit off a piece. The act was purposeful, primitive, and it arrested Fiona's attention for the moment, further confusing her.

Fiona removed her stalk and took a deep sip. It was spicy, a little hot for a Washington-inspired bloody Mary.

"You ever bring this up with Sam?" Fiona asked.

"Absolutely not," Frances said, her eyes squinting over the rim of the glass. "He'd think I was being vindictive." She paused and put her glass down. "About Bunkie."

"And what if he did? What would it matter? You've been divorced all these years."

"It matters," Frances muttered. "I can't bear the thought of what has happened to those women. He must not be allowed to get away with it." Her intense gaze suddenly focused on Fiona. "Not again."

"Meaning me."

"I could never live with myself if I didn't have this conversation."

"Why didn't you have this talk with Helga Kessel?"

She nodded her head, picked up her drink again and sipped, obviously taking the time to frame an answer. Surely she knew now that her credibility was under scrutiny, although she showed no signs of vacillation from her position.

"Don't you see? I was never certain. True, I made assumptions. But I was alone in my theory. After a while I began to believe that I might be fantasizing. Betty Taylor could have run away, disappeared for her own reasons. Harriet could have died from a real automobile accident. Besides, years had passed. I did despise Bunkie. In many ways I blame him for the disintegration of our marriage. But, you see, I couldn't be sure if my idea wasn't being colored by my feelings about him. Also, I had nothing to go on. Not until the death of Helga Kessel put it together for me."

The possibility that Frances Langford was concocting these stories for her own ends had not vanished, but her logic seemed impeccable and her face reflected an uncanny sincerity.

"You don't believe Helga was killed for her jewels?" Fiona asked pointedly.

"A red herring, I'd say. Like the lady. Buried somewhere."

"Why do you think she was buried behind that particular house?" Fiona asked cautiously, studying Frances' face.

"Now you're asking me to get into the man's mind," Frances said. "I haven't the faintest idea."

A line of testing questions was emerging now and the woman was answering them freely. Fiona detected no sign of extreme caution, only openness and apparent sincerity.

"It was a house for sale. Empty."

"Good choice, I'd say. I'm in the business, you know. The neighbors would be used to seeing strange cars near the house. A wooded lot, I suppose. One in which the owners would be reluctant to take down trees and, therefore, leaving the lot undisturbed."

"How would Bunkie know this house?"

"Probably by the For Sale signs. Maybe he was once there. Who knows?"

"Then the rains came and fouled up the plan."

As Fiona said this, she studied Frances' face. There wasn't a flicker of expression that suggested guilt or evil intent.

"Says something, doesn't it? We wouldn't be here if it weren't for that rain. Maybe it's God's way to get even," Frances said. She shrugged, smiled and finished her drink.

The God reference made her seem positively benign, further undermining her suspicions. Nevertheless, Fiona had to move forward with her premise. Her life depended on it. No point in being coy.

"We found Betty Taylor," Fiona said, her gaze two probing searchlights. Frances met them without fear or surprise.

"So you did know about Betty?"

"Same modus operandi. She was buried in a house for sale. We checked that one out. The present owners were building a pool. Then the rains came.

"What did you find?"

"Old bones."

Frances seemed to shiver. She took her glass and gulped down the remaining liquid.

"And from that you were able to—"

"Not really. We got lucky. The killer made a mistake."

Frances' eyes widened. She was reacting now, probing Fiona's face. Fiona let it sit for a while. If she was the guilty party, withholding the information might agitate her, give her away. It didn't.

"What mistake?" The question was logical, merely normal curiosity and, therefore, without relevance.

Fiona did not answer immediately, still hopeful that stalling might set the woman off, ruffle her calm. Fiona played with her drink, brought it up to her lips, put the glass down, fussed with her hair, details designed to throw Frances off balance. She wondered if Frances was passing or failing the test.

"There was an ankle bracelet on her ankle bone," Fiona said cautiously. "A gift from you-know-who."

Frances' reaction was oblique and non-conclusive.

"Maybe it wasn't a mistake. Maybe the killer wanted you to know someday."

"There's a bit of insight," Fiona said. It had not occurred to her at the time. And yet it lay at the heart of the accepted police theory that a serial killer secretly wants to get caught.

"Not really. Years of suspicion has made me an amateur detective of sorts." She smiled pleasantly. "Another drink?"

Fiona shook her head. Her mind was still reaching out to fasten on the flotsam of any idea. Their theory on Frances' guilt was beginning to crumble. It was Frances herself who seemed to kick away the last prop.

"I know I'm the principal suspect, and believe me, I'm not offended."

"Where did you get that idea?" Fiona said, knowing it was a lame try. Who was testing whom? Fiona wondered.

"Look, I understand." Without so much as a glance she literally pointed with her shoulder to the supposedly surreptitious Cates. "Maybe people who follow have a sixth sense about people following them. Who knows? Yet, who can blame you for thinking what you must think. I'm in the real estate business. I therefore know where empty houses are. I'm the ex-wife of a compulsive womanizer and, therefore, a person with a grudge. Long-festering grudges, any psychologist will tell you, make people crazy. Have I got it right?"

"More or less," Fiona admitted, as if she were compelled to defend her integrity. Had they been that obvious?

"I've got the other right, too," Frances said, her eyes narrowing. Only then did Fiona see the passion in her expression. "He's our man, and when he finds out, he's going to make his move. I feel it in my bones." She moved closer to Fiona and put her hand on her arm. "He's gotten away with it three times. He's found a way to beat you people, and I'll bet he thinks he's invulnerable. You've got to be ready for him."

"If he's our man, we will," Fiona muttered. What she needed most was time now to sort things out. She looked toward Cates, who caught her eye. Then she waved. Frances turned toward him and lifted her hand. He cocked his head in surprise.

"I'll get this," Frances said, hailing the waiter.

"I'm glad we had this little chat," Fiona said in a parody of the old cliché. She stood up. Frances put out her hand and Fiona took it. It felt firm, warm, comfortable. Maybe they were allies, after all, Fiona conceded, although she still held back her total surrender to Frances' contention. Not quite total, but tilting toward, she told herself.

"If I can be helpful in any way, please get in touch." She handed Fiona a card.

"One question, Mrs. Langford," Fiona said.

"Only one?" Frances retorted.

"Bunkie is not stupid. He might know that it's a set-up."

"But is it?" Frances said, offering a cryptic smile. "I mean now."

Fiona stood up and walked over to Cates, who had already paid his check.

"What the hell is going on?" he asked as they headed toward the lobby.

She didn't answer, pondering instead a vague sense of failure and humiliation.

"I need to know," he pressed.

"Actually," she said, breaking the silence as she stood in front of the hotel, waiting for her car. "It's a sisterly thing."

XXIX

"First he has to get me in his sights," Fiona explained.

"And then?" Sam asked.

"Two ways to go. The eggplant has a different view than mine."

It was more than that, but she dared not explain. Only Cates was catching on, which was troubling. He kissed her hair and stroked her nipple as she nestled in the crook of his arm. As always, the blinds were drawn but they could see things clearly.

"The point is he has to believe this is . . . well . . . the real thing."

"It is for me."

"Come on, Sam. Don't tease."

"I mean it."

"Bet you say that to all the girls," Fiona said, not liking the idea behind the statement. He probably did. Maybe not all, but most. At least three, maybe more.

"When I say it, I always feel I mean it."

"Maybe you did in a general sense, meaning the whole gender."

"You think that's the root of it? Then you'd have to think I'm an insincere son-of-a-bitch."

"I used to think so. I'm not so sure now. I think you're right. You mean it when you mean it."

"Do you mean it?" Sam asked.

"When I mean it, I mean it," she said, flustered. There was simply no way to adequately rationalize these acts with Sam. Lust. Desire. Passion. Something. He was being untrue to his wife. She to her job. Or was she? Fuck or play gin. What did it matter how she passed the time?

He gently moved her out of the crook of his arm and stood up, showing her his body. He was well made, tall, slender, adequately endowed.

267

He had not asked her to keep her holster on and she had placed it on the floor beside the bed. Now he picked it up and put it on.

"Something about a gun," he said, patting it. He took it out of the holster and hefted it. Then he put his finger on the trigger and pointed it at her.

"It's loaded, you know," she said.

She felt no fear.

"A turn-on?" he asked.

"Not that one. Only the other."

She sat up, reached out and touched his erection. He put the pistol back in its holster and dropped it to the floor.

"Am I really different than other men?" he asked.

"Not to the naked eye," she said, smiling. She embraced him, nestling his penis between her breasts. Her hands grasped the globes of his hard buttocks, pressing him tightly against her.

"You are different from the others, Fiona," he said, caressing her hair.

"Cut it out, Sam. You don't have to."

"You're special."

"Jesus, Sam. You'll have me believing it."

"I want you to. I believe it."

She lifted her face and their eyes met and held for a long moment. His hands reached out and held the sides of her head. Then he gently tilted it and kissed her hair.

Too mysterious to contemplate, she told herself. Go with the flow. Moving back to the bed, he embraced her from behind. Afterward they lay like two spoons.

"Imagine," Sam whispered. "He's down there right now, waiting."

"Have you bought it? The Bunkie theory?"

"Not quite."

Bunkie had come back from California and Sam had, according to their instructions, set it up. "Wasn't hard," he had told them. "Bunkie usually knows my day minute-by-minute. Our people in the office told him that I was spending unscheduled time somewhere. He wanted to know. I evaded the issue. Voilá. Bunkie is very resourceful. I had no doubt he would want to confirm the situation for himself."

Cates, using his car phone, had called up to the room, talking in code.

"He's in his car, waiting," Cates had said. She assumed that Bunkie had followed Sam to the motel.

"No sign of Frances?" Fiona had asked.

"None."

"Ten-four," she had answered, hanging up. "Frances may have it right after all."

"As long as I live I won't believe any of this."

"He'll want to make certain who the new lady is. Figure your charm has seduced yet another canary. We're in Virginia, so it won't be official MPD police business." She twisted her body to face him. "Then he'll confront you? What will you tell him?"

"I'll tell him it's none of his business."

"And then?"

"I'll get the usual lecture about destroying my political career." Fiona saw the evasion.

"Will he believe that I'm the real thing?"

"It's true."

"Stop it, Sam," she said firmly, wanting it to be true, hating herself for wanting it.

"He'll be convinced. He'll also think that by these little meetings in a public place I'm really taking a chance, throwing caution to the winds. Oh, he'll be convinced all right." He stroked her side and kissed her hair. "If Frances is right, I'm setting him up to attack you."

"That's the point."

"Scares the hell out of me," Sam said. He raised himself on an elbow and leaning over her, he kissed her deeply on the lips. "Rough duty," he said when his lips had disengaged.

"We'll get him, Sam. But we've got to get him to crack wide open."

"And Frances is free and clear?"

"Maybe."

It was, the eggplant and Cates had agreed, worth the test. The fact that Frances was not in evidence was certainly a plus for her contention.

"Be a miracle if I can salvage a political career out of this," Sam sighed. "Even a confession has to deal with a motive."

"Maybe he'll cop an insanity plea. Leave a doubt in the public's mind."

"Or he'll deny it. Get a smart lawyer. Go to trial. Put me on the stand. Any way you slice it, I'm in deep shit."

"It was always worth the try, Sam. And the right thing to do."

"I'll buy that."

He slid lower on the bed and embraced her, kissing her navel and her pubic hair.

She caressed his head.

"Maybe we'll find a way, Sam. I would if I could."

She felt suddenly heroic and determined, which triggered an idea. Unfortunately it was morbid, ugly, against her grain. Bunkie would attack her and she or Cates would shoot him.

"My God," she said aloud.

"What is it?" Sam asked.

Should she tell him what was going on in her mind? Before she could act, the phone made them jump. She picked it up.

"He's gone into the lobby," Cates said.

"Can you see him?"

"He's just sitting there, watching the elevators. It's a good spot to observe. You won't see him."

"Ten-four."

She told Sam where Bunkie was at that moment. He reached out to look at his wristwatch.

"Damn. Time goes."

She came back into his arms. It was madness, lunacy for both of them. Once again, old Fiona was trapped by her romantic nature, she told herself. Runs in the blood. The impractical Irish romantic, the worst kind. Maybe she was his counterpart, fated to spread her love over the entire other gender. Yet, she wasn't promiscuous. Certainly not indiscriminate. All right, she could count her lovers on the fingers of both hands. Not quite all the fingers. Was that promiscuity? It certainly was chance-taking in this age of AIDs. A shiver ran through her as she thought of Bunkie and Sam in the way Frances had described them. Oh no. Not Sam, she decided. Hell, was she supposed to cart around condoms in her handbag like some slut?

In his arms she felt safe. More than that? She brushed away the thought. This entire interlude was a travesty, an insult to her job, a violation of all procedures. Wrong as hell. But it hadn't stopped her. Nothing had stopped her.

As agreed, he would be leaving the room first. He prepared to go. They had been together just under two hours.

"Anything happens to you, I'll never forgive myself," he told her.

"I'm a professional," she assured him. "I know how to handle myself. And I've got backup."

"It's not worth it, Fiona. I'm not worth it."

"We're not doing it for you," she said firmly.

"It's me that killed those women," he said. "I should be punished for it." He looked at her, his eyes brimming with tears. "Hell, there's life after politics." Then he opened the door and went out.

She showered and dressed quickly. No point in thinking about anything but the matter at hand. She hefted her pistol, drew it out of the holster and checked to be sure it was loaded. It was.

She did not expect him to make his move immediately, only to make her, identify her. That done, he would act as soon as he determined that her relationship with the Senator was more than casual. But expectations often conflicted with reality. It was his option and he could act immediately. Today.

As if to assure his postponement, she put on her trick brassiere, which she carried in her shoulder bag. Above all, she'd be ready for the son-of-a-bitch. Catch him in the act and loosen his tongue. That was the gamble.

"You get done for nothing, I'll have your ass," the eggplant had warned, still reticent, genuinely worried.

"Nothing's for nothing," she whispered to herself, thinking of Sam.

XXX

A grey-haired couple got on the elevator with her. She smiled thinly, let them push the button, and stood against the rear panel as it descended.

On the lobby floor, she hung back and waited until they got out. Then she moved, walking slowly, exhibiting herself. Her check-in method was to pay in advance and there was no need for her to stop at the desk. This time she did, asking the clerk for the time. Peripherally, she saw Bunkie. He was sitting in a corner, a magazine held up to partially conceal him. When she was certain he had made her, she headed out the side door toward the parking lot.

She pushed through the door, noting as she angled her body that he made no move to rise and follow her. Cates, she knew, was waiting in his car at a point in front of the hotel that afforded him the best view of any of Bunkie's potential actions. She assumed that Bunkie's car, too, was parked at curbside. The objective for Cates was to keep the man in view at all times, while giving him enough distance for him to think he was safe enough to make his move. Apparently, now that he knew who she was, he would save that for another time.

Almost at the moment she approached her car, her cop's sense of things awry assailed her. She slowed her steps, studying the vehicle. Then she saw it. The inside lock button was raised. Had she been careless when she left the car? Highly unlikely. She had equipment in her glove compartment, a walkie-talkie. Under the dash was the police radio and car telephone. No way would she have left the door open. Force of habit. Someone had hooked it open.

Her mind focused on that fact and she could feel the adrenaline pumping. Was someone inside? Who? There was no time to analyze.

She prepared her body, which surged with alertness, every cell ready to react.

Hesitating for a brief moment, she touched the mechanism in her brassiere, felt it activate, then opened the door to her car on the driver's side. Before she slid in, her peripheral vision caught the picture. Someone was, indeed, lying on the floor of the car. It was a tricky moment.

There were no doubts now. Frances had snookered them. Quickly, she noted that there were no people in the parking lot. Only cars. Good, she thought. No interference. The time was now. She bent forward, put her key in the ignition, then straightened, calculating the moment. Her fist went up to her neck at precisely the moment when the scarf swished over her head. She felt the pressure on her fist and windpipe as the scarf was pulled taut, tightening as strong hands pulled at either end of a loop.

She heard the grunting sound, distinctly female, although the grip seemed masculine. Body to body, she had been taught—the key to overpowering an opponent was leverage and concentration. With her free hand, she grabbed a handful of hair, pulled back, heard the squeal of pain. With her fisted hand she pushed, feeling the grasp loosen and scarf loop widen. Then she slid under the loop and twisted her body, both arms free now, as she rose to her knees on the front seat and tightly grasped both of Frances' wrists.

In a quick twist, she reversed the woman's body. Frances was strong. No question about that. But not as skilled in defense. In a few seconds, despite the awkwardness of her position, Fiona had both her arms twisted behind her and was tying her wrists firmly behind her with the scarf.

In a futile effort to get free, Frances had used her head as a weapon. Fiona had avoided it, and after the knot was tied, she pulled the woman's head back until it literally hung over the front seat and the woman was grunting in pain. Then she quickly rolled over to the rear seat, unholstered her pistol, and still holding a handful of hair put the muzzle of the gun against the woman's forehead.

"Give me the pleasure, lady," Fiona said breathlessly. Frances had continued to struggle, but the warning froze her. In the light, she saw the woman's frightened eyes. "Funny how even the worst of them hate to die," Fiona snapped.

She pushed the woman facedown on the rear seat, removed a pair of cuffs from her shoulder bag, closed them on her wrists, undid the scarf, then looped it around the cuffs and, forcing the woman to bend her knees, tied the scarf to her ankles.

Then she pushed the woman on her side, jumped over to the front seat and started the car. Her body was still charged as she backed the car out of its space and headed out of the lot.

"Just you and me, babe," she muttered, angling the rearview mirror to see the woman immobilized on the back seat. To see behind her, she glanced at the sideview mirror. No sign of Cates. He was off following Bunkie. Good. This one was for her. And Sam.

"Real smart-ass," Fiona said, looking at the woman.

"Where are you taking me?"

"Mine to know. Yours to find out."

She headed the car north along Route One toward the District of Columbia. Again she checked the sideview mirror. No sign of Cates.

"Had you going," Frances said after a long and deliberate silence on Fiona's part. The woman needed to simmer. Fiona's own plan was still vague. Above all, she needed the woman to talk up a storm.

"You have the right to remain silent—" Fiona began.

"We're getting formal, are we?" Frances sneered.

Fiona completed the spiel, getting it on tape just in case, knowing that the legal niceties would inevitably be gummed up by the lawyers. Okay, baby, Fiona silently urged the woman. Talk to my tits.

"You people and your little games," Frances said. "Fools, the pack of you."

Fiona let silence do its work. She said nothing for a long time, a psychological ploy, feeding on the woman's natural anxiety. Finally,

she said, "Blaming all this on poor, sad Bunkie." Fiona shook her
head in mock ridicule.

"Not over yet," Frances said. Incredulously, Fiona thought she saw
the woman smile.

"For you it is," Fiona said.

No mistaking it now. The woman was smiling.

"Back to square one, lady. No real evidence." Frances giggled.
"And old hot-cock's career goes down the tube."

"Beware a woman scorned," Fiona said.

"Scorned? Me? You've got it wrong, lady."

"Have I?"

"I was the only one he loved. The first and only."

"That's a laugh."

"They didn't have any rights to him. They were usurpers. Who
were they supposed to answer to?" She laughed. "They deserved it."
Off and running, Fiona thought, relieved.

"Why not Nell?"

"I would never interfere with the sanctity of the marriage bond."
When she said this, there was not the slightest hint of sarcasm in
her tone.

It was convoluted, of course. But the woman was obviously mad,
answering only to her own skewered logic.

"If you didn't miss the ankle bracelet we might never have identified Betty Taylor."

"Nobody's perfect," Frances said. "Little black cunt. She was easy."

"Easy?"

"Got her just like I nearly got you. In back of the apartment
house, where she parked her car. Got rid of everything she owned in
the city dump. Fourteen years and you hadn't a clue."

"You strangled her?"

"She was gone in no time at all. No time at all."

"Swimming pool and the rain fucked you up," Fiona said. She
pressed her breast, felt the tiny recording purring.

"The fact was they came too close to the property line when they built that pool. They were illegal. I measured it."

"There you go. Nobody's perfect."

The road grew more congested as they headed north. She cut into the spaghetti curves at the edge of Arlington and headed past the Pentagon toward Memorial Bridge. Spring buds had just exploded into leaf along the parkland beside the highway and the Potomac was slate grey without its normal muddy brown caste.

"Tell me about Harriet," Fiona asked.

"That pig," Frances muttered. "I didn't even want to dirty my hands. I counted her as an infatuation. I used to think about them together, her stinking of horseshit. I just chased her into a tree. Pure panic. I enjoyed the harassment. Never laid a hand on her."

"But you missed Judy Peters," Fiona goaded.

"I was going to follow her to Europe, the little bitch. But I had a big deal going. I canceled out. Then when she came back, I burned out on her."

"Had to feel the white heat of it?"

"Something like that."

Then Frances grew silent.

"Where are you taking me?" she said after a while.

Fear of death, Fiona thought. She had seen it when she had put the pistol muzzle against her temple. She saw it now. No question. The woman was a psychopath. And yet she feared death. Was that a contradiction? At that point another idea had popped into her mind. Resisting arrest. Bang bang. She tried to will it away.

"Why, after all that time, did you do Helga?"

"Kraut pussy. I thought it was over for old hot-cock. I really did. Then when I saw him and her together I knew it hadn't. She was a greedy little pig. I knew she was in the market to buy. Got it right off the computer. I caught her in the ladies' room they had set up in Mount Vernon and told her I had this piece of property to show her, a real deal, a steal. She liked that. Picked her up a block from the Embassy. Dug the hole the night before."

"In the rain."

"Yeah, the rain, the damned rain. Was good for digging, though. Nice and soft."

Frances began to laugh, a kind of cackle, hardly normal.

"What are you laughing at?"

"She put the idea in my head about pinning it all on Bunkie."

"How?"

"That day when I picked her up—to show her up—on the pretext of showing her some property, we had a real talk, us girls. She told me about her affair with Sam. After all, we did have him in common. All of us. You and me, too."

The remark curdled Fiona's stomach. All of us, she repeated to herself. How could he have loved all of us?

"What about the idea?"

"She told me about how Bunkie had told her it had to end. She was upset about it. But she understood. The thing that upset her the most was being told to do it by Bunkie. It was really just a coincidence."

"What was?"

"Him and me onto the same thing. And just about at the same time." She giggled. "Only I made sure it was permanent."

"Killing them?" Fiona said, mostly for the benefit of the machine purring next to her right breast.

"You got it. And they deserved what they got."

"Then you decided my time had come."

"At first I thought, 'She's just a cop, good for a quirky quickie.' You know, doing-it-while-you-wear-your-gun kind of thing."

Fiona's hand went up to her breast. Shut that damned recording off, she told herself, but she made no move to stop it.

"You've got a dirty mind," Fiona said. Again, it was mostly for the recorder's benefit. Who could possibly understand?

"Do I?"

"You spotted my partner—you knew it was all a scam to flush you out. Motivate you to do what we believed you did to the others."

The woman paused, then giggled again. "Big surprise, huh?"

What did that mean? Fiona wondered, feeling strangely uncomfortable. Had she enough on tape? Enough to satisfy them? Was it time to turn it off? More important, was it enough for her?

She turned onto Memorial Bridge, saw the bronze horses' rear ends glistening in the sun. To reach headquarters she would have followed the curving road to Constitution then headed toward the Hill. Instead, she took another turn, which brought the car back under Memorial Bridge, leading toward Hains Point.

From the rearview mirror, she saw Frances struggling to raise her chin to see out the window.

"Where are we going?" she asked again.

Fiona did not answer. Instead she parked the car in a deserted spot along the curb. Ahead she could see the fountain spraying water in the middle of the Potomac.

"If you knew it was a trap, why did you walk into it?" Fiona asked. She turned to look at the woman, lying awkwardly on her side, her eyes feral and malevolent.

"Because it had to be done," Frances said, as if it was the most elementary bit of knowledge. "You had no rights to Sam. I had to set things straight."

"By killing me?"

"Of course. You know that."

It was getting too close to the bone, Fiona decided. Irrelevant to the confession. Still, she could not bring herself to stop the recorder. Then, suddenly, it was too late.

"You think you could fool me?" Frances chortled with contempt. "You can't deny it, Miss Cop. You and he were getting it on and it was the real thing. That had to be stopped."

"So here you are. Caught in the act," Fiona said with some bravado. Only then did she cut the recorder.

"Your word against mine," Frances said. "Bunkie, on the other hand, is in deep shit."

"What the hell are you talking about?"

"Bring me in. I'm ready to tell my story."

Fiona felt her anger mounting. This was a crazy woman. Why then was she taking so much time with her? She had the confession on tape. Surely it would be enough to put the woman away. A good lawyer could plea bargain her into an institution.

"What story?"

"You'd like to know, wouldn't you?"

"You just told me the story."

She was tempted to tell her about the recorder.

"But not about Bunkie and the jewels," Frances teased.

"What about them?"

"Interested, aren't you?" She giggled again, reflecting an inner hysteria. "I'll make you a deal."

"No deals."

"I'll let you have Sam. Sam forever. Sam your true love. No more Bunkies to give you the old Dear-John."

It was madness talking, spewing out the distorted logic of a twisted mind. And yet, there was something in it that was too compelling to resist.

"And what do you get for your revelation?" Fiona asked.

"I go off into the sunrise."

Fiona paused, continuing to observe the woman. She still lay awkwardly on her side, her eyes wild, her lips twisted in ridicule.

"I'm listening," Fiona said.

The woman giggled again.

"All right then. I know you'll do it."

Fiona did not respond, her gaze drifting. Outside the car, the shadows were deepening. She looked out to the slate grey of the Potomac, which was now turning to black. The woman's voice brought her back.

"Helga's jewels are planted in a flowerpot on Bunkie's front stoop."

"Fascinating stuff," Fiona said, wondering if she really meant it.

"That's not all," Frances said. "I sprinkled some of the dirt from Helga's grave on the floor of Bunkie's car. In those hard-to-find places, as they say on TV."

"The criminal mind at work."

"If we need more I have more."

"More what?"

"Evidence. Isn't that the way police convict people?"

"You're really nuts," Fiona said, embarrassed by her own remark. Of course she was. Off the wall. Then why was she listening? Why wasn't she bringing her in?

"Either you want Sam or you don't. Putting me away won't do it for you."

Fiona paused, then shook her head, but it was the hesitation that gave her away. The light was dimming, although there was still enough of it for her to see the woman's eyes, intense and glowing orange as they caught the last gasp of the setting sun.

"Stick your hand on my chest," Frances said.

"Jesus. That, too."

"Don't be ridiculous. Just put your hand in and pull out the locket."

"You are too much," Fiona said. But her words belied her action. She moved fast, put her hand on the woman's blouse, ripped it open, found the locket and ripped it off her.

"You didn't have to break it, for crying out loud. Besides, you hurt me."

Fiona pried open the locket with her fingernails. Something soft was inside. It seemed like hair. Human hair.

"The black is Betty's. Stands up pretty good, don't you think. The blonde is Helga's. Car was too mangled to get at Harriet."

"A real collector." It was sick, gruesome.

"Got to have something for my efforts," Frances said, giggling again. "I would only use the Helga hair, though."

"I don't get it."

She reminded Fiona of a flawed jigsaw puzzle in which pieces fitted perfectly into an illogical pattern. What was needed was for someone to recut the pieces to make a more understandable picture. The idea had jumped into her mind. What evil alchemy did Frances practice to summon up such bizarre behavior, such weird ideas?

Then it came to her. She saw it with pristine sharpness. She could save Sam, save his career, save his aspirations. Was it possible? She shook away the thought, tried to exorcise the idea.

"You are a filthy little demented bitch," Fiona said, turning in her seat, gunning the motor, starting the car. "It's a lie about the jewelry and you know it."

"The proof is in the pudding," Frances said.

She headed the car back toward Capitol Hill. It was almost completely dark. They would be concerned by now. The eggplant would be fuming, berating Cates. She resisted any temptation to contact them. What was churning in her mind now could not be shared.

Bunkie's townhouse was just a stone's throw from the Ninth Street exit of the 605. She made the distance in less than ten minutes and pulled up in front of it. No lights were visible. It was obvious that Bunkie had not come home. Getting on her knees on the front seat, she bent over and lifted Frances' head so that she could see out of the window.

"The one on the left. Just get a hold of a fistful of plant and pull. The jewelry is in a plastic bag."

Fiona pushed the woman away roughly, got out of the car, its motor still running. She bent over the flowerpot and, as Frances had instructed her, gave the plant a quick pull. It came out in tightly packed earth the shape of the flowerpot. At the bottom of the pot lay a pile of jewels in a plastic bag. She put the jewels into her shoulder bag and replaced the plant.

It was not the time to reflect. Events were simply moving ahead of her. She got into the car again.

"You see them?" Frances asked. Because of her position in the back of the car she couldn't see out of the window.

"Yes."

"You see? I was telling the truth."

"Now Helga's hair. We mustn't forget that. Where would you put the hairs?"

"I'd have to get inside. Maybe put them on a pair of jeans. Something like that."

"See how easy it would be? The jewels, the dirt, the hair. Pin it on the bastard. Put a bullet in his brain. Say he attacked you. Then you find the evidence. Pow. Then it's only a simple case of robbery. No trial. No bullshit."

Fiona turned to look at the woman again. She was smiling.

"Do I get a good mark on that, Miss Cop? Enough to get a ticket out of here?"

"It has its charm," Fiona whispered.

"And we'd save the day for the man we both love."

The idea had an odd fascination. She should run it through her mind, just for kicks, she told herself.

"We'd be framing the man," Fiona said hoarsely, goading Frances to believe in her sincerity.

"Who deserves it more?"

Fiona gunned the motor and guided the car back to the 605. She headed the car west.

"See the beauty of it?" Frances said from the rear seat.

"It does have cachet," Fiona muttered.

Indeed, the exercise did have its own twisted logic. Fiona was putting it in perspective now, understanding her own motives. It might be worth considering, she thought, even if it were only theory.

"Where are we going?" Frances asked.

"Georgetown."

"You taking me home?"

Fiona didn't answer. A matrix was forming in her mind and she was surrendering to the fascination.

She had the jewels. She had Helga's hair. She could find the appropriate places to plant them in Frances' Georgetown house. They would be found later. After.

Take it further, Fiona prodded herself, speculating that Frances was probably still concocting ways to eliminate her. Hadn't that been her object all along?

The scenario spun itself out in her head. She might just give Frances the golden opportunity to achieve her objective. Fiona's mind raced with possibilities. Authenticity was, of course, essential. Frances' modus operandi was fixed in her mind, the use of the garrote, murder by strangulation. Naturally, Fiona would have to make the scarf available. It was right there beside her on the seat.

She would be on her guard, ready to counterattack. There would have to be a struggle, then Fiona would fire her pistol in self-protection. One shot direct to the heart. Maybe two.

There would be a hearing, of course. The jewels would be found. Helga's hairs would be found. Verdict: A homicide detective kills a suspect in self-defense. In the absence of a rebuttal, the suspect is circumstantially guilty. Loose ends would have to be tied. Maybe there would be a period of suspension. Maybe not. They would put the Betty Taylor case on ice.

And Sam would be free to pursue his career without fear. He was finished with that kind of a life, wasn't he? And Fiona would be his secret mistress, his only love, and perhaps someday . . .

XXXI

Would she have, really?

Perhaps it was instinct. But if, at precisely that moment, she had not contacted the eggplant, would she have really gone ahead with it?

"Where the hell have you been?" the eggplant shouted.

His urgent scratchy macho voice pulled her back from the edge of the abyss. She did not have time to answer. His next question, which should have been his first, came too fast: "Are you okay?"

"She had us going. It wasn't Bunkie."

"Did she try to do you?"

"Bungled it. She was waiting for me in my back seat. Amateur job. I got her trussed up and raving in the back of the car. I'll fill you in."

"You should have called in," he said, but there was no bite to his rebuke.

"Bitch kept me busy. Took me more time to get what we needed," she told him. Later, she would use that explanation to absolve herself of the guilt of intention. "I got it all, even a little extra." *Got more than I bargained for*, she thought.

"Our boy has bit the bullet," the eggplant said.

The words panicked her. Our boy? Sam?

"He killed himself?" The question rushed out of her before she could stop it.

"Killed his political career. Held this press conference couple of hours ago. He's not going to go for President and he's not going to run for the Senate after his term is over."

"It's a trick," Frances screeched from the back seat. She had heard it all.

"What was that?" the eggplant asked.

"Lady Macbeth without the guilt," Fiona said.

285

"Smart move on his part," the eggplant said. "No matter what. The shit would slop onto him. Better to leave with dignity at the top of his form. Can't say we didn't try to protect the son-of-a-bitch."

"We tried, all right." *Harder than you think.*

"Kind of a classy thing to do on his part," the eggplant said. "Said he wanted to spend more time with his family. Of course, he had no choice."

"Almost did," Fiona whispered.

"Didn't hear you," the eggplant said.

"Wasn't important." She cleared her throat. "But I quite agree. He is a classy guy." In her heart she said good-bye. All in all, she told herself, smiling, it was worth it, every bit of it.

She turned again to look at Frances, a sad sight, a mind obliterated by hate, committed to vengeance, an ugly and obscene woman. They would put her away in some hospital. Perhaps someday she would walk the streets again. Fiona felt her insides congeal.

"So bring home the bacon," the eggplant said.

"Cates must be pissed."

"He's sitting right here. Followed Bunkie right back to the office. Man was loyal to the end. Stood behind his man at the press conference."

"Say Hi," Fiona said, feeling suddenly cleansed as she turned the car and headed toward police headquarters.

"Had you going," Frances said from the back seat.

"No way," Fiona said, suddenly thinking of her old man. "We FitzGeralds always wind up doing the right thing."

The complete works of Warren Adler are now available in both trade paperback and hardcover. All titles are also available in all formats of e-books at all online retailers.

Mainstream Novels

The War of the Roses

The Roses thought they had a perfect marriage, but discover that their relationship is barely skin deep. This is the acclaimed and best-selling novel that became the classic divorce movie starring Michael Douglas and Kathleen Turner.

Random Hearts

Two survivors of a tragic plane crash discover their dead spouses' infidelity. This best-selling novel of love, passion and forgiveness became a major motion picture with Harrison Ford.

Trans-Siberian Express

American doctor Alex Cousins knows a dark and dangerous secret, and the Soviet Union will stop at nothing to keep him in Siberia on the world's longest and most exotic train ride to prevent him from revealing it.

Mourning Glory

A down on her luck 38-year-old single mother with a dysfunctional teenage daughter snares a rich widower in Palm Beach. But her cynical scheme unravels and she finds herself enmeshed in a self-spun web of deception and danger that threatens to rob her of everything she holds dear.

Cult
A novel of brainwashing and death

The suspenseful story of a man's increasingly desperate attempt to rescue his brainwashed wife from a religious death cult. A thriller with a chilling climax that shows how the power of sinister forces using mind control techniques can turn innocent people into weapons of destruction.

The Casanova Embrace

In this explicit and erotic thriller, a charismatic Latin diplomat cynically seduces three lonely women and uses them as pawns in international terrorism. Discovering his ruthless manipulation and betrayal, they plot every woman's revenge fantasy.

Blood Ties

During a family reunion at their ancestral castle, the famed Von Kassel family—arms dealers for over a hundred years—suddenly find themselves in possession of stolen plutonium capable of creating the most destructive weapon on earth. Secret revelations erupt into violence as the family is torn apart by their acquisition's deadly potential.

Natural Enemies

Pursued by human predators, a young urban couple becomes lost in the Colorado wilderness and is forced to confront the chilling and impersonal wrath of nature in this taut and acclaimed novel.

Banquet Before Dawn

After serving his Brooklyn district for many years, an Irish Congressman is challenged by a youthful and more liberal opponent. In this remarkable novel full of unforgettable characters, the last hurrah becomes a poignant and seething masterwork.

The Housewife Blues

An innocent and naïve young woman marries to escape from her small mid-western town. But her controlling husband moves her to an apartment in New York City and keeps her a virtual prisoner. Her journey of self-discovery from naiveté through disenchantment and eventual wisdom makes for a suspenseful story with explosive consequences.

Madeline's Miracles

A young family falls prey to a woman who convinces them that she is a psychic and can foresee their future in this critically acclaimed and chilling bestseller about brainwashing and superstition.

We Are Holding the President Hostage

When terrorists capture the daughter and grandson of a Mafia Don in Egypt, the angry Godfather insinuates himself into the White House and teaches the President some lessons of the mob. This classic confrontation between two men on utterly opposite sides of the law is laced with humor and illustrates how fierce paternal love can motivate even the most ruthless of gangsters into reckless acts of courage and bravery.

Private Lies

Two Manhattan couples are caught in a complex and emotional web of adultery, sexual obsession and deception that turns deadly on an African safari.

Twilight Child

Readers Digest originally published this acclaimed, heart wrenching novel about the visitation rights of grandparents and the terrible ordeal that ensues between generations locked in a bitter struggle for a child's love.

The Henderson Equation

The people who run the influential newspaper the *Washington Chronicle* have just brought down a President through their damning investigative reports. Now they want to create their own choice for Chief Executive! The power of the press to manipulate comes under the microscope in this tense exploration of the media and the thirst for power.

Undertow

After the beautiful black aide and lover of a womanizing married Senator accidentally drowns, the Senator mounts a massive cover-up of cynical lies designed to deflect the potential damage to his career in this suspenseful tale of adultery, media manipulation, and political chicanery.

Short Stories

The Sunset Gang

With time running short, the retired residents of Sunset Village in Florida continue to thirst for life, love and happiness. In the process, they teach us all a lot about living—a subject on which they are, after all, experts. These critically acclaimed short stories were adapted into a PBS trilogy that won worldwide recognition for its wonderful insights into the aging process.

Never Too Late for Love

The intrepid crew from Sunset Village is back! With sensitivity and humor, these brilliant stories depict the lives, loves, conflicts and trials of the modern senior citizen. This is the complete collection of the classic *Sunset Gang* stories.

Jackson Hole, Uneasy Eden

These acclaimed stories capture the truth, warts and all, of how modern life can both corrupt and enhance a traditional environment. Based on the author's experience as a long-time resident of this pristine valley in Wyoming nestled in the heart of the Grand Tetons, America's most beautiful mountain range.

The Fiona FitzGerald Mysteries

American Quartet

This is the first book in the popular Fiona FitzGerald mystery series. Fiona is a senator's daughter turned Washington, D.C. homicide detective. Four seemingly unconnected murders stimulate Fiona's sense of history as she delves into our country's dark past. In her effort to solve the crimes, she uncovers the twisted sexual and homicidal obsessions of a socially prominent but failed Washington politician. Named by the *New York Times* as one of the top ten crime novels of the year.

American Sextet

Fiona takes us behind the scenes of power and unravels a massive political sex scandal that shakes the Washington establishment to its core. As Fiona investigates, she uncovers a conspiracy involving six men from the highest offices in the country—a great American Sextet!

Senator Love

A seductive and philandering Senator is the prime suspect when bodies begin turning up buried in an upscale Washington neighborhood. Besides solving the mystery, will Fiona submit to the powerful sexual charm of "Senator Love?"

Immaculate Deception

The clock is ticking both figuratively and biologically. During Fiona's pursuit to conceive a child, a powerful female pro-life Senator is found dead. The case gets even more baffling when one shocking clue contradicts the entire investigation.

The Ties That Bind

The daughter of a prominent lawyer is found murdered, and a Supreme Court Justice with a sadomasochistic fetish is the target of Fiona's investigation. This is a case that truly brings Fiona to the dark side of the Washington scene.

The Witch of Watergate

When an infamous and unpopular *Washington Post* reporter whose poison pen has destroyed many careers is found hanging in her Watergate apartment, suicide is the logical explanation. But Fiona won't stop investigating until she uncovers the truth, even as it leads to the corridors of power on Capitol Hill.

**To order any of these titles or
For more information,
Visit www.WarrenAdler.com**

LaVergne, TN USA
02 September 2009
156790LV00004B/109/A